Hollow Back Girl
A Gwen Arthur Novel

Olivia R. Burton

OTHER TITLES

Gwen Arthur Series

Mixed Feelings
Business With Pleasure
Cold Feet
Hollow Back Girl
Change of Heart

~

Bone to Pick
Flesh and Blood
The Writer's Overnighter
Gut Feeling
Suckered In
Split Second

The Preternatural PNW

Rattle
Metal
Knell

~

Throb
Murmur

COLLABORATIONS

Passage Through Moonlight
The Godfather's Naughty Daughter
Song of the Argyle Goddess
Belladonna Clasped
Cash Grab

CONTENTS

THANKS

Thanks to Courtney for reading Gwen's books before they're ready to go, forgiving my dumb mistakes, and helping me correct them. Your help is invaluable and your commentary entertaining!

Thanks to Margaret Bishop: Plot Hunter for all your help with the first draft of **Hollow Back Girl**. Your suggestions for Izzy and the shenanigans he propagates helped me better understand his nonsense and how Gwen would react to his presence.

Olivia R. Burton

One

"You can't make me go!"

"Technically I'm not *making* you go," Chloe said, before bodily shoving me through the doors of SEA-TAC airport. I huffed out a breath, trying to fight her, despite the fact that I knew I was being childish and stupid. Chloe Warren works out regularly and knows her way around a cranky empath; I had no chance.

"Besides, Gwen," she said, her slim arm around my shoulders as we walked ever closer to the serpentine security lines. "This trip was *your* idea."

"Technically," I intoned, mimicking her like I was three instead of thirty, "it was my mother's idea."

"Then blame her. In person, in Montana, later tonight. Now. I've got to leave before the parking fees get to be so high I have to sell my soul." Kissing my cheek and leaving me standing next to a TSA agent who was so bored it was almost painful, she backed toward the exit. "Don't worry about Sonny, either. Just enjoy yourself. Your bird will be fine."

"I can't leave him!" I said, seeing it as the opportunity it really wasn't. "I should stay, he'll miss me."

"If you try to get back in my car," Chloe said with a big smile. "I'll pay Mel a thousand dollars to follow you around for a week, telling you how cute your butt looks in those jeans—even if you're not wearing jeans. Have fun!"

Knowing she'd properly cowed me with the threat of our werewolf work neighbor, Chloe winked and disappeared around the corner. I scowled, already miserable without the idea she'd put in my head. Mel and I were friends—had even slept together one, regretful time—but werewolf emotions can be brutal to an empath and no amount of ogling his sexy abs could overcome the miserable state in which his presence often left me.

Turning, taking a deep breath, wishing silently that I could get back home without the misery of actually traveling there, I scurried into the security line like a rat trying to escape a flood by jumping into an oven.

Bag checked, cup of icy, blended, pink, syrupy goodness in hand, I sat at my gate, glaring at the wall. I could have been skimming social media or reading, but instead, I was trying to decide if I wanted to kill time properly or just pout some more. So far the emotional din of all the other passengers in the airport had made the choice for me.

I like being an empath. It's a useful skill that makes life easier in a lot of situations. I've never been turned down for a date, I know when someone is lying to me, and you cannot bluff me in poker. Cleaning up in Vegas aside, it has its downsides, too. Everywhere I go I'm bombarded by the feelings of other living creatures within my vicinity. Sure, it's cool to always know if there's a particularly aggressive goat at a petting zoo or if someone's planning something dastardly. (No need to twirl your dirty mustache and cackle madly, sir; I already know you're plotting to tie me to the train tracks.) Being constantly forced to, at least in part, experience every emotion of those around me gets tiring, though. It's why I try to keep much of my human interaction strictly internet-based.

Sitting in a crowded concourse, surrounded by cranky travelers, stressed babies, and harried parents was making me kind of want to throw my drink to the ground and have a tantrum like the toddler three seats over. I didn't, of course; not only would the TSA have been on my butt faster than I could yell, "Frappuccino!" but it would have been a waste of perfectly good sugar and I am nothing if not committed to rotting my teeth with sweets.

My phone rang, buzzing against my side insistently, trying to distract me from the cloud of grumpiness swirling around. I dug it out of my pocket reluctantly, fighting my urge to continue to sulk, and put it to my ear without looking at who was calling.

"Yeah," I said, shoving the straw of my drink toward my mouth. Poking myself in the nose because I was too stubborn to tear my gaze away from the spot of carpet I was fixated on did not help my mood.

"Chipmunk, are you at the airport? Are you boarding yet?"

"Mom," I complained, suddenly ten years old again. "Don't call me that."

"So you haven't boarded?" my mom asked, ignoring my protest as she'd been doing for twenty years. I heard commotion in the background, followed by a pair of masculine laughs. I was betting Robin and Jake had already arrived; I refuse to believe my father is capable of laughter, so that left only my brother-in-law Jake and my brother Thomas.

"No, not yet, but soon."

"Eat something healthy," she said, though it had the ring of habit, as if she'd just said it because she'd had to remind me not to eat like trash since I'd gotten old enough to feed myself. "Some nuts or fruit or something."

I glanced down at the pink drink in my hand, shrugged.

"Fruit is involved," was as close as I could get to the truth. My mother sighed, knowing me better than to trust me at my word. Despite being two states away, I hunched my shoulders in shame. "Fine. I'll get an apple. Or something."

"Good. When does your flight land again?"

"Mmm," I mumbled around the straw, taking a guess. "Two-thirty?"

"Robin's going to meet you," my mother said, her tone distracted, likely by the child begging, I was assuming from the nonsense approximation of the word, to be picked up. I'd sent her my itinerary weeks ago and I was sure she'd put it on every calendar she had in the house, overjoyed her middle child was finally deigning to risk life and sanity to come home for a visit. "Let me get her."

Mom called out to my sister, setting off an aural chain of events that made me smile, despite the toddler still having a fit nearby: a young boy shrieked, my brother laughed, my mom mumbled, and Robin made a sound of excitement, before speaking directly to me.

"Hey chipmunk!"

"I refuse to answer to my slave name," I sniffed, slurping the last bit of the liquid out of the frozen slush at the bottom of my cup. Frowning at it, I set it in my lap and shifted the phone to my other ear.

"Don't be callous," Robin chided. "Two-thirty, right?"

"Yes!" I snapped, knowing she didn't deserve the ire but unable to help myself. "Don't bring dad."

"I know better than to lock the two of you alone in a car, dummy," she said with sisterly affection. "What did you want for dinner tonight? We're going shopping before I leave to get you."

"Pie!" I answered without giving it any real thought. My sister, as used to denying me pleasure as my mother, didn't even sigh or seem surprised.

"I meant real food. You're not getting pie for dinner."

"For dessert, then. A light snack. A welcome gift for the prodigal daughter who just braved—"

"Shh," she interrupted mildly. I heard my brother's voice get closer again before it faded away and I heard a door shut. Silence fell and I could almost feel my sister's concern, even though that was physically impossible. "You okay?"

"I mean, I'm at an airport about to come visit dad, so no," I said.

"You're not seeing dad, you're coming to see everyone," Robin chastised, before going quiet again. Then her voice slow and serious, she said merely, "You've been weird the last few months."

"I'm always weir—er, I mean, weird how?"

"I don't know," she said thoughtfully. "I just want to make sure you're still ... you."

"Not at all," I joked. "I'm Ted Nugent now."

Robin only sighed and I could picture her as she'd looked when we'd been teenagers: hand over her eyes, sick to death of my stupid jokes. I snorted quietly, feeling only a little guilty that I couldn't be an adult for even ten seconds.

"I'm fine, Rob," I insisted, before feeling my phone buzz in my hand. I glanced at it, considering the unknown number, and decided to use it as an excuse to get out of this awkward conversation. "I have another call. I'll see you when I land, okay?"

Robin was quiet for a moment before singing, "okay, see you soon, chipmunk!"

"Ugh," I grumbled, hearing her snort out a laugh before I ended one call to answer the other.

"This is Gwen," I answered, expecting to hear a call from one my clients. Chloe had let everyone know I was going to be out of town for awhile, and most of the people I counsel don't need to chat outside of our sessions, but I wanted to be safe. To my surprise, a sexy voice I hadn't heard in much too long slid over the line.

"Hey, Gwen. It's Owen."

"Hi!" I nearly shrieked, startling the kid who'd moved on from screaming over nothing to screaming over Cheerios. "I mean, hey," I corrected, trying to sound cool. Owen laughed, and I was so pleased he didn't find my excitement irritating, I did a little dance in my seat.

"Guess who's coming to Seattle soon," he teased.

"Simon and Garfunkel?"

"Yes, that's why I'm calling," he agreed, going with my bit. "I know you're a huge folk rock fan."

"Well, that's very considerate of you," I said, grinning downward and noticing the cup with its chewed up straw still sitting in my lap, dampening the crotch of my pants in a way I hadn't considered when I'd tucked it there. "When do you think the boys will be in town?"

"With any luck, next week."

"Next week as in, the week after this week?" I asked, feeling my excitement ebb away.

"I ... don't know how else to specify such a date, so yes," Owen said.

"Dammit," I grumbled. "I'm out of town until next Friday."

"How out of town? Could you rush back for just a night? A few hours?

4

Fifteen minutes?"

I laughed. "You sell yourself short, Reid. Fifteen minutes? Come on."

"I could come on in fifteen minutes, if properly motivated."

I giggled, unable to help myself, dirty, messy thoughts of our last encounter making me blush all over.

"Any chance I could entice you to jet over and meet me? Where are you headed? When are you leaving?"

"I'm literally about to board a plane to Montana. I'm going to visit family for two weeks."

"For your birthday?"

"How do you know when my birthday is?" I asked, trying to remember if I'd told him. He was quiet and I shook my head and grinned. "Okay, fine, Mystery Man. You have your secrets. But, yes, for my birthday and then Thanksgiving."

"Where exactly will you be?" he asked slowly, sounding secretly delighted.

"Um, it's a little town no one's heard of: Balanis."

"Balanis?" he asked and I could hear a smile in his voice. "Balanis, Montana. Where you grew up."

"No fair on the background checks," I chastised. "I don't have your resources."

"Well, when I see you later, I can lend you my resources. You can use them for whatever you may desire."

"When you see me *later*?" I asked, suspicious and eager all at the same time.

"That's the plan."

"How later? What plan? Where are you and are we gonna make this work for longer than fifteen minutes?"

"Much longer, since we can start tonight."

"Tonight?" I laughed, sure I was misunderstanding, but enjoying the tingly feelings of anticipation just the same. "I won't even get home—er, to my parents' house for a few hours. Where are you?"

"In a hotel room just outside—drumroll please—Balanis, Montana."

"You are kidding!" I cried, my spine going rigid, wondering if fate had a P.O. box and if it was accepting thank-you gifts. Owen let out a low laugh, pleased at my glee.

"I never kid about my job. Though, I am a little surprised you're happy I'm so close to your loved ones."

"Eh," I said with a shrug. Owen hunts monsters, taking care of problems the police couldn't even begin to comprehend. Balanis wasn't a major city but it was big enough and bordered by enough forest where monsters probably lived that I was pretty sure my kin would be safe. I wasn't thinking with only my hormones, I swear. "Should I be worried? Are you hunting something dangerous?"

"When do you want to meet?" he asked in lieu of answering. I chuckled, used to his avoidance of work-related questions.

"Well, I should spend some actual time with my family, but later in the evening would work. I can sneak out after the kids are in bed." I really didn't want to wait, but I hadn't seen my family in over a year and darting off to get my rocks off first thing after arriving would *so* get me grounded.

"We can get late dinner, catch up in the hotel bar, what do you think?"

"How about we just cut right to the chase. Tell me where you are and I'll meet you in your room and we can get all our catching up done in bed." Owen let out a low purr of a sound, making me bite my lip as I wondered if my cheeks were as red as they felt.

"A woman after my own heart," he said. I let out a quick laugh.

"Let me assure you, that is not the organ I'm after."

"Ten o'clock?" he asked.

"Perfect. Text me your hotel information and I'll see you then."

"Can't wait."

"You have no idea," I said.

Two

"Don't say chipmunk," I ordered as I pulled open my mother's car door and pointed threateningly at my sister. She just waved me in.

"Hurry, hurry. I've been circling and I don't want to get in trouble."

"You won't get in trouble," I said. Hefting my bag into the back seat, I shut the door and hopped forward to the passenger door, sliding in. Robin leaned over and gave me a quick hug and kiss on the cheek before pulling out into traffic.

"How was the flight?"

"Being trapped in a steel box with a hundred unhappy people and two teething babies? Oh, it was great."

"You're fine," she said, dismissively. I scowled, but felt right at home.

Robin looked good. I hadn't seen her since my youngest niece had been born, but she looked much better than she had fresh from squeezing something the size of a watermelon out of her body.

Robin and Thom got my mother's stunning good looks, though she'd been the only one of us to get mom's lovely red hair. I'm average height, curvy with short dark hair, a square jaw, and green eyes, but Robin got the model genetics. She's tall and willowy, with long copper hair and pale skin. Her eyes are hazel, her smile somewhat delicate. She looks extremely similar to our mother, though I had yet to recognize either of my parents in my own face. This is despite the fact that everyone tells me repeatedly that my father and I are the same person in every way.

I looked over her long, soft dress, suspected she'd chosen a pattern jammed with so many angled spots of color to hide the inevitable grape juice stains or toddler vomit. She'd paired it with a cardigan to fight off the chill of the November afternoon.

Glancing down at myself, I wondered if I should invest in more interesting clothing to hide the fact that I tend to eat like her youngest. I'd just settled on jeans with a hole in the knee and a yellow shirt that had a spot of something I couldn't identify on the bottom hem.

"So what's with the cold shoulder?" Robin asked as the silence stretched on. I hadn't really meant to go quiet, but the calm of having only her nearby was such a relief, my brain had gone somewhat numb with contentment. Here and there I could feel some other driver or an animal peak into my empathic range, but mainly it was just Robin. Curious about the sheepish curiosity fizzing within her, I forced myself to focus and be present.

"What do you mean? I'm always dumb like this after a flight."

"Yes," Robin said delicately, giving me a teasing smile. "After a flight." I scoffed and she laughed, shaking her head. "I mean—" she laughed again at the look I kept giving her. "—you used to call at least once a week. Now it's barely once a month."

"I just …" I trailed off, not sure how to explain. "I don't have much to say."

"You didn't before either. Being boring's never stopped *you* from talking."

"I don't know," I lied, looking out the window. Truth was, I didn't know what to say about what had been going on in my life since my last birthday. Something about turning twenty-nine had kicked off a fairly steady stream of strange and unusual circumstances. I had no idea if my family would understand—let alone believe—me if I tried to tell them. I couldn't just calmly explain that I'd been kidnapped by a vampire, attacked by a werewolf, nailed by that same werewolf, snacked on by a giant spider, and bewitched by a succubus. I had scars and bad memories and an ever-evolving set of magnetic poetry that had, at one point, used my refrigerator to cryptically tell me the future. Not to mention that my pet bird knows Morse code thanks to a creature that was dating my best friend.

How do you tell your perfectly normal, sweet, housewife sister that the world isn't about bake sales and play dates?

You don't.

"I don't have your gift," Robin said, "but I know when you're lying. Just tell me what's been going on." She reached toward my hand like she was trying to sneak a squeeze and I yelped, slapping her away.

"No!" I protested through a laugh. "Don't you use your crazy mind control powers on me."

"I don't know what you're talking about," she claimed innocently, even though she knows I can smell a lie. Glancing over just long enough to see where my arm was, she reached for me again. I growled like a threatened animal and smooshed myself as far into the corner of the car as I could get.

"Stop!" I whined, slapping at her when she laughed and reached toward me a third time. We were in grade school all over again. "Get away!"

"I'm not doing anything," she insisted, grasping for my arm. She caught the sleeve of my shirt and I yowled again. The last thing I needed was my sister using her influence to make me spill the truth. She isn't exactly Professor X, but she can make you admit things you kinda don't want to. She could also make you do her chores even after you swore you never would and I was betting she'd used her powers on her husband in more situations than I wanted to think about.

Luckily she could only tug on my sleeve and not get her hand on bare skin; that was when the real problems started.

"I don't want you to—"

"Get the truth out of you?" she asked, letting go of my arm long enough to slap blindly at me.

"Cheater!" I accused. Robin chuckled, pulling her hand away, leaving me to my tantrum as she had so many times before. Finally, I growled, the guilt winning out. "I can't tell you what's been going on in my life. Because I'm in the CIA. If I tell you what I do, you could be in danger."

"Now you're just being silly."

"No! It's a magical CIA," I said, sniffing smugly. "They recruited me for my empathy. I do a lot of field work."

"Oh, sure."

"My partner has a gun and everything." That part wasn't a lie; Chloe really has a gun. She's used it to save my life on more than one occasion.

"Gwen," Robin said. We were finally pulling up in front of my parents' house. The weeping willow in the front looked especially sad in the chilly air. As she turned the car off, she twisted in her seat to stare me down. Despite still being scrunched up in a ball against the door, I felt myself hunch even further.

"What?"

"What's really kept you from calling?"

"Nothing major," I said, feeling uncomfortable for all sorts of reasons I couldn't properly articulate. We had a stare down for a minute or two before I relaxed, bit my lip, and glanced toward the house. While I wasn't exactly eager to get inside and deal with my father, I wasn't enjoying getting the third degree from my sister.

"You're okay? You swear nothing's going on?"

"I swear. I'm perfectly healthy,"—she snorted at that and I pressed on as if she hadn't mocked me—"happy, and in no danger. Everything's cool."

"Okay." I felt her suspicion and worry melt into relief with just an edge of disappointment, and I reached out to slug her lightly on her arm.

"Come on. Now that I've gone a few rounds with you, it's time for the boss fight."

"Dad's mellowed," she claimed, but I could hear the lie in that too.

Despite my better judgment, I followed Robin into the house. She had my bag, after all, and I'd stashed my phone in there.

First things I found were a toy truck under foot and a screaming four-year-old running frantically from the door as if we were viciously growling grizzly bears with a taste for little boys. Robin avoided the truck as if she'd known it would be there, whereas I tripped, toppled, and nearly brained myself with the jut of staircase railing.

"J.J. please be quiet," Robin said. The screaming stopped but I saw a red head poke out from the kitchen doorway to my left and brown eyes watch us mischievously. As I righted myself and kicked at my luggage in anger, I caught my nephew's eye, scowling his way in faux threat.

Instead of being intimidated, he matched my look with his own glare and we held that position for a bit until I saw a slight wiggle overtake his shoulders. Once he couldn't take the stillness anymore, he shrieked loudly and ran off in the other direction. I laughed, feeling his glee burble inside my chest like soda as I grabbed my luggage and took the stairs up to my old room.

My parents have a huge house with a huge yard, but they'd clearly been focused on common areas when choosing the place. Each bedroom is tiny, able to fit a minuscule closet, a double bed, and a dresser at most. You could probably get a queen bed in one or two of them, if you don't mind stubbing your toes a lot. Despite this, I had spent most of my pre-first-boyfriend years locked in my room with books and a Discman, as dull claustrophobia was better than fighting with my father.

Eager to relive that solitude rather than seek him out—I was keeping my empathy as to myself as possible, lest I accidentally poke into his psyche and lose my mind with frustration—I reached the top step, turned toward my room, and stopped.

"Uhhh, mom?"

As far as I could remember, my room had not had a screen door instead of a real one and had not been filled with a bird's jungle gym worth of stuff.

"What happened to my room?" I asked, knowing no one could hear me over Jake Junior's excitement and the whirring dishwasher.

The other two rooms looked as they had when I'd moved out, even down to the Usher poster on my brother's wall. This was an attack, I thought, unable to help myself where the stupid bird was concerned. Grumbling, leaving my luggage where it fell, I stormed downstairs, ready to verbally take someone's head off.

"What's up with my room?" I demanded as I hit the edge of the kitchen. My mother glanced over from the pile of brightly colored vegetables she was dicing and her face lit up. Ignoring my question completely, she set down the knife, sidestepped J.J. as he darted past, and yanked me into a hug. All crankiness melted away upon contact, my mind soothed by maternal love. She was overjoyed to see me, happy and nostalgic and amused, probably at the fact that I'd chosen to bitch rather than greet her.

"Chipmunk!"

"No!" I argued, though it was half-assed, as was my attempt to pull out of the hug. She ignored my protest and squeezed me tighter, kissing the top of my head. While I grumbled and wiggled, mostly for form, she just laughed, kissing me more aggressively, and started rocking back and forth.

"My baby girl," she cooed. "My baby with the big teeth!"

"My teeth are fine!" I insisted. Mom chuckled against my hair, kissed me one last time, and pulled away, smiling down at me.

My mother is gorgeous and well out of my father's league, if you ask any of us kids. She's tall and slim with short, red hair, a bevy of smile lines at the corners of her green eyes, and a core of strength that could stop a charging bull with just a look. Despite her formidable nature, she's the sweetest woman you will ever meet, an amazing cook and baker, and quick with a compliment for anyone at any time.

None of this stopped me from complaining.

"My room!" I accused, pointing at the stairs, as if she would think I mean my room in Seattle.

"It's Dorian's room, now."

"But why *my* room? And where do I sleep?"

"You can sleep in the yard," Thomas said from behind me. I turned to glare at him, but he yanked me into a hug, rocked me like my mother had, and squeezed harder when I started to complain.

My tantrum aside, the mood was pleasant: my mother's love, my brother's mischievous glee, my sister's contented happiness all mixing to threaten my childishness in a way few things could.

"I'm not sleeping in the yard, you sleep in the yard," I argued, shoving my brother away. He let me, looking unkempt and half-asleep as if he'd been the one to just get off a plane full of angry strangers. His dark hair was mussed, curled a bit at the edges, his long face looking tired and a bit pale.

"The kids are sleeping in tents—inside—not you. You get Thomas' old room," Robin assured me, appearing from the living room with my youngest niece in hand. Seeing the baby melted me instantly, my insides turning to goo, my uterus demanding to be fertilized.

"Stella!" I cooed, reaching for the toddler. She bounced in her mother's arms, thrashed a tiny fist in excitement and drooled down her front. I took the drool as a good sign, gripping her delicately under her pudgy baby arms. She let out a burbling goo-goo and I felt a little pop of delight from her young psyche as I yanked her against me. When I layered kisses over her face and sniffed her red hair, she barely even halted her bouncing.

"Ohh," I moaned against her cheek. "She's perfect!"

"Of course she is," Jake said, leaning around Robin to give me a half-hug. "She's ours. How are you, Gwen?"

"Feeling like I want one," I said, letting Stella's innocence and unfettered happiness bleed in through my skin. She gave a spastic dance with her arms, kicked a leg, and then blew a raspberry at me; I didn't even mind the spit all over my face.

"I can't help you with that but any time you want to come out and babysit, just let us know." I smiled up at him, looking him over.

Jake is a bit taller than Robin, which means he's got a full head on me, and he's always reminded me of some surfer-academic type. Sandy brown hair, bright blue eyes, and a slim, muscular build join a perfect jaw line and make him almost a knock-out. His nose is a touch too big, but it gives his face character, making you think he knows a thing or two about chemistry or chess or something. I admit, I have a bit of a crush on the man, despite the fact that I've known him so long I couldn't honestly consider him anything except family.

With his genetics and hers, I had no doubt Robin and Jake's children really would be perfect once they aged past all the screaming and drooling. Just as I started to wonder where their oldest was, figuring Natalie had likely matured past me, even at eight, I heard my nickname sing through the air.

"Chipmunk!"

My eye twitched and I peered past my brother-in-law to the African Gray parrot perched on my father's shoulder. Dorian had been around longer than even Robin, and I was pretty sure my father loved him more than he loved any of us kids. Well, more than me anyway. I gave the parrot a dirty look, wondering why, of all the things I'd been called by my family over the years, that particular name had stuck in his tiny bird brain.

My teeth are normal-sized, now, couldn't he see that? Couldn't any of them see that?

Instantly the emotional temperature in the room dropped about ten degrees. The bird tipped his head at me and my father glanced between it and me. We squared off for a moment, both of us undoubtedly deciding who would draw first, before my mother rolled her eyes and turned toward her husband.

"Marvin, doesn't Gwen look great?"

"Sure," he said. I sighed, cheek still pressed against the baby, using Stella like a shield against my father's annoyance.

He's a touch taller than me, though I've long suspected he's not really, that most of his height is just his unruly, black hair. Dad's a bit portly, with a round face and cheeks that hope to be full on jowls when they grow up. His eyes are a deep, dark brown that I've never once seen sparkle, and he's got a perpetual five o'clock shadow, no matter what time of day it is. Robin got her full lips from him but Thomas inherited what some might call his weak chin.

We sighed at each other, friction arcing around the room as I tried to ignore the annoyance and apprehension bouncing between us. The feeling reminded me of feedback from a microphone and was just as unpleasant.

"Hi dad," I said finally. Jake failed to silence his laugh at our awkward greeting, but stepped aside so we could at least pretend we enjoyed each other's company. I leaned in and we hugged, keeping Stella as a barrier between us. To my surprise, I felt a teeny, tiny, almost imperceptible sliver of affection as my father tugged me quickly against him in what even upper-class, unaffectionate, super white people would consider a pansy-ass hug. I pulled back as fast as I could and went back to cooing at Stella, who blew a raspberry right in my eye.

At least it was better than having to have a full-on conversation with dad.

Olivia R. Burton

Three

"Where are you headed?" Thomas asked as I hit the bottom of the stairs. I glanced over at him, wondering if he'd meant to startle me. While that was usually impossible, considering my gift, he'd managed it a time or two in the past when I'd been distracted. He was just too damned lucky for my own good.

"Out," I said, suddenly feeling like a teenager again. Dancing forward, he grabbed at my hand, managed to catch the loop of the key fob on my mother's car keys and yank them out of my hand. Dancing back, he twirled them around his index finger once. "Give those back!"

"You can't make me!"

"Oh my god, Thom," I sighed. He laughed, holding the keys above his head, knowing full well I couldn't reach them.

"Why must you leave us so soon?" he asked, masking his face in dramatic sadness. "We just got you back, Gwen."

"*Jeez*," I said, snorting out a laugh. "If you really missed me that much, you would've visited like you promised."

"Oh, I was gonna," Thomas said, lowering his arm, suddenly conversational. "Carter needed help at the store, though, so I'm covering."

"Doesn't he have his brother for that? The kid, right?"

"He's not a kid anymore, he's barely younger than me." Ignoring my look, Thom pressed on. "Plus, he's real sick, remember? They're both not doing great."

"Still? Jesus, it's been a month. Is he dying?"

"I hope not," Thomas said earnestly. Biting my tongue, feeling bad for being so flippant about his friends' health, I went quiet, reconsidering the

15

grab I'd been planning to make to get the keys back. Thomas watched me in the dark for a bit, before breathing out a quiet laugh and handing them over.

"Does mom know you're taking the car?"

"Yes, because I'm an adult," I lied.

"Only in height. Will you be home late?"

"Uh," I grunted, unsure of my answer. I had considered just sleeping at Owen's hotel all night, but it occurred to me in that moment that I hadn't thought to pack any sort of overnight bag. It wouldn't be the first time I'd slept over with just the clothes on my back, but it really would have been smarter to be home before breakfast, if only because my mother would ask all sorts of questions if I wasn't.

"Probably," I said after a long pause. Thom tipped his head and I felt curiosity burble out of him.

"Are you seeing a *boy*?" he asked, drawing the noun out like warm taffy. I rolled my eyes, heading toward the door.

"No, that would be creepy. He's a fully-grown man. A very sexy, fully-grown man. Now go to bed."

"Okay. Well, have fun," he said, as if unsure what else to say.

Immediately, embarrassment flooded through us both as I turned, halfway through the doorway. We met each other's gazes for a moment, both considering that we knew exactly where I was going and what I was planning to do to my fully-grown man friend.

"I mean ..." Thomas said, trailing off. After a second, I held up a hand.

"Stop. Stop talking. Just lock the door behind me and never speak again."

He mimed locking his lips up and tossing away the key while I rolled my eyes amiably, shook my head, and fled.

Owen's hotel was only about twenty minutes away from my parents' house, but it was about nineteen minutes too far for my hormones. I pushed through the doors into the lobby, strode straight to the counter. The woman there looked up from a book she was reading, gave me a practiced smile. I felt an arc of annoyance jolt out of her and it kicked up a funny sort of nostalgia; I remembered the joy of customer service jobs all too well.

"Hey, my name's Gwen; I'm supposed to pick up a package from a friend here?"

"Oh, okay," she said, getting to her feet. She dug around behind the counter for a second, pulled a fat envelope out, gave it a once-over. Tossing away the post-it on the front, she looked back up at me. "Can I see your ID?"

"Yep," I pulled it out of my bag, handed it over. She gave it a pretty thorough examination, tilting it in the light before handing it and the envelope over. I thanked her, yanked open the envelope and laughed, making my way toward the elevator. Owen had left me a note and a candy bar. Of course, I tore into the candy first, but it was just as well; the note was simply his room number.

I was halfway through the candy when he opened the door to his room and I got a look at him. It's a testament to how attractive he is that I chose to grab him and yank him into a kiss rather than finish my chocolate. I watched his blue eyes drift shut as our lips met, felt his hands come around my back to press against my spine and pull me into the room. Once over the threshold, I dropped my bag, made a happy sound against this mouth. Affection, arousal, and delight burbled and tumbled through him, tinged with an edge that made me want to bite him, to scratch my nails across his bare skin. I felt his fingers dig into my hip as I slid my arm from his shirt around to grip his hair just this side of too tight.

"Your candy's going to melt," he murmured between kisses.

"Still edible," I responded, wrapping my other arm around his neck, despite the fact that it was still clutching the chocolate bar. He chuckled against my mouth and, much to my dismay, pulled back. I did my best to give him a chastising glare, but I couldn't quite make it happen; my body was just too damn happy to be so close to his.

"Hey," I said conversationally. He pulled away further, straightened up.

"Hey," he said back. I looked over his narrow face, wondered briefly if I'd managed to get chocolate in his blond hair. I bit my lip, figured neither one of us really cared that much, and looked over to the bed across the room. He followed my gaze and I felt another swell of arousal run through him.

"Down girl," he purred, his tone oppositional to his words. I blinked up at him, trying to decide which of his mixed signals I should heed. His body and brain were not in agreement and, in the end, I just giggled, took the final few bites of the chocolate. Giving me a quick kiss on my forehead, he pulled away, looking me over. I did the same to him, enjoying the thought of what I had planned for his slim body.

"Down, eh?" I asked with a lascivious eyebrow wag. "I can do that."

He laughed and twisted to walk toward a small round table at the back of the room. I noticed two covered plates set out alongside an open bottle of wine. I squinted at the wine as I crumpled the candy wrapper and tossed it toward the small garbage beyond the table.

"What's that for?" I asked. The last time we'd had wine, it hadn't ended so well for me.

"Oh, the hotel sent it up. I still don't drink, but I thought you might like it."

"I don't know if I trust it."

"Don't worry," he said, stepping close and removing the lids of the food. "I checked it for puncture marks."

One plate held a thick cut of steak, a large portion of vegetables and a small roll with a little, foil-wrapped pat of butter. The other plate held a giant slice of cheesecake. I smiled, turned my gaze to his and felt suddenly swamped with affection and pleasure.

"You are getting so laid tonight," I declared. A laugh rumbled through his chest as I hopped forward, pulling him down into another kiss. He indulged me briefly, but spun me around, aimed me at the chair in front of the cheesecake.

"At least let me build up my strength first," he said, stepping away. I took a seat, watched him do the same, and then grabbed the bottle of wine to inspect it. He watched me with a half-smile as I poked at it, peeled back the label and aimed the cork at my face like I was planning on shooting out an eye.

"Hmm," I said cynically, before setting it aside. "I think I'll stick with the cheesecake."

"At least take it home with you?"

"And drug my family? I—" I paused, considered life at home with my parents. "Actually, that might not be such a bad idea."

Owen snorted, cut into his steak, and scooped it up along with vegetables. After a bite of the tasty cheesecake, I lifted a brow, caught his eye.

"What's with the late night meal?"

"I haven't eaten all day. I figured you wouldn't be hungry, but I also figured it would be rude to eat in front of you. Plus, I know you can't say no to sugar." Several dirty and possibly sexually improbable thoughts crossed my mind at that moment, but I just smiled, held my tongue. We watched each other for a bit as we ate, before he spoke again.

"What've you been up to?"

"Not having sex, that's for sure," I grumbled. Owen winked, stretched his leg out knock his toe against the side of my shoe.

"I'll fix that."

"That's the plan." I stuffed more cheesecake into my mouth, made a happy humming sound.

"So you're chaste now; anything else interesting? Any more succubi hanging around?"

"Just Madeline. It's been boring, mostly. I mean, there was the week I spent with Mel and the giant spider thing, but that's about it."

"Are we talking *Arachnophobia* or *Eight Legged Freaks*?"

"Ah." I considered his question, waggled my hand in the air as I crammed more cake into my mouth. "Somewhere in the middle. It was called, ah," I tried to remember the pronunciation as I swallowed my food. "Unktomi?"

"Ah. Fuckers," he grunted around a mouth full of meat. I nodded.

"Yeah. Caused me these." I held up my scarred arm, realized I had a long-sleeved shirt on, and frowned at it. Owen watched patiently as I set down my fork, yanked my sleeve up to show off the rough, shiny lines along my skin where I'd been attacked by a confused werewolf. Owen lifted a brow, gave an impressed nod.

"Damn. The spider did that?"

"Oh, not exactly. Mel did, but only because he thought I was the spider at the time."

"You survived a werewolf attack?"

"Er," I mumbled, feeling my cheeks go a little pink. Owen's lip quirked as he realized there was something there I didn't want to admit. Knocking his foot a bit harder against mine, he jerked his chin at me, took a bite of vegetables. I rolled my eyes, slumped a little further in my seat.

"He … We'd had … He didn't really try to kill me. Past the first bite, that is. He … knew what I tasted like."

"So you *have* been having sex," Owen chastised, shook his fork at me. I shook my head rapidly as he continued. "You little minx."

"Bad sex doesn't count."

"Bad sex with a werewolf?" Owen asked; I felt genuine confusion bubble out of him. "Did he think you were the spider while you were having sex?"

"Not … that I know of. Though, that would explain a lot."

"I just can't think of any other reason for bad sex from a werewolf."

"Oh my god, don't you *start*." Owen stifled a laugh around the food he was chewing, pulled the cover over his plate and leaned back.

"Don't start what?"

"Everyone's always telling me, 'oh sex with Mel is *great*! It's wonderful! Best you've ever had!' Well, excuse me, but you are all crazy, it was dreadful."

Owen shook his head, amusement warring with confusion for the top spot in his psyche. "I'm sorry to add to the chorus, but I've had sex with several werewolves and it's just hard to believe."

"Well, believe it." Still grumpy, I stabbed into the last bite of cheesecake, pulled it to my mouth and bit into it hard enough that I dinged my tooth on the edge of the fork. This did not help my mood.

"So you got attacked and then what?" Owen asked. I let myself glare at him as I finished chewing, shoved the plate petulantly aside.

"Then Mel and his sister killed it. I just sort of hung back and waited. I mean, there was all the throwing up I did just being next to the damn thing, but mostly I did a lot of waiting." After a second, I added in a cheerful voice, "also bleeding."

"But you're okay now," Owen stated, pushing to his feet. I watched him as he stepped around the small table and stood in front of me. I smiled at him and nodded.

"Peachy," I said. He held out his hands, pulled me upward when I took them.

"Good."

I stood on tiptoe and he bent down and we met somewhere in the middle, arms coming around each other tightly. I hummed eagerly into his mouth as he pulled me back toward the bed, his hands slipping under my shirt to rub roughly along my skin. My fingers got straight to the point, moving to unbutton his jeans, tug his shirt free so I could feel his belly, scratch at his back. He smiled against my lips, pulled my arms away just long enough to spin us both and push me back a step. The backs of my knees hit the soft bed and I dropped onto the blankets.

The look in his eyes was intense as he crawled over me, bent down to press his lips against my throat. I sighed out as he bit my collarbone, his hands shoving my shirt up. I twisted under him, helping him tug my shirt up and over my head, but quickly pulled him down against me, wrapping my legs around his hips. Our kisses were frantic as I ran my fingers through his hair, my other hand slipping under his shirt to scratch along his back.

His phone beeped from his pocket as I made my move to get him topless. I loved his shoulders, the look and feel of them. I wanted to drag my teeth along his skin, grip him tight and taste him. I got the shirt pulled up enough to bunch under his arms but he didn't help me along like I'd done for him. I felt a tension run through him, resignation flooding his psyche, overtaking the arousal. I caught sight of the light from the phone when he held it up near my cheek, pulling away from me enough to look at the screen. I knew the second the resignation and disappointment took over.

"I have to go," he sighed.

"By go, do you mean come?" I asked, turning his mouth to mine. I got another kiss but it was slightly marred by his grin.

"This time, no."

I sighed, letting up my grip enough that he could pull back. He sat up on his knees, glanced down at my legs wrapped around his hips, ran his eyes over my body. The sigh he let out perfectly encapsulated the disappointment and slight hint of irritation that ran through him. I lifted a brow, watching him.

"Is someone dead?"

"Likely, but that's not why I have to go."

Fighting the urge to pout, I loosened my thighs' grip on his hips, gave him the chance to move away. He didn't for a second, watching me.

"I'm sorry. Believe me, I'd rather be here with you than traipsing through—actually." He paused and I felt delight snap through him. I smiled, wondering if I was going to get lucky after all. "Maybe you can help me."

"Damn straight I can." I reached up, looped two fingers through his belt loops and tugged. He snorted as he leaned over me again, let me wrap myself around him for another kiss. He played along briefly as I slid my hands from his hips to his hair, doing my best to entice him to stay. After a few moments, he turned away from my mouth, ignoring the pain it must have caused him with my fingers tangled so tightly in his hair, and spoke quietly against my ear.

"Can I borrow your empathy for an hour? I promise we'll come right back here after, and finish what we've started."

"You need my help?"

"Need is a strong word," he said, pulling back to catch my eye, "but I could use it."

"What are you going to do?"

"I have to … meet a source."

It wasn't exactly a lie.

Olivia R. Burton

Four

"It. Is. Freezing!"

Owen glanced over at me with a small smile on his face.

"Well, you didn't bring a jacket."

"Even with this," I flopped the arm of the over-sized, zip-up hoodie he'd lent me. "It's cold as hell."

"I don't think that's a thing."

"You don't know. Maybe we've got it all wrong and Satan digs the arctic."

Owen rolled his eyes over a smile, shook his head. Then, after a moment, he said, almost as an aside, "I don't believe he actually goes by Satan."

"You can't blame me for not bringing a jacket," I griped, not jumping on that tangent. "I thought I was going from the car, to your bed, back to the car, and then to my bed. I didn't know we'd be—how'd you put it?— traipsing through the forest at midnight."

"It's not midnight yet," Owen said, stepping close. I felt the net bag of loose, raw produce he'd brought bump my arm and I glanced over.

"You still haven't told me what those are for."

He laughed and I felt it. "Man, you get cranky when you haven't had sex."

"And whose fault is that?"

"Mel's?"

"*Dammit*," I snarled, suddenly angry all over again that Mel was a crappy lay.

Owen threw back his head and laughed, stepping around to my other

23

side so he could wrap his free arm around my shoulders. Despite my attitude, I leaned into him, looked about. The moon was bright through the autumn-bare trees.

"What are we looking for? Who are we meeting?"

"Just keep an ear out. Or, well …" He trailed off, turning to look down at me with a lifted brow. "What do you keep out, anyway?"

"What do you mean?"

"Your empathy. Do you consider it a muscle, a sense?"

"Uhhh." I considered his question, tried to decide if there was an applicable comparison. "I don't really keep anything out. I mean, I guess I always do. I can't really turn it off."

"Well, then just be quiet."

To placate me before I could growl or fight or make a smart comment, he squeezed me against him, dipping low to give me a quick kiss. I sighed but did as he asked and stayed silent. We'd been walking for what felt like an hour, after having driven for at least thirty minutes toward the hills around Balanis.

We'd pulled up near the edges of a forest I hadn't been in since my father had taken us all camping when Thomas was little. Then, without pretense or camping supplies, we'd just traipsed on in. Owen hadn't explained what we were looking for or where we were going or even why he had a bag of onions, potatoes, cauliflower, and a handful of other root vegetables that I couldn't have named even if you'd pointed a turnip at me and threatened to pull the trigger.

I'm just guessing here, but you can shoot a turnip, right? That's a thing.

"You *still* haven't told me why you brought all that." I elbowed Owen and he smiled, but it was just a show. Something in him had changed from easy amusement to wary calm.

"In case we get peckish," he said distantly, pausing. I stopped too, stepped out of the circle of his arms and reached up to scratch at an itch along my skull. Much to my dismay, it was one of those irritations that presented in one place but actually needed to be scratched in another. As I rubbed my nails vigorously over my skull like you do to a happy, excitable dog, I watched his face.

"What's up?"

"You feel anything?"

"My head itches," I said, as if he hadn't noticed. He watched me passively for a moment.

"That's it?"

"Uh," I said, shrugging my shoulder before realizing that too itched. "No, my … actually I itch all over. Dammit. Did we walk through—*whoa*."

This wasn't poison oak.

We weren't alone.

24

Owen watched me as I froze in place, trying to ignore the itching along my skin in favor of going perfectly still like a frightened bunny. He hadn't made it to worried, but there was caution in him.

"What's going on?" I whispered, giving in and scratching the wriggling line of irritation attacking the back of my ear.

"You feel something?"

"I think so," I hissed, looking around. As I turned, the itching along my scalp moved to my forehead. I blinked into the darkness, considering that this wasn't just itching, it was emotion. Something in front of me was feeling nervous, unhappy, concerned. Something—multiple somethings, if I wasn't reading my empathy incorrectly—here didn't want us so close. "There's something out there."

"Perfect," Owen said before dropping the sack of produce to the ground. I yelped, jumping away from it as if it might explode, my nails still scraping along my face and neck. Owen held both hands in front of him and started making complicated hand gestures out into the air. I turned to watch him before half-grinning and jerking my head toward where I felt the emotions originating.

"They're over there, slick." A needle-thin line of embarrassment oozed out of Owen, followed by a hot arc of annoyance. I hugged a little closer to him, his very human emotions helping—though only a bit—to combat the vicious disquiet tearing through my skin like graboids trying to eat Kevin Bacon. Owen turned, repeated his hand motions and then pointed at the bag of vegetables on the ground.

Silence tried to fall but my fingernails still rasped loudly over my skin as I continued to fight the discomfort of being so close to whatever was out there. The emotions in front of me shifted slightly, calmed, and then I was staring at a group—a pack? A pride? A bushel?—of sasquatches.

Sasquatches!

There were sasquatches right in front of me, possibly even a whole family. I could see six or seven, but the emotions my empathy was interpreting as itching made me think there were several more that I couldn't see. My brain and my eyes were disagreeing over what was going on, but my skin didn't care about their argument. It knew these weren't imagined; I could tell this wasn't a pack of kids stacked on top of each other, wearing a gorilla costume.

These were the real thing; I was actually close enough to a bigfoot to see the rough fur along its grumpy face.

I'm clearly not versed in sasquatch biology so I couldn't tell you if the two standing over the three little ones were a mother and father or if baby bigfoot has two daddies. Regardless of their gender, they were staring at me, the one on the left watching me scratch my head as if I was completely crazy.

Maybe I am crazy; maybe all the things I've seen in the last year have been just figments of my imagination and I'm actually locked up in a loony bin with Buffy Summers and Sam Winchester. In that moment, though, it felt pretty damn real.

The creatures were possibly twice my height and wide enough that you could easily hide two of me behind each furry back. Shaggy shadows in the forest, they had wide foreheads, heavy brows, and thick upper lips. Their short chins and heavy overbites made them look obstinate, as if no matter what I asked of them, they would refuse. Judging by the fat tusks tucked under their droopy upper lips, I wouldn't be risking asking anything of them any time soon.

One of the taller pair stepped forward a bit and, yes, its feet were gigantic. Had they shoes, I could have worn each one backwards on my shins and walked around easily on my knees without getting my pants dirty. They had massive hands, too, but Big-Feet-and-Hands just doesn't have the same ring to it, I guess.

The creature pointed at the sack near Owen's feet and then pulled its hand back to make motions similar to the ones Owen had signed. Delight and a little bit of relief flitted through Owen before he returned the hand gestures with some new ones of his own.

The sasquatch made a grunting sound that may have only sounded happy because I could feel the emotion behind it. His hands made one quick gesture and then I watched Owen grab for the sack and step forward.

"What are you doing?" I hissed toward him, still scratching the top of my head.

"Paying them. You don't have to whisper; they can't understand us," he said, holding his arm out. The sasquatch took one giant step forward and grabbed for the bag, lifting it up in the moonlight. I let out a small, nervous giggle, but no one seemed to notice.

"Are you speaking … er, I mean. Are you communicating in sign language?"

"Yes," Owen said, before rolling his hands out toward the sasquatches in more signs and gestures. Standing there shivering, rubbing at my skin like a junkie, I considered the fact that even mythical forest creatures had more skills than me. I was probably not even that well versed in my own language, whereas these fuzzballs knew at least two.

Owen and the sasquatches continued signing as two of the smaller creatures came forward, grabbing for the bag. The taller one grunted at them, before lowering the bag toward them slightly. I jumped when one of the furry kids let out an excited sound that was somewhere between a toucan's scream and a puppy's bark. It grabbed for the bag, tried to yank a carrot through the hole in the side of the fabric mesh, and found the fattest part of the carrot was caught. A third child appeared from behind the parent holding the bag and thumped its sibling on the head, before tugging gently on its parent's wrist.

The taller creature ignored the little ones, still watching Owen communicate with its mate.

Still itching, I watched the kids fight and tug on the bag, each of them grunting with frustration and annoyance. Their grunts took on a pattern that I couldn't help but feel I recognized from interacting with my own sister and brother as a child. It seems sibling rivalry is a universal language. It made the side of my mouth tug up in a half-smile.

Meanwhile, one of the older kids who was hanging off to the side just watched, amused and somewhat anxious. This bigfoot was about my size, though beefier through the shoulders and waist. It probably could have fit into the sweatshirt I was wearing, but it would have been a stretch. The possibly-teenaged sasquatch kept a bead on me as I stepped around Owen's side to move into another position. I wanted to help the kids get to the carrot and the onion they seemed to so desperately desire, but the parents were making me nervous.

I elbowed Owen gently and, when he turned to me, I jerked a chin at the bag.

"Can you ask them to let the kids have a snack or something?"

Thoroughly distracted, Owen blinked at me but didn't agree or acknowledge me otherwise. Annoyed that he'd gone back to signing with the adult sasquatch, I stepped closer to the family, pointed at the bag. I tried to catch the teen bigfoot's eye, but it turned its head deliberately away as I did, snubbing me.

Sighing, I waved an arm, trying to get the attention of one of the parents instead.

"Hey! Hi. Um. They're hungry," I offered, hoping they'd figure out what I was saying if I gestured vaguely toward the kids. The adults ignored me but the little ones turned to look me over, hands still on the edges of carrots and clutching the papery skin of an onion they couldn't free. I took another step forward and they grunted disparagingly at me before turning back to the bag, tugging, grabbing, yanking. Still, they were ignored. They just couldn't reach the opening of the bag, but I figured I was tall enough.

"Owen, can I help them? Will they be mad?"

"Yes," he said, still signing.

I took another step, turning to face him as I did, as I reached out toward the bag.

"Yes I can help or—" I was already flying through the air before I realized what happened next.

Fur and a knuckle the size of a doorknob had hit my chest, sending me back into the leaves. A chorus of outraged grunts flooded out with an itchy wave of anger, fear, and shock. I wheezed out into the cold air, trying to clutch my own heart and make it stop hammering a dent into my ribs. I wanted the thing to keep pumping enough for me to stay alive, but good god it didn't need to be such an overachiever about it.

As Owen stepped between me and the shadows moving closer, I felt his frustration, heard the angry growls being leveled toward him as he thrashed his arms in communication. He was probably signing something apologetic and explanatory (or possibly agreeing with them that I'm a complete moron; I wouldn't blame him.), but I was too busy coughing into the leaves to pay any attention. Finally, as I was able to take one full breath, I felt a hand on my arm. Owen yanked me upward, turned me to face the creatures. I coughed, doubled over, pressing a hand to my aching ribs.

"Oh god." My voice was strangled as I tried to decide if I wanted to vomit or breathe. Another angry chorus of grunts paired with madly shifting moonlight and I peered up to see both the taller creatures gesticulating wildly.

"Sorry," I wheezed, trying to make them understand that, while I wasn't entirely sure what I'd done, I was damned well never going to it again. "I'm sorry!"

I coughed and Owen grabbed my shoulder, straightening me up. He pointed at me, then at the produce, and finally at the little bigfoots (bigfeet?) clinging to their parents' legs. Then, he made one quick gesture toward them and stopped moving completely. Everyone went silent and I tried to do the same, despite the fact that I was still fighting irritated skin and a pair of lungs that apparently wanted to crawl through my throat and go for a brisk jog.

Finally, as I gave in and coughed, the taller of the two parents lifted its head skyward and let out a series of grunts that sounded like Tim Allen impersonating a gorilla. I lifted a brow at what I recognized as amusement and gave a nod.

"That's right," I said, before groaning at the pain speaking caused. "Laugh at the stupid human. Better than beating her to death, right?"

Owen stepped past me, gestured back toward me, and then signed something quick and concise. The shorter parent signed back, pointed unhappily at me, and then every one of the creatures disappeared from view. I knew they remained there, as my skin still felt like I'd been dunked in cayenne pepper, but I was guessing this meant the meeting was over.

Five

"I think all my ribs are broken," I whined. Owen smiled next to me, but his emotions didn't match the look. He was being nice, but he wasn't exactly happy with me. I turned to point at him accusingly; the motion only made my entire torso ache more.

"Don't pretend this is entirely *my* fault," I snapped. He turned to me, stopped walking. He watched me for a moment and I felt the annoyance within him build. When he spoke, his voice was much too calm for what I felt stirring.

"It isn't?"

"No! You didn't tell me what we were doing or why. You just plopped me down in the middle of a bunch of bigfeet—"

"Bigfoots."

"Shh! In the middle of a group of creatures that could probably eat me alive and then left me to my own devices. You know I am not to be trusted! With anything! Especially not vegetables! Don't put me near those! Come on."

Emotions easing, Owen's lips tugged up in a grin and he stepped closer to wrap his arms around my shoulders. He hugged me as gently as he could and then pulled back to look me over.

"They wouldn't eat you; they're herbivores. But, you're right. I shouldn't have assumed you would be competent."

"Exactly. Now, I need a hospital."

"I don't think so," he said, sliding his hands down my arms.

"But my everything is broken!"

"I'm sure that's not true." Hands on my hips, he dropped to his knees,

29

before reaching up and tugging down the zipper I'd yanked up to my throat.

"If you're trying to seduce me, I have to say your timing is terrible."

He laughed but ignored my unhappy whine as he shoved the hoodie aside and slipped his cold hands under my shirt. Head turned to the side, eyes unfocused, he felt along my ribcage gently. I allowed myself a few whimpers as he prodded, one whine when he pushed gently against my kidney, and a very offensive string of cuss words when his hand hit the space just above my left breast where the sasquatch's knuckle had hit me. Lowering his hands and my shirt, Owen looked up at me.

"Nothing's broken, but I'm sure you're pretty badly bruised. Unless you want to explain this to your family, I'd stick to turtlenecks."

"No hospital?"

"If you really think you should explain to the nice doctors and possibly police officers that you were attacked by a bigfoot because you tried to get to close to their offspring, I guess I can drop you off at a hospital."

"You wouldn't even go in with me?"

"Haven't you even seen an episode of Grey's Anatomy? The first thing they'd do is assume I was abusing you."

"Making me stomp around the woods in this flimsy thing? You kind of are."

"Shh," he chastised, a smirk on his beautiful lips.

I glared down at him, my hands resting on his shoulders. When I didn't have any further smart remarks, he pushed to his feet, catching my snarling lips in a kiss on the way.

"Come on. We can go back to my hotel and I can get you out of that jacket, show you a good time."

"In my state, only cookies and a nap would constitute a good time."

"Are you seriously turning me down for sex?" Despite the shock in his voice, I knew he was teasing. I thought about it. I had shown up two hours before specifically to get laid; was I really about to turn that down because my torso was turning the color of an eggplant?

"Yes," I admitted, my voice small. "It just hurts too much, right now."

"Well, then we'll have to buy you some cookies."

Owen stayed true to his word and bought me cookies, effectively making me forget that he'd been meeting the creatures for an actual reason and not just to get me knocked around. I'd finished off half the plastic tray of chewy chocolate chunks before he'd walked me to my mom's car and kissed me goodbye.

We'd agreed to meet up the next day and I'd promised to get hold of painkillers of some sort to ensure that we could finish what we'd started.

Now that it was morning, I was craving the other half of the tray of cookies, as well as the painkillers that I hadn't figured out how I would procure. I was also hoping that the skinny arm draped over my face would move itself and that the body attached to it would let me free.

"Move," I grunted, still half-asleep. I heard a delicate snort from the person sharing my bed but that didn't faze me as much as the fact that said person had cookie breath. Someone had taken half—make that three quarters—of my bed *and* eaten my cookies? That someone was going to die.

"Hey!" I said, shifting to shove at the narrow ribs pressed against my chest. The arm over my face shifted downward to yank me into a choking hug. I recognized the smell of Chloe's perfume along with a slightly musky body odor that I knew but couldn't quite place.

"Hey," I said again, panicked this time. My brother, having been a teenage boy the last time he'd slept in this room, had put up a pretty heavy-duty pair of black-out curtains; the room was too dark to see much of anything and, unless I was going to shove my guest off the bed onto the floor, I was effectively trapped.

The bony-armed hug let up as a hand reached out to swat at the curtains next to the bed. Light streamed aggressively into the room and I let out a growling yelp, clapping a hand over my eyes and then moving it to clutch at my sore ribs.

"You're making it worse," a voice said. I squinted against the light, recognized the dark hair flopped over the delicate features inches from my face.

"Izzy?"

"Uh huh," he grunted through a giant yawn, before he reached for my arm and pulled it away from my torso. "Don't prod."

"Where—" I looked around the room, suddenly wondering what the hell had happened in the last few hours to make me wake up next to my best friend's boyfriend. "What?"

Izzy shifted to let my arm free and fling his limbs outward in what might have been a stretch, but *could* have been a seizure. I wasn't versed enough in him to know if that was a danger, but I was pretty irritated and told myself I wouldn't have helped if it had been.

"Who, why, when?" Izzy asked after a moment, laughing at his own joke.

"What?" I asked, jerking my head back to avoid another spastic arm flail.

"You said that already. Are there any more cookies?"

"You ate all my cookies!" I accused, reaching out to slap at him. He managed to hop to his feet and avoid my attack at the same time and I grunted painfully as I rolled to follow his movement.

"I figured you left them for me."

"Why would I leave you—what are you *doing* here?" I asked, pushing myself gingerly into a sitting position. Izzy shrugged.

"Was in the area."

"What area?"

"Here," he said, rolling his eyes. "What other area? Jeez. You think there's waffles yet?"

Leaning to the side, Izzy yanked open the closet door, and dropped his narrow butt to the ground as he made a grab for the shoes there. He pulled one bright red sneaker on over his left foot, grabbed a brown, leather loafer and pulled it over his right foot. Lying back, he wiggled his feet up in the air, snorted like something was hilarious and then looked up across the small room at me. I realized he'd put on two left shoes.

"So, you think there's waffles?"

"Do I what?" I asked, shifting against my body's discomfort. My ribs ached and I tugged down the neckline of my sleep shirt to look my chest over. Purple, blue, and deep shades of magenta decorated my collar, breasts, and upper ribs like a smoggy sunset. I winced, barely noticing that Izzy had gotten to his feet to stroll over and look down my shirt at my naked chest. I'd spent enough time around him and could read his emotions well enough to know there was nothing sexual in the glance. Izzy and I could not have been less sexually interested in each other if we were two rocks.

I squinted up at him and let my shirt drop back against my chest. Being Izzy, he bent at the waist, grabbed my shirt and yanked it up so he could see my belly.

"Not so bad down here. You'll be fine in a week or so."

"Why are you here?"

"Depends on when here is," he said, dropping my shirt and grinning into my face. I sighed, already sick of his confusing turns of phrase, even though it had been awhile since I'd last been subjected to them.

Despite his dreadful manners, Izzy is quite a looker. He's small, with fine bones and big eyes; his lips would make any model jealous and the awkward way he carries himself probably would, too. Sometimes he reminds me of a baby deer just learning to walk; other times he kind of looks like an excited puppy taking its first steps on slippery linoleum. Right now, he just reminded me that Chloe probably had no idea he'd come to harass me.

"Does Chloe know you're here?"

"Maybe. So—"

"Don't ask about waffles again. Focus!" I snapped, pointing at his face. His expression got serious, but the gooey emotions in his inhuman mind oozed toward mischief. Despite that, the globule of hunger at the forefront of his mind was still jiggling wildly.

"Like a microscope."

"Why are you here and why were we sleeping together?"

"You were sleeping, I was napping," he said, as if that was a thing. "And there's gonna be waffles. Just maybe not today."

"Gwen, your father said—" I heard mom call from the staircase. Izzy shifted positions, grabbed for a robe hanging next to my brother's bed and tossed it at me. It covered my face and head, making me breathe in my own morning breath. I heard the door creak open, felt my mother's shock and Izzy's delight.

"Cora!"

I yanked the robe down just in time to see Izzy wrap his spidery limbs around my mother and yank her into a hug. I think he started purring, but my mother just looked calmly down at him for a moment, before turning to me curiously.

"Gwen?"

"Ah," I said, clutching the robe close to cover the bruises along my neck. "This is my friend Izzy. He came to visit."

"Oh, all right." My mother nodded, hugging Izzy back absently. When he didn't immediately pull away, she patted his head like I'd seen her do with the kids, and then looked back to me. "I'm not sure we made enough batter, but I can make more. Izzy, do you like waffles?"

"I love waffles," he moaned, bouncing back to clutch his hands together in front of his chest. I glowered at him, feeling lost and out of place, as had become common since Izzy had shown up. Mel and Chloe often treated him like his strange outbursts and excessive energy were normal, leaving me to look like a mad woman when I questioned them. Mom seemed to be in their camp, unbothered by Izzy's weird behavior, acting like he was just another one of the little ones.

"Excellent. I'll go start another batch. Get dressed, chipmunk," she told me. Izzy snorted, pointed at my teeth as she continued. "We'll start eating in about ten minutes. Everyone's already up."

"Ah. Kay," I grunted, still glowering at Izzy.

"Waffles!" he announced, before padding after my mother toward the stairs.

"Marvin, we need to make another batch!" mom yelled. Even from so far away, I felt the spike of annoyance from my father in the kitchen.

"That's what I told you," he groused. As Izzy disappeared down the stairs, I glared after him.

"This is ridiculous," I said to no one, heaving to my feet, and yanking at the robe until I could figure out which part of it was a sleeve. "Crazy fairy … thing … guy, showing up in my room, eating *my* cookies. Stupid Chloe's stupid boyfriend, stupid—"

"Gwen?"

"Ack!" I cried, the picture of grace and poise. Whipping around, I found Natalie peering into the bedroom, watching me have a breakdown. I hadn't even noticed her approach, too caught up in my own rage and pain.

"Are you okay?" she asked. I blinked at her, found that she was mildly concerned about my state of being, but didn't have enough life experience to really recognize insanity well enough to be bothered by it.

"Yeah, I'm okay. My … friend just showed up out of nowhere and I didn't expect him to …" I realized she didn't know what I was talking about. Tugging the robe closed, I smiled, sat on the edge of the bed. "Are you okay?"

"No, what happened to your neck?" she slipped in through the doorway, shoved at her un-brushed blond hair, and came to stand in front of me. We were almost eye-level and I realized that I found her somewhat intimidating.

"Nothing hap—" Cutting me off, she reached out, tucked her small hand under the fuzzy robe and into the neckline of my shirt, pressing warm fingers to my collarbone. I grunted as she did, gasped when I felt the sensation of *healing* seep into my bones. Her narrow nose wrinkled as she leaned into me, as I felt a determined sort of annoyance rattle around inside her. Shocked, I put my hand over hers, felt the heat coming off her knuckles.

It took a few seconds but, when she pulled her hand away, the bruise along my neck had faded. I could barely see it anymore. My ribs and breasts were still tender, but Natalie had managed to take away the marks that would be visible to anyone who wasn't trying to take off my clothes. It seemed that no one would have to know about my injuries except Owen and me. And Izzy, apparently

"Wow," I mumbled. Natalie swallowed thickly, her eyes unfocused for a moment. After a second, she looked into my face.

"Were you hurt by a monkey?"

"Was I?" I asked, my brows shooting up. Exactly what powers did she possess? Robin had never even mentioned to me that her children had inherited the super power gene.

"There's a furry hand when I touch you."

"There is?" I asked, staring incredulously. After a second, Natalie lowered her head and I felt nervous shame flood through her. I reached out, grabbing her shoulders and shaking my head. "No, you're not in trouble. Thank you for helping me. I was … I got too close to an animal's baby and the momma got mad at me. She was just trying to protect her baby, like your mom protects you."

"You're okay, now?"

"Yeah, I'm all better. That was pretty cool, kid."

Natalie's narrow lips split in an adorable grin; I caught sight of a missing tooth off to the left side of her mouth and it made me smile back. All annoyance at Izzy and worry about hiding my injuries flooded away and I yanked Nat close into a hug. She giggled against my cheek and squeezed me back.

"Can we keep this between us?" I asked. "I mean, if your mommy asks you, I don't want you to lie, but I don't want anyone to worry about me."

"Okay," she agreed. I pulled back, looking into her eyes. She wasn't lying, but there's something inherent in the agreement of children that isn't ever quite commitment. Continuing to smile at me, Natalie stood there in her tiny, fuzzy slippers and pink sleep pants.

"I hear there's waffles," I said after a bit. "You in?"

"Okay," she said again, stepping back. Checking myself once more to make sure all signs of sasquatch attack were hidden, I took her hand and led her toward the stairs.

"So, Izzy," Jake said from across the table. "What do you do?"

I could feel his discomfort as he watched Izzy shovel bites of soggy, syrup-soaked waffles and fruit into his mouth. For such a skinny person, he had a really big mouth. People had probably said the same of me, actually. Well, minus the skinny part.

I glanced down at my own syrup-soaked waffles and, despite the weirdness of the situation, felt a little bit of kinship with the gooey-brained creature.

"Dunno," Izzy responded with a mouthful of food. After chewing once and swallowing, he waved his fork around in the air spastically. The only reason sugary, maple-flavored product didn't go everywhere was that he'd slurped it all off the tines.

"I walk. Sometimes I run. I like to play with dogs and meet pigs. Occasionally I'll visit a pub or something." He stabbed at the last giant bite of waffle and stuffed it into his mouth just as my mother approached with another tray, scooping his fourth helping onto his plate. He grinned up at her and I felt a little puff of affection cloud around her. Mom's happiest when those around her are well-fed and joyful.

"You don't have a job?" Jake asked. I felt a rope of frustration whip out of my father and slap against my chest.

"He's obviously not human, Jake. He doesn't have a job."

"He's what?" Jake asked.

"I have a job," Izzy groused. I flinched at the shock crackling out of my brother-in-law, but I reached out to touch his arm, jolting when his anxiety seemed to leap from him to me. It wasn't conscious, but that happened occasionally, emotions seeming to flee their owners as if I were shelter from a storm. Jake seemed to relax, but only minutely, and I jerked my hand back, unwilling to let any more of his panic take up residence in my gut.

Izzy continued eating while those around us seemed to wait for him to elaborate. Only the sounds of munching filled the air for about a minute until I realized he wasn't going to explain. Jake's shock was burbling into worry, which made me feel bad, even though we weren't touching anymore.

"He's harmless," I offered, hoping to ease Jake's mind. Izzy snorted at my words, but kept eating. I glared but continued. "He's dating my—Chloe, you know Chloe! He and Chloe are going out."

"Then why is he here with you?"

"Um," was my only answer. For another minute, silence struggled against the crisp shrieks of utensils scraping against plates as Izzy, Natalie, and Jake Junior finished up. Finally, Stella burbled spit across her plate and Robin snorted out a nervous laugh.

"Is he why you haven't been calling much, lately?" she asked. I turned to her slowly, partly to keep an eye on my uninvited guest and partly because I didn't know the answer to her question without lying.

"Ah. Sort of?" I turned back halfway, tried to catch Izzy's eye, in hopes he'd help me out with the familial interrogation. Mostly he'd proven useless, but there had been a few times when he'd effectively saved the day. As it was, I really only needed him help me save face.

"Izzy helps me out with my clients," I finally said. My father barked out a laugh, like he could tell I was lying, but I ignored him. "I've been taking on … more than just my usual type of clients. Izzy helps out with that."

Izzy finished eating, leaning back in his chair and catching my eye, before jerking a thumb toward my dad as if he had something to say. He didn't speak, but Robin stood up to grab Stella and carry her toward the downstairs bathroom, and dad grunted unpleasantly.

"What?" I demanded. He refused to meet my gaze and I struggled against the crackle of tension running between us. Jake spoke up, getting back to the main problem that we were all really having, whether we were aware of it or not.

"He's not human?" Jake repeated.

"It's okay, daddy," Natalie announced, reaching to pat her father's hand. Jake turned to look helplessly down at her and then up at me. I shrugged.

"I don't know—he's—uh, harmless."

Rather than mock my assessment of him again, Izzy hopped to his feet, singing Chloe's name eagerly. Mom skirted him calmly as he whooshed past, barely noticing. As he disappeared through the kitchen, she came to sit down at the table next to my father.

"You should tell us when you're inviting friends into our house," my dad said, his unhappy gaze leveled at me.

"I didn't invite anyone!"

"Marvin, *listen* to her," my mother murmured, patting his hand. My father rolled his eyes, shaking his head rapidly as if he wanted to continue to argue, but went quiet.

"Hi all," Chloe said from behind me. I whipped around, smacking my leg into Robin's empty chair, and bit my lip before I could cuss in front of the kids. I hadn't even noticed she'd arrived. The crackle of antagonism between my father and me was only partly to blame. There were so many people in the house, I couldn't barely pick anyone out—though I can always recognize my father as the most unpleasant man in the house—and Chloe's low level of apprehension was unusual, at least for her.

"What are you doing here?" I asked, getting to my feet as Chloe leaned in for a hug.

"Later," she whispered almost imperceptibly into my ear, before moving back and reaching a hand out to Jake. "You're Jake, right? I think we met once, but it was—"

"Online," Jake said, controlling his distrust of Izzy in order to be polite. "And I think I was covered in baby vomit, so I'm sure the resemblance to my former self is hard to grasp."

"I'm Jake, too!" my nephew announced, before folding a piece of waffle the size of the Chrysler building into his mouth and chewing with his mouth open.

"Nice to meet you, Jake-two," Chloe shifted to hold out a hand to my father, who was watching her with a fair amount of suspicion. It annoyed me.

"Dad, be nice."

"I'm being nice," he argued, his annoyance arcing out to whip me across the cheek. "Considering there are a hundred people in my house and some of them weren't invited."

"Hey," Izzy said, sliding Natalie's waffles off her plate and into his. "I invited Chloe."

"He did," she said, her lip tugging up as she watched Natalie try to be secretive about sliding a bowl of fruit out from in front of her father and over toward Izzy. "But I should have called first, I'm sorry."

"I know you are," dad said, sort of dismissively, before going back to the last few bites of his waffles. Chloe hooked an arm around my shoulders, tugging me subtly the way she'd come. "Come, G, let's talk."

Olivia R. Burton

Six

"Sonny's fine," Chloe said as she led me out through the front door. "And so is Rupert, though I know you'd never ask."

"Ugh," was all I could manage. Without asking me, Chloe had adopted a giant, grumpy-faced, ginger cat to live at the office and terrorize me on a daily basis. Most of the clients were thrilled with her presence, despite her misgendered name, but I didn't see the appeal. Cats and I generally don't get along.

"Betty and Mel are feeding her, though I'm assuming Betty's doing most of the actual work. Sonny and Poopy are staying with a friend of mine—a bird expert," Chloe said, anticipating my argument. "He's likely better off with Lydia than with me, in fact."

"No, I get it. I trust you," I admitted. Chloe's been vegan since well before I'd met her and she puts little above animal welfare. "Did he miss me?"

"You should ask Izzy, he'd know."

"I'll pass," I said, not thrilled with the prospect. "What's he doing here, anyway? And you, what made you come? I begged you to join me for weeks and you kept refusing."

"I wasn't going to set aside my whole life just to babysit you in front of your family, but Izzy asked me to come, said I should bring some things. He said some stuff's going on and you're gonna need my help."

"How does he know?"

"What do you mean? You know what he can do."

I grunted at her; I did know. For the last year, Izzy had become somewhat integral to solving my problems, even though I hadn't known it until a few months ago. He could see the future, despite the fact that he never quite seemed clear on it. Sometimes the things he'd told me were incredibly useful, like when he'd pointed out that my ex-husband's stalker was the same killer Owen was hunting. Other times, his insights were fairly useless, like when he'd told me that one day I would have babies and that they would be adorable.

Of course my babies would be adorable; look at the genetics I share.

"That still doesn't explain why you two are here. Though, I bet it explains why Owen's here."

"Owen's here?" she asked, alarm bells jangling through her. They weren't the size of church bells or anything, but I could feel apprehension and nervous energy clattering and it made me tense. "Did he say why?"

"He's not really the sharing type, but we did go meet some," I wiggled my fingers, "*sources*, which turned out to be sasquatches who hated my guts."

"You?" Chloe asked, making it clear her over the top disbelief was false. "But you're such a delight!"

Resisting the urge to sock her in the arm, I pressed on. "He talked—well, I guess they don't talk, but they … uh, signed, a bunch of stuff and then they hit me."

"Just out of the blue?" Chloe cocked her head, clearly suspicious of my version of events. "You wouldn't have been trying to steal their food, so I'm guessing you got too close to one of their kids?"

"How could you *know* that? Any of it!"

Chloe just shook her head, laughing quietly to herself before patting my shoulder and taking a deep breath. She paused for a bit, looking like she was thinking about something, before I felt that apprehension back.

"Owen didn't mention anything about why he's here?"

"Once I got punched in the boob by a fist the size of my head I lost interest, honestly. Why?"

"You said he was a mercenary," Chloe said, and I felt the barest sliver of dishonesty slicing at the end of the last word.

"I did?"

"Um," she corrected, "well, you said he hunts things. He was there to kill Norma, right? He doesn't work for the cops and kills things for money. Pretty sure that's the textbook definition of mercenary."

"Yeah, okay," I agreed, though it did make my stomach do a little jump to think I was dating a mercenary. It sounded so dangerous and like it could one day involve a lot of jungles and maybe the Italian government.

"So, he's here for something dangerous, Izzy's here and wanted me here, so we have to figure something's up. Has anything been going on?"

"I just got here, I don't know. Why would Izzy want *you* here, anyway? Just to protect me? Because I've got Owen if I need my body closely guarded."

"We can ask him," Chloe suggested. I gasped, an idea suddenly coming to mind.

"When I asked why Izzy was in my bed this morning, he said he was in the area. What if he's what Owen's after?"

Chloe's snort of derision burst out of her like an exploding watermelon, making me step back and try to rub away the heavy, thick feeling before it could disappear from my chest. As I grunted against the false feeling of being pelted with wet fruit, she shook her head.

"No, he's not that stupid."

"Izzy? I beg to differ."

"Owen," Chloe corrected, before hooking her arm around my shoulder and leading me back toward the house. "Come on, let's get you dressed and ready for the day. You can come with me to check-in to my hotel, get you away from your dad for a bit."

I wanted to press harder on the Izzy thing, but the idea of getting out of the house for an hour or so was so appealing I let it go.

"Hey, this is Owen's hotel," I said as we pulled up outside. Chloe nodded, as if that were obvious to everyone.

"Well, it's the only one in town."

"It's not the *only* one," I argued, though I hadn't been around in awhile and I had no way of verifying the others I remembered from childhood still existed. Chloe gave me a look that took me a moment to decipher. "I mean, is it?"

"It's not the *only* one, but it's the only one that wouldn't make me bunk with roaches."

"But you love all creatures!" I teased.

"Not believing we have a right to kill them and wanting to have them crawling all over me are two entirely different things." Chloe paused and then chuckled to herself. "It's like you and Mel."

I wrinkled my nose at the idea of him ever crawling all over me again.

"I'll be right back. You two make nice," Chloe said as she opened the door. Then, quickly, as if tossing a live grenade, "There are chocolates in the console!"

"Chocolates?" Izzy and I both asked at the same time as she slammed the door and scurried off. I didn't even get a chance to search for them; Izzy snaked his hand over, yanked open the lid, and grabbed the bag before I'd even finished speaking. I glowered at him, but it was a bag of dark chocolate so I could probably survive if he refused to share.

Around the fourth time he'd stuff a whole square into his mouth, I jerked my chin at him, my curiosity getting the best of me.

41

"Why were you in the area?"

"Just sorta worked out that way, I think." Izzy frowned, considering as he chewed. "Is it Thursday?"

"Does it matter?" I asked, genuinely curious whether or not that mattered to whatever he was. Absently, still frowning at the ceiling of the car as if it had wronged him, he handed me a small stack of foil-wrapped candies, delighting me and ending my train of thought. We snacked in silence for a moment, before I considered the scene as a whole. The hotel seemed quiet, though I couldn't feel the far end of it. The whole town felt quiet, actually, which was strange. Sure, it could have been that I was used to the emotional hustle and bustle of Seattle, but something still didn't feel right to my empathy.

Holding my hand out for more candy, I jerked my chin at Izzy.

"What's up? Why are you here? Why's Chloe here?" Reconsidering, lifting a brow and hoping for the best as he set two more chocolates in my palm, I pressed on. "Why's Owen here?"

"He likes you," Izzy said, as if it were the most obvious answer.

"He's not here for me," I said, stuffing both chocolates into my mouth.

"No," Izzy agreed, before scrunching up his face as if trying to remember something. "But you're the deer with the bullethole."

"What?" I demanded, horrified by the mental image. Izzy shook his head.

"No, that's not right. What'd she …? The—you're the whatzit. Um." He seemed to genuinely consider his words for a while, but Chloe's reappearance distracted him and he grinned at her with chocolate-stained teeth as she climbed back in.

"I knew the candy would keep you two from coming to blows," she said, pleased at her genius.

"It's dark chocolate, though," Izzy and I said at the same time. I glared his way, not sure if our shared reaction had been genuine or some trick he and his foresight were playing. Chloe laughed, starting the car, and pulling out of the temporary spot.

I didn't dare head upstairs with Chloe and Izzy, even though she swore they were just going to drop some stuff off and be right back down. I hid in the car with the rest of the chocolates rather than risk seeing them give in to their constant desire to get carnal. I'd accidentally walked in on that show one time too many already.

They were back before long—though not before I'd eaten way too much of the chocolate, according to Chloe—and we were on our way. I'd been somewhat disappointed to not feel Owen's low-key emotions from my seat in the car, but it hadn't really surprised me. He was there for work, not just to be ogled by me and my hormones, despite what Izzy had suggested.

Around the time we were in a normally crowded section of downtown, I looked around, curious about the lack of activity. Balanis had never been a bustling metropolis, but it had its share of activity, if only kids skipping school and hanging out in parks or in front of convenience stores aiming to buck expectations and flaunt their rule-breaking prowess. Since getting back, though, it all seemed off, slower somehow.

"Is it quiet or is it just me?" I asked, not really expecting Chloe to know the answer, but feeling the need to vocalize my question regardless.

"I don't know, it seems like a typical small town to me. Why?"

"It just … it feels weird."

"Maybe you're used to Seattle," Chloe suggested, before slowing slightly and leaning forward to scan one of the buildings across the street. "Should we get your mom flowers?"

"Why?" I asked, still stuck on the idea that maybe I'd just gotten so used to Seattle's constant emotional hammering of my empathy, wondering if it was just that simple.

"Because she's a lovely woman and she had to feed Izzy this morning."

"Hey," Izzy said, though he didn't sound insulted exactly, more like he was concerned she'd misunderstood the situation. "She didn't have to, I can survive without food."

"You can?" I asked, shocked both because that in and of itself was a revelation and because Izzy had a nasty habit of eating everything in sight as if he'd wither up and die the instant he didn't have food in his guts.

"I'm getting her flowers," Chloe said, pulling into a parking spot with an adeptness that never failed to amaze me. The rental car was compact, but she managed to fit into a space that looked like it would have had trouble accommodating even a fat Labradoodle. "You coming in?"

"Sure," I said, as Izzy announced, "nope." He got out of the car alongside us, but veered off toward an alley down the way, perplexing me as he always did. Chloe ignored his strange behavior, and headed straight for the florist. We got all the way to the door before Chloe noticed the small, hand-written sign on it that said, "Closed due to family emergency. Thank you for your understanding," in bright red marker. The writing was just barely legible, a downward-sloping scribble on a piece of printer paper that looked like it had caught the edge of a coffee spill at some point.

"Aww, man," Chloe said, genuinely bothered by the fact that she couldn't bring my mom a gift. "I can probably grab something from the grocery store, you think?"

"Yeah, probably. I wonder what the emergency was," I considered aloud, turning to look at the street with the same concern I'd churned up when we'd been driving. "You think it's the zombie apocalypse?"

"Starting conveniently here in your home town?" Chloe asked, leading me back toward the car. "Maybe that's why Owen's here."

"You think?" I asked, alarmed. She laughed and shook her head.

"No, I think someone's dad had a heart attack or someone's mom fell down some stairs. Come on, show me where a grocery store is."

Izzy was already back in the car as if he'd never left, whistling a tune I didn't recognize, and didn't acknowledge us as we climbed back in. I didn't say anything as Chloe pulled away from the curb, still lost in my worried suspicion that something was fishy in Balanis.

Luckily for all of us, my father had disappeared out into his shed, which he'd configured years before as his own, temperature-controlled man cave. I'd never ventured inside myself, but Thomas had assured me it's basically just a television, a comfy chair, and a perch for Dorian.

Mom loved the flowers, hugging Chloe tightly and showing them off to everyone as if they were made of platinum and not petals. When Chloe offered to help out with cleaning the kitchen and making lunch, mom got excited, diving into a deep discussion of Chloe's veganism and healthy eating—blaming me for her knowledge of both. She didn't outright *say* I'd complained ad nauseum about Chloe's insistence on feeding me vegetables, but the implication that I whine about it a lot was there.

No one except Jake and me seemed to mind Izzy's presence; in fact, the kids loved him. Not only could he make interesting sounds and voices, but he also didn't mind the fact that half their toys were sticky and smelled funny. In fact he probably added to both, which made him an ideal companion for children.

I got a call from Owen around noon and I was only too happy to escape the emotions of the house and flee out front to speak to him in private.

"Please say you're calling to tell me you're on your way to pick me up," I answered. Owen chuckled, and I had no doubt that his aforementioned resources had already fed him my parents' address and, hell, maybe even their favorite foods and social security numbers.

"I was, though not for what you'd hope. Unless something changes, I will be free for that tonight, but in the mean time, I have some things to take care of. I'd still like to see you, though, and you've got that helpful skill so I'm hoping you'll join me."

"What is it this time? More mercenaries? Another succubus? Shoe-cobbling goblins out to destroy every high heel in the land?"

"Goblins don't—"

"Hush," I warned. His laugh was low and it made me think sexy thoughts. I hadn't found any painkillers, but I was sure my ribs wouldn't bitch too much if I just stayed on top during sex.

"I'm just going back into the forest," he said after a moment.

"Brushing up on your Swahili?"

"I don't believe I know Swahili, nor any creatures that speak it. I've got a hypothesis to test."

"Well, that doesn't sound dangerous at all," I said, considering his offer.

"Thus the invitation. I like to live on the edge and danger follows you like toilet paper stuck to a shoe."

I sighed dramatically, making it known the accusation didn't exactly make me feel charitable. He laughed again and I had to admit he was right. Even at work it seemed I was running into open drawers and clipping doorways with my shoulders more often than I had throughout my entire childhood.

"Fine. Can I meet you at your hotel again?"

"No need, I really am on my way to pick you up."

"That might be a bad idea," I said, thinking of my mother's penchant for interrogating any men in my life. Robin's three kids are not enough for her; my mother wants a hundred grandbabies to spoil and I just happen to be of childbearing age. She was still unhappy that I'd let my ex-husband Stan slip away; if she caught sight of Owen's blue eyes and straight teeth she'd be three florists and a caterer deep into planning the wedding.

"Let me know when you're close and I'll meet you on the corner."

"You have to sneak out at your age?"

"Pretty much, yeah," I admitted.

"Well, we can work out a complicated series of signals. I'm sure I can find a flashlight to blink through your bedroom window—or maybe I should bring some flags? Can you understand semaphore?"

"If that's not a delicious chocolate dessert, I'm not interested. Just send a text when you're nearby."

"Are you sure? I *may* be able to get hold of a carrier pigeon."

I hung up on him.

Olivia R. Burton

Seven

As I buckled myself into Owen's car, he reached a hand out, tucked it into my jacket and tugged the fabric away from my chest. I blinked over at him as he inspected the skin beneath.

"That's looking suspiciously good," he said as he shifted to put the car into gear. I grinned.

"Oh," I breathed. "Thank you, Doctor."

"I was talking about your bruises, but your knockers are nice, too."

I chuckled, shifted forward to turn the heater up. Owen ignored my action, driving us out of my neighborhood at a nice, grandfatherly pace.

"My niece is apparently a healer."

"Nice. Which type?"

"What do you mean?" I asked. He glanced over at me long enough to see if I was serious.

"I'm surprised you don't know."

"I've only met two. There isn't exactly a clubhouse where humans with minor powers go to hang out and talk shop."

"Of course not; that would make it much too easy to take you all out at once."

"Ha ha," I said, squinting over at him. His smirk turned into a full on smile when he realized I didn't find his joke funny.

"There are, as far as I've come across, two types of physical healers. There are psychic healers, but they don't apply here. One takes on the pain that they heal, though not the injury itself. So, if you break your leg and they fix it, they feel the pain for a few hours—sometimes days. They are much better at healing and can often handle much more, but it takes its toll. The

47

other sees the injury they fix and experience the emotional impact of what it was to get hurt. They can generally sense when those around them are hurt, too."

"That one, I think." I jabbed a finger into the air next to him, as if that would help make my point. "After she healed the bruise at my collar, she said she could see a furry hand hit me. She didn't seem too bothered by it, though."

"Were you?"

"Bothered by being beaten down by a sasquatch? Damn straight I was."

"I mean," he said through a laugh. "That you were more shocked than anything. Did you even realize what had happened as it hit you?"

"Ah," I murmured, thinking about it. "I guess not."

"Well, there you go."

"And where we go?" I asked, deciding it was time for a change of subject. "What are we doing today?"

"Like I said, we're investigating."

"What are we investigating? Is it dirty?"

"Not in the fun way." Owen went quiet for a bit, before looking over at me with a lifted brow. "Can you be discreet?"

"Who am I going to tell?" I asked, throwing up my hands. "I haven't even told my sister I work in the same building as a werewolf, and my father and I can't even look at each other. Your secrets are safe with me."

"Hmm," he considered, as if he didn't believe me. Then, after another few seconds, he continued. "About three months ago, four campers went missing. One was found a few days later, but he *conveniently* had amnesia."

"Conveniently?"

"For him and the doctors trying to figure out what's wrong with him, no. For me, yes. It's sometimes how you know something otherworldly is up. Recently, another pair of hikers disappeared, though no one's shown up with missing memories, yet."

"So we're going to search for an amnesiac wandering around the woods, alone and confused?"

"Alone, yes; confused, hopefully not. If I can get someone to just tell me what I need to kill, we can just go straight back to the hotel and do that catching up we missed out on last night."

"I'm not completely healed, Romeo." When he looked over and gave me a small pout, I grinned. "But I'm sure we can work something out."

"Well, then keep your empathy out for any half-dead hikers."

"Sad image," I said. "But good band name."

Half an hour of walking through the woods had netted us nothing. I felt the usual bunnies, birds, and other small, furry creatures around us, but there was no sign of a befuddled backpacker or malevolent monster that I could pick up.

"What do you think this thing is?" I asked. Owen shrugged, the picture of nonchalance, even as a slice of worry cut through him. He grabbed my arm and tugged me away from a patch of leafy plants before I could put my sockless, loafered foot right down into them. I eyed the mess of leaves as we walked by, deciding I'd almost stepped in poison oak.

"I have a few theories, but without knowing more, I can't pick one. Hundreds of things live in the forest and eat humans if they get a chance. The only reason we know it's not a mountain lion or a bear attack is that one person survived with amnesia."

"What did the bigfoots say about the situation?" Owen shrugged but before he could answer, another question popped into my brain. "And how do they know sign language?"

"As far as I know, one of your types taught them in the seventies—eighteen-seventies, that is."

"An empath?"

"Not necessarily," he said, stopping for a moment to grab a metal bottle out of his backpack. He took a swig and offered it to me. He waited for me to finish drinking before speaking.

"Just a human who could sense them. Here, they're ASL exclusive, though; as far as I know the sasquatches in other countries wouldn't be able to understand me."

"That's nuts," I said, thinking about the fact that a human had just decided one day to teach a bigfoot a new skill and the bigfoot had been not only keen enough to learn, but game enough to teach others.

"It's not that unusual. All sorts of fae creatures who can't speak like humans learn how to communicate. Some are multi-lingual, some learn the basics and just flail through getting their point across. Sorta like you when you're sleepy." I ignored the dig.

"So don't travel to Austria and try to talk to a Chupacabra, got it."

"There aren't any—"

"I don't care," I said, leaning close with a smile. He let me kiss him but finished his sentence before he let me pull completely away.

"Chupacabras in Austria."

"What if one is on vacation?"

"Then it's going to have a hell of a time getting directions to the bar."

I shook my head at him before stepping back and turning to survey the area around us. He grabbed the bottle from my hand and stuck it back into his pack.

"Have you done your testing yet?"

"In a manner of speaking," he said, without elaborating. I waited a moment, before realizing he wasn't going to.

"Okay. Should I be looking for something specific?"

"Just evidence that someone was here. I don't know the exact trail the hikers may have taken, but I know from their friends that they usually entered the forest somewhere around where we did."

"So we're hiking blind?"

"I will be able to get us out. Don't worry."

"I'm going to keep worrying. The outdoors and I don't get along so well."

"Is that so?" he asked, turning a smile on me that probably read as condescending but that I chose to take as curious.

"It is. Last time I was left alone in the forest I ended up glued to a wall with spider poop."

"Stop, you're getting my engine revving."

I laughed at his deadpan tone, whacking him with the back of my hand lightly, and he chuckled, catching my hand and giving my knuckles an absent-minded kiss.

"You feel anything?" he asked after a moment. I shrugged a shoulder and he pressed on. "Just uh—feel out, see if something reads off one way or another. If something's eating people, it probably doesn't garner the love and trust of other creatures. Good chance that wherever it hangs out will be pretty empty."

"Nothing's really empty," I argued and he glanced my way as if expecting me to explain. "There are always … things around. Birds, gophers, moles, bugs, you know."

"That's my point," he said, his speaking slowly as if talking to a child. "If this thing is grumpy and angry, it could scare off anything that might normally hang out. Look for empty pockets that should have some sort of life but don't."

"Oh," I said, getting it. "Right, okay." Then, because he looked too smug for my liking, I jabbed my finger into his ribs. "You are going to owe me so much sex for this."

He just wagged his brows and winked.

Closing my eyes, I took a deep breath, did my best to extend my mental feelers out as far as it could go. My range isn't incredible, but I can usually catch emotions from one end of a large house to another if I'm really trying. Focusing my attention on my empathy, I did my best to ignore my other senses. I breathed through my mouth, concentrating on only what I felt through my empathy rather that smells and sounds.

There were birds, small mammals of all types, a deer off in the distance—bringing up the unpleasant image Izzy had conjured earlier. I made a mental note to ask Owen about that later, though I could probably be certain he'd have no idea what I was talking about.

None of the normal forest dwellers seemed scared or nervous; none of them struck me as though they feared for their tiny lives. I couldn't feel any creatures out there slavering over my organs or any people desperate for rescue. Something felt off near the river, but that was about it. Opening my eyes, I stared off into the distance where I'd felt one slimy jolt of surprise from a fish as it had swum into my psychic range.

"I'm getting something strange over there, but I can't really tell what it is."

"Let's go, then." Owen hooked an arm in mine and we started moving closer to the water. As we did, I caught traces of more fish feelings and a few frustrated squirrels. We stopped near the edge of the river and I looked up, trying to figure out what I'd found. Something breezed into my brain from above, but my eyes couldn't see anything. In fact, I wasn't even sure I was feeling anything strange at all.

"I may just be cold," I admitted.

"You're sure?"

"No," I reconsidered, feeling pressured, second-guessing myself. I did my best to prod further into the leaves above, trying to dislodge any feeling, trying to make something nervous or curious enough to know for sure if there was anything there to make nervous at all.

"I don't know. There could be something there, but … I don't know, maybe it's something but it's just not feeling anything. Or maybe it's nothing and I'm just hungry."

"Hey!" Owen yelled suddenly, his booming voice making me jump.

"Jesus!" I snapped. "What—"

Then, looking back up into the trees, slightly to the left of where I'd been looking before, I got it. There was something up there and Owen had startled it, ever so briefly. Following my gaze, Owen stepped forward, keeping an eye on what appeared to just be leaves and silence.

"I don't see anything," I whispered, "but there was something there for a second."

"Do you know what it was?"

"No," I said, shaking my head. Still, nothing appeared to us. "Just that you startled it for a second. Now I feel almost nothing again."

"Hmm," he said, still as stoic as ever.

"Did I do good?" I asked. He stayed in place, staring upward, foot just at the edge of the river.

"I'm going to need more than just you, I think," he said, finally. Turning bodily toward me, he glanced around the forest again, his strong jaw locked as if he'd made a hard decision.

"We good?" I asked, bracing in case he yelled again. He gave it a beat before looking to me and smiling, the appearance of it genuine, even though there was nothing behind it. While I'd never felt honestly threatened by or worried about Owen, the smile reminded me how good he was at faking emotions out in the real world. As he slipped an arm around my shoulders and led me back the way we'd come, I looked up at his pretty face, wondering how much of his daily emotional displays were nothing but habit and how many were real. I wondered as we moved in silence what that must be like to have to hide yourself from the world around rather than risk your life being honest.

Eight

"You're bringing me to a bar? You don't drink." Owen smiled at me, reached out to unbuckle my seatbelt.

"Bars are a great place to hear crazy stories. Plus, I think if I liquor you up, having sex with you might not hurt your ribs quite so much."

I laughed, watched as he got out of the car. He probably had a point, though I usually avoid drinking in the presence of others because of how it so unpleasantly magnifies my empathy.

Not So Sober is a tidy sports bar tucked into a strip mall lot toward the edge of town. The building itself had been around much longer than the strip mall, though they kept the inside up well enough that you couldn't really tell. It got business this early in the evening by serving hot wings and fries and, of course, copious amounts of beer. I reached the door as Owen pulled it open for me and stepped into a thick, slightly woozy emotion soup.

Among others, there were a few drunks, a couple depressed layabouts, two men who were clearly there solely to get laid, and the waitresses who were sick of being hit on. It wasn't overly busy for three o'clock, but there were enough people in the building that I knew I didn't really want to be there. As we stepped in, Owen looked around, lifted a brow at the sign on the wall stating that the establishment refused to serve bears.

"What's that about?" he asked. I shrugged a shoulder, put a hand to my temple as if I could shove the pain out if I pushed hard enough.

"Old story, not even sure if it's true. Apparently when it first opened, a bear just wandered on in one afternoon, sat down at the bar."

"Did it order anything?"

"If I had to guess, I'd say fish sticks."

Owen put a hand around my back, settled his palm on my waist, and pushed me in toward a table near a window, pulling out my chair and scanning the people at the bar as if he were the Terminator. After a few seconds, he turned back to me, still close. I felt a bit of pity slide into his psyche and figured I must've looked like shit.

"What's your poison?" he asked as the door to the bar creaked noisily open and shut.

"This place, I think," I said, putting a hand to my forehead as I dropped into the offered chair. "I don't really do bars."

"I'll try to make it quick." He leaned down, gave me a quick kiss on the knuckles, stood, and then turned to go. Immediately, he was stopped by a brunette who smiling pleasantly at Owen as if they were old friends. Despite the expression, she was raring for a fight, her insides crackling and hissing like a cornered cat.

Owen slammed to a halt, surprise and annoyance arcing through him like electricity. Quick as a coiled snake, malice swiped, raking out of him like a lasso coated in razorblades. I felt myself shrink back from the pain of his emotions before my eyes flicked from the woman's face to the side of his. If I hadn't been an empath, I would have had no idea he was unhappy with her; his body language and expression were mild as he looked down at her.

"Veronica," he said quietly. She continued to smile up at him, but tipped her head slightly.

"Who?" she asked. Slivers of annoyance crept out of her meant for him, but her mask was just as convincing as his. I considered her as they squared off, running my gaze from her sturdy but well-worn leather boots to her sensible, fitted jacket.

She was thick, but I could tell from the way her pants hugged her thighs that it was all muscle. She had dark brown eyes and deep brown hair shaved along the sides, left longer atop the middle. The tip of her short Mohawk was the same shade of purple as my fresh bruises, barely brighter than the rest of her hair in the dim light. She wore almost no makeup, but had curved black eyeliner across her eyelids to curl at the corners. Her lips were parted just enough that I could see a slight gap between her two front teeth; it did nothing to detract from her looks and, in fact, made her face more interesting.

His smile grew, as if he could tell he'd gotten to her.

"Kincade," he said after a moment. Her smirk sharpened and she lifted a hand to touch his arm. He let her but I had the feeling he wouldn't have if they'd met anywhere other than a public bar.

"How are you, Owen?" she asked, leaning up to kiss his cheek. Again, he let her, but it felt like she'd have been on her ass if she'd tried such a thing anywhere else. Squinting up at them, I wondered about their history. Stepping to the side, Owen deliberately pulled his arm away from her, turned so he could easily see us both at the same time.

"Gwen, this is Kincade." His tone indicated he was bored, but the malice was still there under the calm surface.

"Hello," she said, her eyes darting to me. She gave me the once over, eyes sliding across me with a slight look of disgust. I could tell she meant it to appear as if she was judging whether or not I was a threat to her socially, but that wasn't it. She wasn't worried I was going to steal her boyfriend or hit on her husband; her curiosity was selfishly motivated, maybe wondering how I might affect her conversation with Owen, or if I might offer her the same malice he was so easily hiding.

"You two friends?" I asked, knowing the answer. Kincade's smile returned and she looked back up at Owen.

"What do you say, darling? Are we friends?"

"We've had sex, but it was never exactly friendly."

"And I tried to kill you," she said with a wink. "Don't forget about that." Owen shrugged, loosely.

"You were hardly threat enough to remember."

She threw back her head and laughed, her other hand coming up to touch his arm again as if she found his comment so endearingly amusing she couldn't help but flirting. Underneath it, anger boiled. I made a small groaning sound and brought my other hand to my head.

"Your girlfriend's got a hangover, darling," Kincade said. I ignored her, but Owen seemed to find her comment funny.

"Hair of the dog. What are you doing here?" he asked. I peered through my fingers and found that she'd shifted positions, hands loose at her sides. Her expression was still flirty and cocky, but she was annoyed with him again—or possibly still.

"Just in town visiting friends."

"You don't have friends. You on the job?"

I felt a bit of surprise blossom in Kincade and I watched her lift a brow, turn her attention fully to me as if she suddenly found me interesting.

"What does your friend here know about you exactly?" she asked. Owen shook his head, still looking as if she was no more interesting than an ant on his boot.

"Enough."

"So she's not on the job?" she asked. Owen snorted, shook his head. When he didn't explain, Kincade glanced at him, then back to me. "Fuck buddy, then?"

I decided I wanted her to go away. Her frustration that she couldn't get a rise out of Owen was beginning to make me feel ill. Pushing to my feet, I got as in her face as I could manage, grabbed her hand and pumped it up and down.

"Gwen Arthur, Fuck Buddy. Nice to meet you. Wonderful lay, isn't he? Really sticks it to you good."

Kincade's emotions shifted slightly, leaving the burning landscape of passion and hate in favor the cooler, more temperate terrain of amusement and delight. I sighed a bit, dropping her hand as I turned back to Owen, giving him my full attention as if she no longer existed.

"I know your whole plan was to get me drunk, but really, I'll fuck you sober. I mean look at you. I don't have a quarter, but trust me: I could bounce it. Come on, sunshine. We can go back to my place and I'll show you a good time."

"I guess we're leaving," Owen said, nodding to Kincade curtly as he bumped her slightly so he could lead me toward the door. I didn't look her way as we exited and neither did Owen, but it didn't aggravate her as I'd expected it to.

"I'll see you again soon, lover," Kincade called as we hit the door. "You too, Owen."

"Well that was incredibly unpleasant," I said once we were in the car and driving back toward the hotel.

"Indeed," Owen said. I turned to him and realized he wasn't listening. I poked at his emotions and tried to discern what was going on in his brain. After a few minutes he turned to me as he pulled up to a red light. "Sorry, what?"

"I said that sucked."

He smiled, turned his attention back toward the traffic ahead, and tapped his left foot. "What about it sucked for you?"

"She hates you," I said. "Like a kid who hasn't studied hates a pop quiz from their meanest teacher. No, worse. Like I hate being forced to eat a plate full of steamed broccoli." Own laughed, but a small bubble of surprise burst inside him, splashing me lightly and making me absently rub at my skin.

"Really?"

"You didn't know?"

"I know we don't get along, that there's a …" Hesitation covered up a slight river of dishonesty. "Professional rivalry, but I didn't realize it was broccoli strong."

"You don't hate her?" I asked, laughing lightly at his term

"I want to punch her, but I don't hate her."

"Huh," I said, my laughter died down as I wondered if I was really enlightened enough to be okay with Owen wanting to hit a woman. He seemed to sense my thought process.

"She'd hit me first if she had the chance. I promise you."

"Hmm," I grunted, refusing to agree or disagree.

"You're not mad at me for saying I'd hit a woman, are you?"

"I'm not sure," I admitted. He sighed, irked. "It's just weird. I guess it makes sense; if she had different genitalia, it wouldn't bother me. I'm not sure if that makes me sexist."

"The only reason she didn't kill me was that I got lucky," he explained. I grinned.

"You bribed her not to shoot you by nailing her?"

He snorted, laughed a bit. "I didn't mean it that way; we'd already slept together. I honestly mean that it was only luck that saved my life. She tried to blow me up."

"No wonder you want to punch her."

"She's not that handy with explosives. Or, she wasn't back then; she's probably gotten better."

"She looked pretty handy with other things, though," I commented, thinking about her physique. "I'm surprised she didn't take you out with those thighs, just suffocate you dead or break your neck."

Owen laughed and his amusement rolled through me like a steam engine. By the time his voice settled, I had joined him, giggling despite the fact that I hadn't found my own joke all that funny. As we pulled into the hotel parking lot, I asked the question knocking around in my head.

"Why'd she try to blow you up?" Owen backed into a spot, glanced out at the sprinkling rain starting to come down. After a few moments, his gaze fell to me and I gave a small smile, hoping to encourage his explanation rather than his habitual evasion.

"She was hired to." He unbuckled my seatbelt again and I wondered if he thought I was too stupid to figure out such complicated puzzles as seatbelts or if he just often thought I took too long to get out of the damn car. As his hand went to his door latch, he smiled a bit. "Madeline hired her, actually."

My brows shot up and Owen twisted to get out. I shoved out after him, slamming the door and yanking up the zipper on my jacket to my neck. Madeline was a friend of mine who had been recently suspected—by Owen—to be murdering random citizens of Seattle. She'd been innocent, which I'd been thankful for; the homely succubus owns my favorite café and keeps me in chocolate cake and donuts.

"Madeline? My Madeline?"

"Your Madeline? Has your relationship changed since I was last there?"

"You know what I mean," I said as we hit the back door. Owen bounced his key into and out of the card reader, pulled open the door. When I didn't go through, he gave a small smile, enjoying my confusion, and pressed a hand to my lower back. Shoving me into the warm stairwell, he stepped in after me, nudging me toward the stairs.

"Yes, your Madeline. I'm assuming she told you why."

I thought about it for a second, trying to remember everything we'd talked about the few times we'd seen each other outside of The Internets. Halfway up to the second floor, I whirled on him, pointed accusingly.

"You killed her mother!" He nodded, rolled his eyes at my volume. I darted my gaze around the second floor landing when we got there, hoped no one had heard me. As if it would convince anyone I was kidding, I continued with, "In that video game you play. About the … zombies and stuff."

Owen snorted out a laugh and shook his head, pushing me up another flight of stairs. I briefly wondered why, if he wanted to get laid, he was wearing me out by making me climb stairs. We went the rest of the way up to the fourth floor in silence, though I was huffing and puffing a bit toward the end. As he shut the door to his room, I went to the little sink in the bathroom, ducked down, and turned on the tap, slurping water. Owen waited silently for me, sitting on the edge of the bed. After I'd had my fill of water, I turned back to him, yanked the zipper down on my jacket. I spoke again as I pulled it off and tossed it vaguely toward the chairs by the table.

"What'd she do to deserve a bullet in the brain?"

"Do we have to talk about that now?" he asked, making a show of looking me over. I smiled at him, stepping close and running my fingers through his hair. It was soft and a little damp from the rain. Watching his eyes as he looked up at me, I moved my hand to cup the side of his face.

"Just tell me real quick."

He rolled his eyes, but it too was a show. I felt his hands move up my hips to tuck under my shirt. I jolted when his cold thumbs hit my skin, which amused him. Determined to keep me from asking any more questions, he slid his hands further under my shirt, placing his icy palms on my skin. Giving in, I squealed, squeezed my eyes shut.

"Come on, no fair."

"I'm just icing your bruises is all," he said, feigned innocence softening his voice. I sighed and shook my head.

"Still looks like Harold and his crayon used my body as a canvas."

"Aww," Owen cooed, sliding my shirt up. His brows lifted as he looked over the welts along the right side of my ribs. Gently, he ran his fingers over the bruises there, before leaning in and kissing me gently. "I'm sorry."

"It's not your fault. I'm the idiot that walked straight into it."

He kissed me again, a little higher this time. His hands stayed tucked under the edges of my shirt, his lips remaining just as gentle as the first time they'd touched my bruised ribcage. But the atmosphere changed in an instant. As he moved his mouth up for another kiss, he rolled his gaze up to meet my eyes. Lust flooded my body, filling me up and making my insides tingle.

I decided I didn't need to hear about Madeline's mother right then.

Pushing my fingers further back into his hair, I watched him as he kissed me again, his nose brushing the underside of my breast. After a moment, he pulled back enough to shove my shirt up. I let him pull it off, drop it to the floor.

"Now you," I murmured, unzipping his coat. He held his arms out to the sides like I would pat him down for weapons and I grinned. After I tugged his jacket off, I took a step back.

"Problem?" he asked. I waved a hand around in the air, gesturing to all of him.

"I know better than to assume you're not packing heat, Reid. Come on, disarm."

He gave a little chuckle and a nod. "Fair enough."

He held up a finger to indicate he'd be quick and got to his feet, stepping around me. I turned to watch him go to a suitcase laid out on a little stand by the bathroom door. He draped his jacket on one side, then lifted his ankle to pull a gun and holster out of his pant leg. All in all, he took off two knives, two guns, and a slim leather pack from under his shirt that I couldn't figure the point of. It looked too thin to hold anything useful, but he laid it out gingerly, before turning to face me again.

As he pulled his shirt over his head and dropped it on top of the suitcase, I heard his phone beep from his pocket.

"Son of a bitch," I growled, knowing exactly what that meant.

Olivia R. Burton

Nine

"Hey," Chloe said from the easy chair by the fireplace. "I figured you'd be gone all night."

"Gwen!" mom cried from the kitchen as she noticed me. I winced at the tone and turned to smile innocently at her. "Where have you been? Chloe said you went to meet a friend, that it was an emergency. Is everything okay?"

"Yeah, it's fine," I said, eyes darting between her and Chloe. I caught the curious look on Chloe's face before I gave a minute shake of my head. Pity rolled out of her and I sighed, turning back to my mom. I'd taken the coward's way out and half-assedly mentioned to my brother that I was going out instead of telling mom anything directly. Apparently I was going to pay for my secrecy.

"I was just helping a friend with something."

"A friend from school?"

"N—yes," I amended, giving one small nod.

"But everything's okay?"

"Yeah. What's for dinner?" I asked, changing the subject. I heard a yowl from the living room and peered through the kitchen and dining room to see what was going on. It looked the same as it always did, so I turned my attention back to my mother and her array of food. My mood fell instantly as my brain caught up to what was going on. "Augh, are you making vegetables again?"

"You are your father's daughter," my mother mused. Chloe snorted from the doorway, leaning against the jamb.

"I'm your daughter, too," I said. When my mom just lifted a cynical

61

brow, I rolled my eyes. "More yours, in fact. *He* didn't bake me for nine months."

"Speaking of baking, what do you want for your birthday?"

"Cake. Pie. Cookies."

"Pick one."

"Um," I said, scanning the food my mom had laid out; I noted there wasn't a single piece of meat in sight. "Can you bake a pie into a cake and put cookies on top? I've seen it on the internet. It's a thing."

"No," my mom said, simply. Chloe laughed, stepped forward to rub a hand on my back.

"I have a present coming for you, so don't choose cake."

"You bought me a cake?"

"I didn't say that," Chloe said. My mother went back to chopping.

"So what do you want to do on Friday?"

"Ah, whatever. I don't really care."

"Do you want to go out?"

"No. I mean, if you don't want to cook we can, but I don't care either way."

"You are impossible," Robin said, entering the kitchen behind Chloe. Stella yawned an adorable baby yawn in her arms and I made a happy sound in my throat.

"Stella!" I squeaked, stepping forward. Without hesitation, Robin handed her over, turned to mom to look at what she was making.

"Pasta?"

"Yeah, Chloe's got a vegan sauce for me to make."

"Oh!" Robin said, turning to Chloe. "That reminds me! I wanted to get that recipe from you."

"What recipe?" I asked, eying Chloe suspiciously. Stella kicked me in the ribs, making me grunt. Luckily my sister was already heading toward her old room.

"You sister wanted some vegan recipes," Chloe said. I glanced back toward the living room.

"Does Jake know?"

"I don't know," Chloe said with a shrug. Another shout and the sound of mouth-made gunfire came from the living room.

"What is happening over there?"

"Izzy and the kids set up forts," mom explained. "He's been great, keeping them busy all day."

"You should check the living room out, it looks really cool," Chloe said.

"Dad doesn't mind?" I asked. Mom's amusement burbled out and I took that as a no before she even spoke.

"He's been out in the shed for a few hours. I think Izzy is a little much for him to handle." After a moment, she turned to me, lifted a brow. "How do you deal with him?"

"Uh," I said, wondering if we were headed down a path that could enlighten me on my father in a way I wasn't ready to deal with. "Dunno."

Turning on my heel, I carried Stella toward the living room, stepping to the edge of the ugly dining room tile and looking out over the thick carpet at a sea of tiny pillow forts, blanket tents, and shirt flags among the two real tents set up for the family. J.J. shot out from under one of the blankets draped between the back of the couch and three dining room chairs. Stumbling in a run, he turned and shouted something I couldn't understand in a voice that was trying its prepubescent best to approximate a pirate's growl.

Natalie popped out of another tent further back, tried to call her brother over. Suddenly, Izzy swung out of the fort J.J. had vacated, hopped onto the back of one of the dining chairs and pointed at him with both index fingers, making laser sounds. J.J. let out a long, high-pitched death scream and flopped onto his back dramatically.

"Wow," I said. Baby Stella squealed, blew a raspberry, and grasped the air toward Izzy.

"You won't get away with this!" Natalie yelled from the corner, ducking back into a pillow fort. Izzy crossed the backs of the chairs—how he didn't tip them right over, I have no idea—and hopped onto the seat of another chair near J.J. He snatched the shirt pinned to the side of the bar, held it up into the air.

"Victory!" he yelled.

"But I'm a *zombie* now!" J.J. announced with a long growl. Izzy yelped, genuine surprise wiggling around in his psyche, and tumbled off the side of the chair. He landed hard on his bony ass and watched as J.J. made childish groaning sounds and pretended to claw his way out of the earth.

"This is about the sixth time he's been a zombie and Izzy acts surprised every time," Thomas said from next to me. I turned to glance him over.

"Why aren't you playing?"

"I did, but Natalie kept overthrowing my kingdom and J.J. shot me into space." I blinked at him and he shrugged. "I'm lucky, but I've got nothing on a zombie astronaut pirate."

"Well, who does?" I asked, turning back to the action to find J.J. had clawed his way to Izzy, trying to bite his bare foot. Izzy squealed and dove for the fort he'd erstwhile evacuated. Jake growled again and got to his feet, pulling his arms in close. Natalie pointed at him with a sparkly wand that matched the princess hat threatening to slide off the side of her head.

"He's a zombie dinosaur! Save the princess!"

"Is she the princess?" I asked Thomas through the side of the mouth.

He shook his head. "No, Izzy is."

"No, yeah, I get that," I admitted.

When Stella burbled out another saliva-drenched squeal and reached toward her brother, I stepped into the room, set her down on the carpet. She rocked spastically on her hands and knees twice before shooting off at a cheetah's pace. J.J. gaped down at her when she grabbed for his foot and then hoisted her up around the belly, carrying her awkwardly toward Izzy's fort.

"I have a machine gun!" he announced, aiming Stella at the dining chairs. As Izzy demanded he not shoot, I turned to leave.

"I don't know if I can handle this much excitement."

"This is why dad's outside," Thomas said. "So, what did you want for your birthday?"

"You already flew me out here, you don't have to get me anything."

"I know," he said. "But everyone else will be giving you presents; I don't want to be the only jerk who doesn't."

"Buy me a box of fruit snacks and call it a day."

"Easy to wrap," he said. I nodded.

"Exactly."

"You screwed up getting laid again?" Chloe said as I shut the door to Thom's room. I threw her an annoyed glance and shook my head. She took a seat at Thom's rickety desk and crossed her legs.

"I didn't screw anything up. I was raring to go, bruises and all, and he got called away again. Something about a police contact or blah blah. I don't know."

"Aww," Chloe said as I took a seat on the bed. "How're your bruises?"

"The same. We checked out the forest some, where we came across *something* and then we went to a bar."

"Didn't you say he doesn't drink?"

"He doesn't, but he said he wanted to listen to crazy stories and get me liquored up."

"You seem completely sober, so I'm guessing it didn't quite work out?"

"No, he ran into an ex or something."

Shock blew out of Chloe in a prickly cloud. "Really?"

"Not ex-girlfriend, as far as I can tell, but ex-something."

"What makes you think that?"

"Just the way they—well, and they admitted they'd slept together. Though, it came about like she was trying to get me riled up, jealous maybe."

"But you're not?"

"Nah, I know what's up with me and Owen. Plus, I couldn't blame him for being into her. She was cute, though the mohawk did nothing for her."

"She had a mohawk?" Chloe asked, as a sinister sort of disgust burbled through her, like it had been her ex who had shown up to taunt Owen and not a stranger. She was quiet for a bit, her expression unreadable before her lips tugged and her disgust shifted toward joy. "And you said they didn't like each other?"

"Yeah, they acted that way, sniping in that super cool way badasses do. I probably wouldn't have known anything was going on if I couldn't read them both like billboards."

"So, no drinking and no sex? Poor baby."

"You know what would cheer me up? Cake."

"I'm not baking you a cake. Just wait until your birthday," she ordered. Then, excitedly, "the big Three-Oh, eh? You nervous?"

"Not really. Same as all the other birthdays. Maybe Mel will send me more of Sarah's cupcakes. Like, more than he did last time."

"I'm gonna have a big blow-out for mine. I've got a few years to plan, but I think we'll hit Vegas or Venice or something."

"Venice and Vegas aren't exactly close," I said. Chloe shrugged a shoulder.

"No big."

"The cost is a bit different, I think." Again, Chloe shrugged as if it wasn't an issue. I rolled my eyes at her and leaned back on the bed. Pressing a hand to my sore side, I rubbed a bit.

"My life is weird," I decided aloud. Amused again, Chloe got up, came to stretch out next to me.

"How so?"

"What do you mean, 'how so?'" I asked, turning to her. She tucked an arm under her head and watched me as I explained what shouldn't have needed any clarification. "Vampires, werewolves, spiders, fairies, Izzy. All weird stuff."

"Zombies," she added, like it was just another thing to add to a grocery list.

"Yeah exactly. It's all weird and it all happens to me. I don't know what's up with that. I mean, why'd Laurel and Hardy come to *me* instead of … absolutely anyone else?"

"Right place, wrong time, maybe?" Chloe asked, patting my thigh. She rocked up to her feet and turned to face me. "You and Owen got any further plans tonight, or are you just staying here?"

"No plans. He wasn't sure how long he'd be busy, so he said he'd call tomorrow."

"Well, Izzy and I were thinking of going to the movies later, smuggling in copious amounts of candy, sharing a giant soda. You in?"

"You said the word candy and I lost track after that."

"Perfect, then I get to choose the movie."

"Nothing with subtitles."

"Spoil-sport."

"Fine, if you buy me my own box of Cookie Dough Bites and my own pretzel you can have your filthy subtitles."

"I never said I was paying."

The movie was ridiculous, the candy options a perfect mix of chocolate, tart, and gummy, and I got my pretzel. Chloe and Izzy dropped me off at home before heading back to their hotel to, undoubtedly, have sex loud enough to disturb the neighboring rooms and possibly all the neighboring businesses.

I woke up early the next morning, though I don't know why. One minute I was dreaming about explosions and zombie princesses, the next I was staring at the dull green glow of my brother's bedside clock.

Deciding to blame my bladder, I got to my feet, padded down the hall toward the bathroom. I caught sight of Jake and Robin snoozing in their room, glared at Dorian as he snoozed in mine.

Hoping the flushing toilet and hand washing didn't wake anyone up, I grabbed my phone from my room, tucked it into the only pocket my pajama pants offered and headed downstairs, aiming to smuggle some chocolate milk down my throat before my mother woke up and made me drink carrot juice or eat some plain oatmeal.

I don't know how my empathy missed the fact that my father was sitting alone at the dining table with a cup of chocolate milk of his own, but I slammed to a halt when I saw him. For a merciful few seconds, the only emotion I felt was my own shock. Then, as he glanced up at me, his surprise joined mine, followed quickly by a rumble of unhappy irritation.

We stared at each other, unsure what to do.

He was already sitting comfortably reading the paper and drinking in peace; getting up and leaving would be downright rude. I had come into the kitchen with a purpose and turning to pretend I forgot something would be just as bad. It was possible we were going to actually have to talk to each other.

Ignoring the crackling of nervous unhappiness between us, I cleared my throat, tried to give him my best politely distant smile.

"Morning," I said, moving to pull open the fridge door and poke around inside for the milk. I didn't even have the luxury of taking my time; he'd left the glass bottle right there at the forefront. With a sigh, I pulled it out, carried it to the counter under the cabinet of mugs and poked around for one big enough to sate me.

"Can't sleep?" dad asked. I glanced over at him, tried not to snarl at the accusation I swore I could feel stabbing me in the spine.

"Slept fine. I'm just up, is all," I said, unable to keep the petulance out of my tone. My dad grunted once in response and went back to reading his paper. I grabbed a squat, fat mug from the back of the cabinet and dumped milk into it hard enough that a bit sloshed over the side. I opened my mouth to growl out a swear word and felt my father's eyes on me.

Instead of cursing, I took an annoyed breath, pressed my lips shut, and turned to take my mug to the microwave. As I waited for it to warm up, I heard my father grunt as if trying to get my attention. I turned to him sharply and he pointed at the milk.

"Don't leave that out."

"I wasn't going to," I insisted, though I had actually forgotten about it. Grabbing the milk and shoving it back in the fridge, I hopped the two large steps to the microwave, jerking the door open before it could scream out a beep. I burned my hand a bit on the mug but the smell of chocolate powder as I yanked the top off the plastic container made it worth it.

After dumping way too many spoonfuls into the cup, leaving chunks of powder at the top for a special, gooey treat, I twisted back to face my dad at the table. Now came the big decision: did I stay and continue the awkward stalemate, or did I go hide in my room until everyone else woke up?

"Come sit," dad said, surprising me. When I just stood and stared, he kicked his foot into the chair next to him, knocking it back. "Now."

"Jeez," I hissed, stomping toward him as hard as I could without risking my cocoa. To spite him, I took a seat across the table, ignoring the chair he'd kicked out for me. He watched me for a moment before I felt amusement burble around us both. I couldn't help but smile and he did the same. Closing the paper, he jerked a chin at my drink.

"Your mom buys that in bulk and we still run out."

"Well, don't eat so much sugar," I said, fully aware of the irony of my statement. Anger snapped back and forth between us, and my father's brow furrowed.

"Don't be smart."

I bit my tongue, choosing to take a sip of my scalding treat instead of making a remark I would probably regret. After a moment, he jerked his stubbly chin at me.

"Your mother says it doesn't have to be this way, just because we're both empaths."

I choked on my chocolate. Shock and panic broiled around us as I wheezed and hacked into the sleeve of my shirt. After a few seconds, my dad got to his feet, coming around to my side to clap me on the back hard enough that it knocked me into the table. When I finally got my coughing under control, he moved back to his chair, slid my mug across the way. He dumped half of what was left into his cup and, when I glared at him, he just pointed at me as if cowing me into not complaining.

"I don't know," I said finally, rubbing my eyes to get rid of the tears. "It was just always a thing, you know? I thought everyone did it, and then I found out it was only me, and maybe you, but you never brought it up and we were—are always fighting. So I figured maybe it was wrong—that you—I mean, that I was alone and maybe you did something else."

"Something else? What something else? Jesus, Gwen, you didn't even ask."

"You didn't ask, either!" I argued, feeling that horrible feedback of irritation and insult arc between us like lightning. It made me chest hurt, tightened my jaw, and made me want to hit something. "That's your job! You're the parent."

"Your mom didn't tell you?" he asked, voice strained. I fought the urge to bite his head off for throwing mom under the bus, even though part of me knew that probably wasn't his intention.

"Don't make this her fault!"

"It's your fault!" he argued. Then, like it physically pained him to say, "and my fault."

"Damn straight. You knew what I was feeling, what I was going through as a teenager and you never even tried to help!" I accused, my level of anger rising to combat the embarrassment making my cheeks go pink. Dad tapped his head and then pointed at mine.

"Don't be a brat, you know exactly what I did for you."

Unsure what to do next, unwilling to admit I had no idea what he was talking about, I lifted my mug, downed the last of the liquid, realizing in an instant that it was still too hot. Glowering his way, I got to my feet, stomped to the sink and dropped the cup inside.

"Rinse it out," my father ordered.

"I know!" I growled. "You don't have to be a jerk. "

"Neither do you. You're a grown damn woman, you should be able to control your own emotions. I shouldn't have to do it for you. "

"What are you talking about?" I all but screeched.

"You know what I'm talking about!" he boomed, getting to his feet. Mimicking my action, he sucked down the last of his milk and thumped over to me to slam his cup down in the sink. "You play dumb, but the only way you haven't figured out how you got through your teen years so happy—" I scoffed, but mostly just to needle him. "—is if you're an idiot. And you're my daughter, so you're not an idiot."

"Apparently I am because I have no idea what you're talking about." I was on the verge of yelling, though I probably wouldn't have been if I'd been arguing with anyone else. My father threw up his hands in frustration and then clapped them over his eyes. It was a gesture I'd done myself a time or twelve. He took a second to breathe heavily into his palms before forcing himself to calm down.

"Talk to your mother. I'm going to wake Dorian up."

"Of course you are," I snapped. To my surprise, I felt a stab of hurt inside him as he twisted and plodded toward the stairs. I watched him go, my jaw set, before turning and heading for the living room. I could hear J.J.'s open-mouthed breathing from inside one of the blanket forts and Natalie was stretched out on the couch. Sighing that there was nowhere for me to sit, I glanced around the room before deciding to crawl into the fort Natalie had holed up in the day before. I stretched out, tucked a knot of blankets under my head and tried my best to calm down.

Olivia R. Burton

Ten

I woke up an hour later with my mother laying next to me, watching me sleep. I jolted as soon as I saw her, swore an oath that made her roll her eyes.

"What are you doing?" I demanded.

"Watching my baby sleep."

"Thomas is the baby! Go watch him sleep!"

"He's awake, making breakfast. You and your father woke the whole house."

I grunted in response, leaned slightly away as I worried I might still have chocolate breath. Mom reached out and rubbed a hand over my arm.

"What were you yelling about?"

"I don't know; he was bitch—complaining that I'm ungrateful or something. That he's the reason I was happy as a kid. I think never being here with him was the reason I was happy."

"Well, to be fair, that was partly his doing."

"No," I argued, unable to keep the pout off my face. "That was Stan's doing; as soon as I started dating him, I was over at his house *all the time*. That wasn't because of dad."

"Well," mom drawled and shifted a bit. Discomfort and embarrassment puffed out of her and I felt my pout slide toward a frown.

"What?"

"He did convince me to *let* you to go over to Stan's so often."

"Because he didn't want me here?" Mom rolled her eyes at that.

"No, because he remembered his own teen years. He remembered being able to feel everything going on around him, especially when your

71

grandparents..." Mom trailed off, rolling her wrist to gesture toward me with an open palm; I continued to frown at her. Apparently she also thought it was impossible for me to be an idiot; she shifted to repeat her gesture toward me, but slower as if that would help me understand what she was hinting at.

"What?" I finally demanded. My mother let out an uncomfortable laugh and then sighed.

"Once we realized you had his power, he was terrified of..." Her voice slowed, as if her words were warm caramel, half stuck in her throat. "Of...of getting to ... *know*. *Me*. With you in the house."

I blinked at her, still completely clueless. Exasperation exploded from her limbs as she shoved at my shoulder.

"Sex!" she finally snapped.

"Ahh!" I howled, shaking my head. I suddenly hated this conversation. My mother's discomfort deviated toward amusement and she reached out to pull me into a hug.

"No!" I whined, though I didn't shove her away. When she pulled back, the blush on her cheeks had disappeared.

"We went so many years only having sex while you were at school or over at a friend's house," she griped. "Let me tell you."

"I will not let you tell me! Stop telling me!" I rolled onto my back, pressing my fingers against my eyeballs. "It was bad enough feeling Robin *getting to know* Jake, or Thomas *getting to know* himself. I don't want to think about you and dad *getting to know* anything."

"Robin and Jake?" mom asked, hand clutching my arm "In my house?"

"Uh," I groaned, peering out from under one hand at her. "No?"

She slapped my arm lightly, shook her head. Her despair was mild but apparently I'd spilled the beans on something.

"She swore to me they'd never have sex without talking to me first."

"They've had three kids. It's time you knew. Mom, they've had sex."

Mom's eye-roll was immediate, her breath a quick hiss. "But she didn't come talk to me about it until after she'd moved out. I assumed they were chaste while living here. I swear you girls were so secretive."

"Well, you *need* to be more secretive; promise me you'll never bring anything like this up ever again. As far as I'm concerned, you and dad have never had sex."

She lifted a brow at me, her expression wry. "Gwen, we had three kids. I think it's time you knew—"

"We all budded asexually off your arm!" I interrupted, my voice breaking. "That's how it happened. End of story."

Mom shook her head, grinning. While we sat in the blanket fort in silence, something else occurred to me. I dropped my arms.

"What did you mean about dad making sure I was happy before Stan?"

"You know," she said, as if that explained it. I shook my head.

"Stop talking to me like I'm *not* an idiot. Explain what you guys are talking about." Mom sighed.

"He absorbed your emotions when you were feeling down or angry or, you know, *teenaged*, that's all. He made sure he took on some the garbage feelings so you didn't have to live with it. He did it for all three of you, though you were the biggest challenge."

"Absorbed?" I was lost. "Like a sponge?"

"Yes," mom said plainly. "Why, do you do it differently?"

I stared at her. My father could take emotions? That was on a different level that I was. No wonder we had so much trouble communicating; his powers apparently outweighed mine. He was not only feeling irate at me, he was absorbing the irritation I was putting off, which meant I was feeling his emotions and mine, and putting it right back on him.

"I've never done that," I admitted. Mom's brows went up and I felt disbelief crowd her.

"Not on purpose, you mean?"

"Not at all."

"Yes you have. You take everything everyone else is feeling. That's why you're so cranky. When you were young, your father would help, make sure you weren't overloaded. Once you grew up we assumed you'd learned to control it. He was hurt you never thanked him—or even brought it up, by the way."

"Well I didn't even know he was doing anything!"

"Breakfast is ready," Thomas said from outside the fort. He crouched down to pull open the sheet-door hanging over our exposed legs and look us both over. "Your friends are back, so I made waffles again."

There was a bit of confusion there as Thom looked between us, but he didn't address it. He just gave a small smile, dropped the sheet, and walked away.

The morning went about the same as the one before, though with no more surprise visitors. Izzy disappeared back into the fort city with the kids, wearing the princess hat this time; the rest of us scattered around the house. After ignoring me at breakfast, dad disappeared with Dorian into his shed and Chloe and I went into the yard to sit in the sun.

"I still haven't gotten any straight answers from Izzy on what I'm doing here," she said, her eyes closed as she faced the sky.

"That doesn't surprise me. It annoys me, but it doesn't surprise me."

"Owen told you anything?"

"Nothing new."

"What did he learn from the sasquatches?"

"I actually have no idea," I realized aloud. Crossing my legs, I twisted in my chair to face her, tugged the blanket over my shoulder to compensate for my back no longer being pressed against the body-heated cushion. "I asked about them and then got distracted. Being Owen, he just didn't tell me."

Chloe smiled and there was a nostalgic amusement there that I didn't quite understand.

"So ask him again and don't get distracted this time."

I thought about how I'd been thwarted twice in my efforts to have sex. "I can't make any promises, but I'll do my best."

Chloe cracked an eye open, tipped her head to look at me.

"When was the last time you had sex, anyway?"

"It barely counts but it was with Mel," I said. Chloe made a humming sound like she disapproved and then closed her eye, rolled her face upward again.

"You could always go back to him, ask to try another position or something if you're desperate."

"Bite your tongue," I said. She giggled, shook her head.

"I'm just surprised; with how little restraint you have when it comes to things you like, that you don't use him for sex all the time."

"I like sex but I didn't like sex with Mel; that's what you're forgetting."

"So give him another chance, school him. Really whip him into shape. He's tough, he can take it."

"I don't have the patience for that. I'd be old by the time he learned, too old to enjoy it."

"Well, then just sit around alone eating cake every night for the rest of your life waiting for Owen to happen by."

"I will," I snapped. Chloe grinned and I felt a knowing sort of mischief around her before she spoke again.

"Or I could always lend you Izzy if you're that hard up."

For the second time that day, I nearly vomited into my own mouth. "Auugh! Stop! I'd rather have sex with you."

Chloe laughed, lifting a hand to shield her from the sun as she turned to me again.

"What's wrong with Izzy? He's adorable."

"Yes, but... I don't know. His brain is like Jell-O."

"You love Jell-O!"

"But that's not even it! I don't know. I just...I could not be less attracted to him if we were dead. It would be weird and I...I don't know why."

"You're too similar, maybe. You'd spend all your time arguing over who gets to eat the last slice of cake."

"Forget the last slice; we'd get in a fist fight over who gets the whole thing."

"Slap fight, more likely. I've seen you punch and it's a mess."

"Whatever." As I glared her way, wondering where my dignity had gone, I heard my mother call from the kitchen. I glanced across the porch, wondering if I could see her or politely communicate with her from under the warm blanket.

"What?"

"I said come here!" mom demanded. Chloe did almost her best to hide a smirk. Grumbling, I wrapped the blanket as tightly around me as I could, got to my feet and dashed into the warm house. Mom looked over at me under the cabinets hanging above the stove.

"Can you run to the store?"

"Me?"

"Unless I have another middle daughter, yes. List's on the fridge."

I gaped at her, confused, but I didn't consider it worthwhile to argue. I could hear Thomas, Izzy, and the kids in the living room, yowling and growling and possibly deciding the fate of an entire, imagined world. Robin and Stella were probably napping and I had no idea where Jake had gone.

"Yeah, okay." Leaning out the door, I yelled for Chloe. "Come on, we're going to the store."

"Okay," she said, tossing away the blanket and getting to her feet casually, as if she wasn't exposing herself to cold and wind. She smiled at my mother when she came in and went straight to the fridge. Mom glanced back to see Chloe grab the shopping list and then turned to me.

"Take my debit card; my purse is in my room."

"That's okay," Chloe said. "I got it."

"No, no," mom started. Chloe patted her on the shoulder and then turned to me, jerking her head to the side to indicate we should leave.

"You're feeding us and putting up with Izzy; it's the least I can do," Chloe told my mom.

"Nonsense, it's my pleasure to have you."

"But it's not Marvin's pleasure," Chloe pointed out. Amusement bubbled through my mother and she nodded, gave a half-shrug.

"That's true. Don't buy this one any more sweets. I've already confiscated the candy in her bag."

"Hey!" I snapped, wondering if she was bluffing. "I paid for that!"

"You really want to go that route? Because I could bill you for all the diapers you used and, let me tell, you, it would not be pretty."

Chloe let out a snorting laugh, repeated her head jerk. "Come on, Gwen. Let's go before she remembers all the money you owe them from raiding their change jars."

"How did you know about that?" I asked, moving through the kitchen. Chloe stuck out her tongue.

"Trade secret."

"Where are the beans?" Chloe asked me. I shrugged.

"I don't remember. It's been ten years since I shopped here. Over there, maybe?" I didn't gesture. Chloe had already turned and pushed the cart down the aisle closest to us; it held chips and junk food. When I paused by the rack of bagged candy, I felt a slap of irritation from Chloe.

"Come on," she demanded, grabbing my arm. "Don't make me put you in the cart and push you around."

"I don't think my legs would fit in the little holes."

"Yeah, because you eat so much candy." She smiled at her own joke, pulling me around the corner and down another aisle; this one had mostly condiments, oils, honey, etcetera. I did eye the honey jars but Chloe gave me a stern glare.

"Keep up. For all we know, Izzy brought me here to protect you from a horrible grocery store accident."

"And what exactly would that entail?" I asked. Chloe shrugged a shoulder, scanned the list my mother had given her and grabbed a few things off the shelf.

"An entire row could collapse and crush your legs unless I'm here to stop it." She scanned the back of one of the cans, before setting it in the cart and turning back to me. "Or maybe there's a robbery and I have to take a bullet for you."

"It's empty in here, I doubt they have any cash to rob," I said, before actually considering the scenario. I'd seen Chloe in scary combat situations and I had no doubt that, if anyone could jump fast enough to get between a speeding bullet and me, it would be her. But the idea made me sad.

"No," I reconsidered, "if anything, Izzy would want me to take a bullet for you. He worships you."

"Well, then keep an eye out and get ready to dive."

Before I could argue, I felt an intrusive sort of confusion behind me, mixing into shock and then delight that splattered across my back like Gatorade on a winning coach. I turned to find a woman I vaguely recognized standing down the aisle. She was holding a sack of flour in one hand as if she'd forgotten about it, and there was a little girl bouncing in the front of the cart. Our eyes met and her expression opened up.

"Gwen!"

"Yeah?" I said, still trying to catch her name among the fluttering confusion dashing around the inside of my memory.

"Meghan Chatterton!" she said, before realizing she was still holding the flour. She did a little back-and-forth before setting it back on the shelf and pushing the cart closer. "How are you?"

"Good, how are you?" I recognized her, probably from high school, but that was about as far as my brain could go. I looked her over, tried to capture a stray bit of realization from her appearance. Her face was round, her dark pixie cut hair revealing a broad forehead. Smile lines bordered her brown eyes and her nose was wide but short. Her outfit was sensible, jeans and a T that showed evidence of young children or mild stomach flu.

Another woman came around the corner behind her, half-paying attention to a can of soup in her hand, and suddenly it all came back to me.

"Oh my god, hi!" I said, interrupting Megan before she could quite answer my question. The other woman, Ashley Wolitzer looked up, startled. She looked older than I remembered her, of course, but the years had been good to her. I remembered baby-fat cheeks and acne distracting you from her great smile and pretty eyes. She'd thinned up, grown out her dark curls, and aged out of the acne. When she met my eyes, she smiled, but it was tired, exhausted.

"Gwen?" she asked, her voice strained as if through the dregs of a head cold.

"Yes! How are you guys?" I looked between them, then at the little boy who rounded the corner behind Ashley and climbed onto the side of the cart.

"We're good. Haven't seen you since high school. I thought you moved to Oregon?" Ashley asked, rubbing the little boy's head in a motherly way that exasperated him.

"Washington, actually. I moved to Seattle for college and just stayed there." I glanced between them, unable to keep the smile off my face. "You two together?" I asked before I could control myself.

Delight puffed out of Meghan and she turned to give Ashley a slightly shy smile. I felt Chloe's curiosity as she stepped up next to me. Ashley looked between us, surprise sparking mildly, having trouble getting through a haze of discomfort and exhaustion I recognized as sickness.

"We are. What about you two? No more Stan?"

"Ah," I said, glancing at Chloe. "No more Stan, but she's just a friend."

"Chloe Warren," she said, leaning forward to shake hands with each of them. "Nice to meet you."

The little boy on the side of the cart shifted his grip to stab pudgy fingers through the grated side and push himself back and forward rapidly. I felt impatience within him and it made me laugh. The little girl in the cart's seat was unbothered by the delay.

"You back in town for Thanksgiving?" Ashley asked. I nodded.

"Yeah, it's been awhile since I visited; everything's so different—quieter even, you know?"

"Mommy!" the little boy demanded, cutting me off. Ashley glanced down, patted him on the head again, making him jerk away as if she'd slapped him.

"Shh," she admonished quietly. He yanked himself closer to the cart and obeyed, but he wasn't happy about it. After a moment, he dropped down, stuffing his hand in his pocket and pulling out a little gold disk.

"How's your family?" Meghan asked. I shrugged.

"Pretty good. Robin has three kids, now, Thomas is … we're not really sure what he's doing."

"And you?"

"Oh," I said, shaking my head. "I'm a therapist. Nothing too exciting."

"That's great!" Meghan said. "Not married?"

"Ah," I said, not wanting to go into the details of my sordid past and why Stanley Sneedley was my *ex*-husband. "Nope."

"Do you keep in contact with Stan? We've read his books and they're really good. The new one's out this week, I believe?"

"I think so, yeah." I nodded. I had no idea, to be honest. Chloe piped up.

"Yes! *The Floating Airship* is supposed to be really good. I'm pretty excited." Confusion tinged her psyche as she glanced down at the little boy. Following her lead, I gestured to the kids.

"And who are these little ones?"

"This is Penelope and that's Samuel."

"Aww, they're adorable. How old?" I glanced over to find Chloe had crouched down and was speaking quietly to Samuel. He wasn't sure if he appreciated the action, but I got the feeling that was part and parcel when it came to Samuel.

Meghan, Ashley, and I all chatted for a bit longer, catching up in that somewhat impersonal way you do when you run into people you knew as a kid but have nothing in common with as an adult. Ashley was a trooper, but I could tell without even asking that she felt like hell the whole time.

I cut the conversation short for her sake, making excuses about needing to get back home, but Ashley was polite, not looking thrilled to end the conversation or anything. Samuel, on the other hand, wailed a frustrated, "finally!" which made us all laugh.

"That was nice," Chloe said, once we'd finished shopping and gotten back to the car. "You knew them in high school?"

"Yeah, we had a LGBT club that some kid started and then never actually attended. Meghan had the biggest crush on Ashley, but I don't think she knew it. I could always feel it, but she never said anything and always had a boyfriend. I'm glad to see she figured herself out."

"You were in the club?"

"I was, but it wasn't really a thing. Mainly it was six of us and we'd just hang out at a fast food joint around the corner after school once a week and rail about the unfairness of discrimination—as if any of us had any idea what we were talking about. I don't even really remember doing anything useful. We didn't change lives or anything."

"I don't know; I bet they'd disagree. They probably found each other through the club."

"Maybe," I said, leaving the parking lot. "I stopped showing up a few weeks after, when I started dating Stan, just because being with him was more fun."

"I'll bet," Chloe murmured. Ignoring her teasing, I changed the subject.

"What were you and the kid talking about?"

"Oh right," Chloe said, shifting. She tucked a finger into her pocket, slid out the gold coin Samuel had been fingering. "Got this from the kid. Do you know where he got it?"

"One of those treasure bins in the toy store?"

"No, from a friend of his, whose dad got it *in the forest*."

"So?"

"So, this is real gold. I mean, the genuine article. Samuel said his friend had a bunch of them and he took one."

"He stole it from his friend and you stole it from him?"

"I didn't steal it," she said, though she wasn't feeling entirely honest. I lifted a brow, gave her a cynical squint as we waited for a red light to go green. "I bribed him."

"With what?" I asked, laughing at her embarrassed admission that she'd had to hoodwink a kid.

"A piece of candy."

"Oh sure, you'll let him have candy. Wait, you said forest?" I asked, memories of what Owen had said poking eagerly into my consciousness.

"Yeah, why?"

"There are people missing, people who went camping in the forest. Maybe it's related."

"Maybe. I grabbed it figuring we could get Izzy to look it over, tell us what he thinks of it."

"If there isn't chocolate inside that gold coin, I doubt he'll be interested."

"Maybe. But we have to try. It could be a clue."

"Did I tell you about the camping before?" I asked, lost, wondering why she'd thought to grab the coin from the kid at all.

"Owen's here, right?" she said, though a bump of frustrated regret nudged my elbow, confusing me. "It looked legit, like something a kid shouldn't have. I figured, you know, maybe this is a clue as to what he's here after?"

"You …" I trailed off, trying to parse why her words felt weird. She wasn't lying, but something wasn't right. "How did you know it wasn't—oh, wait, my phone's ringing." I fished it out of my pocket, glancing at it, but unwilling to fight with it while driving. "Looks like it's Owen."

Chloe grabbed the phone, answering eagerly.

"Hello darling," she purred. I felt amusement roll out of her, though I couldn't hear what was going on at the other end of the phone.

"No, she's here but she's driving." Chloe paused, shifted in her seat. "Is That so?" Annoyance flashed but her posture and expression remained mild. "Yeah, okay. I'll let her know. Any particular time?"

"For what? What's going on?" I asked, turning down my parents' cul-de-sac.

"Okay, I'll tell her. Bye." Chloe hung up, handed the phone back.

"He's not going to be able to meet you as soon as he thought; he's got more sources or something to meet this afternoon, but he's hoping he can get away in time to take you to dinner."

"Hmmph," I groused, turning off the car. "That was not the answer I was hoping for."

"Yeah, that's what I figured." She patted my knee, shifted to grab the grocery sack out of the back seat. "On the plus side, that gives us more time to interrogate Izzy and see if you'll actually be bringing anything useful to Owen."

"I'm bringing me; I'm useful."

"Yes, but not in a way that helps him keep his pants on."

Eleven

"Izzy, the coin isn't made of chocolate."

Izzy turned to Chloe, staring blankly as if processing her words, and then slid the coin out from between his teeth. He frowned at her and then shook his head.

"I know *that*. I'm just checking it out. It's gold."

"Yes, we said that," I pointed out. "We need to know where it came from."

"Looks like you got it from a kid named Samuel James Chatterton-Wolitzer. That's a mouthful," Izzy explained, tucking the coin back between his teeth as if to demonstrate. "He had Frosted Ducks cereal for breakfast." Izzy's eyes went a little blurry as if he could taste the sugary, puffed wheat cereal that claimed to be a healthy choice for breakfast.

I've had those things and I love them so you know they can't be good for you.

"So, where did Samuel get it from?"

"Hmm," Izzy said, pulling the coin back to look it over again. "Beckett Franklin Farrell. That kid's gonna be trouble." Izzy handed me the coin, not bothering to wipe his spit off the side of it first. I rubbed it on my shirt, tucked it into my pocket.

"And where did that kid get it?"

"From his dad, who got it in the forest."

"He just found it?"

"No, he was lost. Are we playing more dinosaurs versus pirates now? I was winning."

"I thought you were the Princess," Chloe asked, shifting in her seat. Izzy shook his head.

"Queen, now. Got promoted."

"Hmm," Chloe gave a quick nod. "Before you go back to playing, can you tell us anything else about how the kid got hold of a solid cold coins? Seems like something you'd want to keep your kid from losing or giving away."

"Eh," Izzy shrugged, shook his head. "Not really my place."

"Why?" I complained, sitting up further, exasperated. I was huddled on one of the couch cushions that had previously been the wall of one of the fort buildings, though, and the movement made me feel like the whole mess was about to collapse under me. "You said you and Chloe are here to be of help and now you're being the opposite of help."

"I said *Chloe's* here to help. I said nothing about me." Rolling his eyes, he felt around under a pile of pillows and pulled out a crumbled crown cut crudely out of pink construction paper. "Besides, you want help, ask your brother about Owen," he said before vaulting himself over the back of the couch and diving into the blanket fort they'd made of my father's bar.

I turned to watch him and caught sight of my nephew crossing the kitchen, his mouth open in an uneven yawn. He stopped at the step leading down into the living room and looked around.

"Where's Izzy?" he asked. I pointed at the bar fort and J.J. nodded, moving calmly to the opposite side of the room. Izzy let out a high-pitched giggle as J.J. dug into the giant basket in which my parents kept all the kids' toys. When he came out brandishing a bright blue, plastic sword, he let out a battle cry and turned toward the fort. Izzy popped up through an opening in the top wearing an eye patch that was clearly meant for a much smaller eye and pointed an action figure at J.J. like a weapon.

"Come on," I mumbled. "I think it's about to get loud again."

"You go," Chloe said. "I think I want to play, too."

I shrugged a shoulder, moved around the action to head through the kitchen, through the entryway, and into the sitting room. Mom was tucked onto the couch with her tablet computer, wrapped in the blanket Thomas had been sleeping under.

"Where's Thom?" I asked. She held up a finger, ran her eyes over the screen twice more and then looked up at me.

"I think he went out after you went to the store. Why?"

"Just wondering. Robin, Jake? Dad?" I realized I didn't feel any of them in the house. My father was probably across the giant backyard in his man cave, but Robin and Jake should have been within range of my empathy and they weren't.

"They took the girls to see a friend of Robin's, I think. Your father's out back. Did you want me to go get him?" The smile on her face and the mischief in her told me she knew my answer. I just sighed. Chloe yelled something in what may have been French from the living room and Izzy responded in what sounded like Italian. J.J. shrieked out a laugh that only a young boy having the time of his life can produce and I winced.

"I'm gonna go see what Thom's up to. Chloe and Izzy are keeping J.J. busy, but I can bring them with me if you want?"

"It's fine. I like the commotion."

I just shook my head, moved to grab my coat from the closet and my bag from the table by the door. I rubbed a hand over the coin in my pocket for a second, wondered if I should leave it at home in case some other enterprising young boy was feeling criminal while I was out and about. I decided to keep it, telling myself it was just in case Owen called and wanted to meet.

I stepped into Stripped Teas and glanced around at the rows of pots and cups and at the two cozy chairs by the front window. I didn't see my brother, but a little poking around with my empathy told me he was in one of the supply rooms at the back. I let the door shut, felt a puff of curiosity from the other side of the store and moved toward the back.

"Thom? Carter?" The curiosity turned to a slight embarrassment and I couldn't help but smile. My brother's friend had always had a bit of a crush on me, despite our age difference. He came out of the back room first and I grinned wider. "Hey Carter."

"Hey Gwen, Thomas said you were on your way. How are you?"

"Pretty well. The place looks good. What's on tap?" I asked, moving to the counter. Peering at the three glass pots with little tea lights burning under them, I pointed at the pinkest one. "This one good?"

"You wouldn't like it," Thomas said as he exited the storage room. "But the one next to it is more your speed. Think fast." He tossed me a little shaker of raw sugar. I caught it awkwardly and set it down on the counter. Next to me, Carter let out a hacking cough, tucking his chubby face into his elbow. I winced at the distress and pain boiling through him.

"Jeez, you sound terrible," I said. Figuring he wasn't in any shape to go near the delicate teapots, I moved around the counter, grabbed a mug with a sunflower on it and poured my own, shaking the sugar over the cup. Thomas hopped forward and grabbed the shaker before I could sweeten it too much and I glowered up at him.

"Yeah, I just can't shake his cold. Thom's been helping a lot with the store, though. My brother comes by every so often, but he can't get away from the kids too much."

"How many did Karen rope him into having?" I asked, blowing on the pale beige tea. The mug was a touch too hot against my palms but I was willing to ignore it; the tea smelled amazing and I'd left my gloves at home.

"They're up to five now, but it's not Karen."

"But she was always talking about wanting a hundred babies."

"Well, she was fine with three, but Bobby wanted six."

"You are *kidding* me," I groaned, taking a slow sip. It burned my tongue a little, so I sucked cool air in, causing it to burble in my mouth,

"Yeah, but she loves it. I think your sister's over at their place now, actually."

"Yeah, Rob and Jake are there with Stella and Nat." Jerking his chin at me, Thomas leaned against the counter. "You and dad get into another fight?"

"No, I just wanted to ask you something. Carter, you mind if I talk to him alone for a second?"

"Oh, sure," he said. Clearing his throat wetly, he pointed at the row of narrow doors along the wall. "I'll stay out here; you guys can go in the back."

"Thanks." Thomas led the way into the little closet that, at one point, had been a dressing room. Before Carter's parents had bought the storefront thirty years ago it had been a little clothing boutique. Thomas and I crammed into one of the small rooms, doing our best not to accidentally slosh my tea all over my hands.

"You know Izzy?"

"Your weird friend," Thom stated. I nodded.

"Well, you know he's not human, but what you don't know is that he can kind of … he can sort of tell the future. Not every time and not about important things, apparently, but he said that I should ask you about something."

"Ooookay," Thom drew the word out and I felt his confusion; it was edged with discomfort. "Shoot."

"You know my man friend?"

"I don't think so."

"The one I went to see the other night."

"Oh yeah, him. No, I definitely do not know him."

I let out an annoyed chuff of air, rolled my eyes. "You don't even know who he is! You could know him."

"Exactly, I don't know who he is." Thom grinned at me, socked me lightly in the arm. "But maybe if you tell me, I can say if I know him."

"Um, his name's Owen."

"Mathers?"

"What?" I asked. "No, Reid. He doesn't live here; he's just visiting."

"Only Owen I know is Mathers. He was a grade below me. Kind of a jerk. He's got whatever Carter's got, though, so at least maybe karma's on his ass."

"He's sick, too?"

"Yeah. He's Troy's brother. The guy who's got amnesia?" Thom pushed the door open enough to peer through at Carter and I felt worry cloud his brain. "Owen went to see Troy at the hospital, because, I mean, he's not *that* kind of jerk and came home and got the whole family sick."

"Is everyone around here sick? Is that why half the town's shut down?"

"Maybe," Thom said, before considering my suggestion as if hadn't occurred to him to connect the dots. "Could be Owen's fault, actually—not your guy pal, I'd assume. But, once he was starting to feel better, he came in—well, he was *sent* in by his mom for tea but, being an ass, he coughed on a bunch of the teapots. Could see him doing that all around town because he hates being ordered around but won't, you know, move into his own place or anything."

"Sounds like a peach. And you think he got Carter sick?"

"Well, Carter had to clean everything up so no one else would get sick, but I think he probably got hit."

"Just Carter?"

"I think so. Karen and Bobby are fine, though they don't come in much. Ginger—the girl Carter was seeing for awhile—hasn't been around much, but I just figured things had fizzled."

"Have you been to visit the guy—Troy, was it?"

"Nope. I didn't really know him and once his family all got sick, rumor got started he caught something from wandering the woods in the cold and no one wants frostbite or dysentery or whatever."

"I don't think frostbite is contagious."

"No, I know," Thom said with an eye-roll and a grin. "But no one really knows what he's got, just that everyone in his family has caught a bad cold or the flu or something. Plus, like I said, Owen's sort of a dick, so I can see him scaring everyone off just by being himself."

"You hear anything else about any of Troy's friends, the other kids who went missing? No one's found them or anything, right?"

"Not that I know of," Thom said, his shoulders slumping. "I hope they're okay. There were search parties for awhile, but no one can find any trace of them, and Troy can't even remember where they camped. They only guessed where to start looking cuz they always took the same path in, you know? And they can't even be sure they didn't, like try a new site or something."

"So everyone could be looking in the wrong spot?" I asked, worried Owen had been on the wrong trail when he and I had gone a-wandering.

"Maybe. I heard that Troy had maps of different areas and stuff, like maybe they were gonna head to another section of the forest, but no one can be sure. They can't even find their car."

"Who'd you hear that from?"

"Since when do you care about all this home-town gossip?" Thom asked, frowning my way, before leaning in close. "Are you really in the CIA?"

"Come on, Thom. What's your source?" I punched him lightly in the shoulder. "Don't make me rough you up."

He laughed at the image and stood up tall. "Carter heard it from someone who heard it from someone, you know? You'd have to talk to the family or the cops to find out for real."

"So you don't believe it?"

"I hadn't really thought about it, to be honest. It's just sort of something to chat about during downtime. And lately, there's a lot of downtime. We had a run for awhile, lots of people in buying herbal teas and honey stuff but that's mostly slowed down."

"Okay. Well. I've gotta make a call, but you stay safe."

"I'm sorry?" Thom laughed at my dramatics, pushing open the storeroom door to let me out. "Is something out to get me?"

"I hope not. Just take some vitamin C or something. Echinacea, or whatever it's called. I'll see you at home. Carter, go home if you're sick," I called as I passed him. Instead of the response he meant to give, a hacking cough exploded out of his throat, making me wince as I fled.

Halfway down the block to my car, I yanked my phone out of my jacket pocket, held it up so I could get a better look at it against the glare of the bright, autumn sun. Unfortunately, it looked like the buildings or my phone plan or maybe even a plate in a passerby's head was killing my service.

"Ah, dammit," I grumbled. I couldn't call Owen and tell him what I knew. I couldn't even call Chloe and tell her what I knew.

I paused near the passenger side of my mother's car and wondered what exactly I did know. We'd learned that the forest was an odd place lately. Campers and hikers were disappearing, little kids were snaking lumpy gold coins from their parents, and people—lots, and lots of people were getting sick.

I unlocked my phone again, hoping I'd left whatever dead spot I'd been through, but found it was still useless.

"Dammit," I mumbled, tucking it into my pocket. I felt a flash of amusement from my left as I moved to step off the curb, and then a hand grabbed my arm, holding me in place.

"Phone, please," a familiar voice said. I turned to find Kincade standing next to me, a pleasant smile on her strong face.

"Hi?" I asked glancing around. She didn't let go of me, didn't change her position. I felt a certain smugness in her and it made me glance down the line of her free arm. She was holding it in front of her belly, something clutched in her grip. It took me a moment to understand that I was seeing a very small knife protruding from her fist.

"Your phone, if you please."

"You need my cell phone?"

"I'm assuming you don't carry around a rotary phone, so yes. Your mobile, please."

"Why?"

"Because otherwise I'm going to stab you with this knife and you'll be poisoned."

She was dead serious and enjoying herself to boot. I tried to take a step back, but she gripped my arm harder, leaned slightly forward.

"I have no interest in keeping your phone," she lied. "You'll get it back once we go somewhere to have a talk." That, perplexingly, was the truth. I swallowed thickly, glanced at my mother's sedan as if it would turn into Bumblebee and save my butt. When nothing transformed or ground out a metallic battle cry, I sighed.

"You're not going to hurt me?"

"Probably not," she said. It wasn't exactly a lie, which led me to believe she wasn't planning on hurting me but she wouldn't shy away from it.

"Shit," I sighed. She laughed, but kept her eyes on mine. Slowly, I slid my hand into my pocket and pulled out my phone. The few people who passed us barely noticed; we were just two women chatting on the street. She pocketed the phone and then shifted her footing.

"I'm parked a bit down the street. Shall we walk?"

"I'm assuming I have no choice."

She cocked her head at me, her dark eyes sparkling. She was enjoying herself too much for my liking.

"Come on." She tugged my arm a bit to turn me, fell into step when I started walking. Remaining silent for a few stores, she waited until we'd rounded a corner down an alley and paused. "Now the keys."

"Ahh," I groaned. My phone was one thing, but I didn't want to hand over my mother's keys. If I lost the car, I'd be in trouble. Dad would give me so much hell. "Do I have to?"

"I'll give them back, of course. Unless I have to kill you."

"Goddammit," I groaned, forking over the keys. We started walking again, the blade still a threat to my life. We crossed through the alley, across a gravelly parking lot, and she led me to a white SUV parked rear-in. The doors unlocked with an audible *thunk* and she pulled open the back door. I sighed.

"You're seriously kidnapping me?"

"I have some questions for you is all."

"Why me?"

"Because Owen doesn't just sleep with someone for no reason. He's in town on a job, possibly related to the job I'm here doing. If he's spending time with you in a bar while doing that job, you know something about it. Get in; buckle up. We're going for a drive."

Olivia R. Burton

Twelve

"So," Kincade said from the driver's seat. Her voice was conversational, her expression mild as she glanced at me in the rearview mirror. She'd handcuffed me to the handle jutting from the roof and I was watching the scenery pass, fearing the worst. "What can you do?"

"What can I do?" I repeated, lifting a brow. "I eat a mean cake, but that's about it. I'm not terribly skilled."

"For Owen," she said. "What good are you to him?"

"Ah," I grunted, hoping she wasn't asking about what I thought she was asking about. "Like you said, fuck buddy. It's sort of a mutual benefit, actually."

"I can't tell if you're being deliberately dim but, if you are, I'd advise you to stop." We turned another sharp corner and I watched the last of the buildings on our path disappear behind a copse of trees. We were headed into the forest where the people had gone missing and where Owen had taken me to investigate. She let time stretch on, maybe enjoying my unhappy expression as I watched us drive toward unpopulated nature.

"If you're just trying to get information out of me, why are you taking me to the forest?" I asked finally. I couldn't see her whole reflection from my position, but I could see the smile wrinkling her eyes.

"Once you tell me what you do for Owen, I'll tell you what you can do for me."

"That sounds ominous and vaguely rapey," I said. She snorted.

"I promise you, I have zero sexual interest in you. Now," she said, as she pulled over to the side of the road well away from where Owen and I had parked before. Yanking up the e-break, she turned, produced a small gun from somewhere and aimed it at me. "Tell me what it is you do or I shoot you in the kneecap."

"I don't like this game," I said. She waved the gun slightly to the left, talking with her hands.

"You're human, but that's not all. You a healer? Mind reader? A telekinetic?" Her eyes lit up. "Pyrokinetic? What can you see or sense or do?"

I didn't want to tell her everything. I don't know why, but the idea of letting her know the full extent of my powers scared me. I'd seen Owen kill a succubus and feel nothing; if Kincade was in the same league, I wanted her knowing as little about me as possible.

She'd been telling the truth when she'd said she had no interest in sex with me. I knew Owen had no interest in hurting me, partially because we were sleeping together and partially because he would gain nothing from it. He knew about my empathy, but I'd only used it to help him.

I didn't want Kincade expecting me to help her; I doubted she'd persuade me in quite the same way Owen would.

"I can …" I trailed off, trying to decide what to say. I went with a partial truth. "I can sense when there are creatures around."

"Creatures? What types?"

"Um. Fairies, werewolves, vampires, that sort of thing."

"Interesting!" Her voice went up an octave and she smiled. "That must be handy."

"It's pretty useless, actually. And kind of a pain in the ass with some creatures."

"No, I have just the use for that. You got your walking shoes on? We're going for a stroll."

"I'd rather not," I said. "Haven't eaten in a few hours. Feeling a little faint. I'll stay here, you go ahead. Just leave the radio on, will you? Maybe some smooth jazz?"

Climbing out of the car, Kincade moved around to my side, yanked the door open. Somewhere around the rear of the car, she'd holstered the gun under her own jacket, produced a tiny key. She unlocked my cuffs, stepped back.

"Come on, lover. Let's go."

"You can call me Gwen," I said. She lifted a brow and I felt a bit of amusement come. "Otherwise I'll just get my hopes up."

As I dropped out of the car, Kincade grabbed my wrists, cuffed them together behind my back. She gave me a little nudge, started walking as if she expected me to follow. When I didn't, her disappointment pelted against me like a rotten apple, making me sigh. Without looking back or stopping, she yelled over her shoulder.

"Your brother's pretty cute. I may have to go introduce myself later, get a little side dish of my own in the area."

More and more, I was starting to feel like a character in a cheesy action flick. Unfortunately, I didn't have any hidden fighting skills or a giant, impressive gun collection. In that moment, I didn't even have a snappy comeback.

"Yeah, all right," I said, pushing on. She continued walking, her eyes scanning the forest as she did.

"Let me know if anything comes around."

"Like what?"

"Like anything that isn't a deer or a bunny rabbit. Like something that might want to eat your face, or offer you a deal you just can't refuse."

"So I'm looking out for Dracula and The Godfather?"

"Yes," she deadpanned. "I'm extremely concerned we're going to be attacked by a rabid pack of Coppola movies."

Like the last two times I'd been brought out into the forest, it was awhile before I saw anything except trees or felt anything except normal wildlife. Kincade seemed content to walk, not bugging me or rushing me to find something I had no control over. I kept poking at her emotions, trying to dislodge something that would give me an edge or tell me something about why she'd picked me of all people to drag out here, but nothing came except a faint whiff of boredom.

"How'd you know where I was," I asked finally, my gaze on the ground, watching for poison oak. She glanced over, a spurt of pompous amusement hitting me as she did.

"You gave me your name, you idiot. It wasn't hard to find where you live and check in on you until you did something interesting."

"Going to see my brother was interesting?" I skirted around a low bush, wished I had my arms to help me feel more balanced; they were starting to get a little sore cuffed behind my butt.

"Not in an of itself, but you seemed distracted, like maybe you *knew* something interesting. I switched on my phone jammer, waited for you to get far enough away that no one would notice, and here we are."

Cell phone jammer: genius. I sighed, wondered why movie villains never thought of that one.

"How did Owen figure out about you?" she asked. I eyed her for a second, discerned she was genuinely curious.

"Pretty much the same way as you. He observed...something different going for me, asked about it. Although," I grumbled. "He was a lot nicer in how he asked."

"I don't doubt it. While he's no sucker for a pretty face, he likes the ladies." Hooking a hand onto the trunk of a skinny tree, she swung around it, paused when she was facing me. "You're far from the only woman he's seeing; I hope you know that."

I lifted a brow, watching her blankly for a moment. Was she trying to make me angry, trying to get me to turn on Owen in some way? Dropping her hand from the trunk, she continued to watch my expression intently. On a sigh, I shrugged.

"I know. He's not the only man I'm seeing, either. It's mainly just an excuse for the two of us to have sex."

When her smile grew and her curiosity abated, she turned to start walking again.

"What about you?" I asked. "When you two knocked boots did he claim you were the love of his life?"

That she found genuinely funny. Tossing a smile my way, she shook her head. "Not at all. Neither one of us is that naïve. It was just, like you said, an excuse to have sex."

"Well, then we're even. You can stop with the attempts at mind games."

"Mind games?" she asked, still facing forward. "I'm just wondering about you, that's all. You're taking this remarkably well for someone who's been threatened, handcuffed, and dragged out into the woods." An annoyance was growing inside of her, but that wasn't the only thing I felt. The closer we got to the river, the more I could feel a familiar, faint emotional signature. When she twisted to put her back to the sound of the water to smirk at me, the emotions beyond her started vibrating.

I stopped walking; she didn't.

"You've got something going for you other than an awareness of other creatures, Gwen Arthur. I can—"

The tree to her left *moved* when she crossed its path. A great creaking sounded as the bark of the ancient fir tree twisted, pulled away from itself. The moss along the bark shifted and I caught sight of amber eyes before one of the lower branches swung around in a swish of needles. Kincade caught something telling in my expression and threw herself into a roll, diving away from the tree to come up in a crouch. She lifted her right hand, causing the hard-edged, steel rings on her four fingers to glint a bit in the light. A smirk tugged at her lips before she yanked something out of her pocket and threw it at me.

"Ow!" I cried. Something hard hit the edge of my brow, not quite breaking skin but hurting enough that I felt it into the bone. Before I could demand to know what she'd done, I heard more creaking, turned my gaze back to the tree.

A womanly creature had pulled away from the trunk. It was a bit taller than me, but otherwise just about my size, with long limbs and wild hair made of pine needles shiny with moisture. Had it not been made of bark and moss, I would have been pretty damned jealous of the lady tree's vivacious bod.

The tree bark curved in all the right places, forming perky mounds where a human would have breasts, sloping away from a small waist into wide hips and shapely thighs that met under a mossy knoll. White fungus grew from her strong calves, further lines of bright green moss decorating her wooden flesh like decorative tattoos. Her face was angular and beautiful with thin scars in the wood where eyebrows would be and dots of amber resin making up her eyeballs.

As the curiosity and irritation of the tree creature joined the smarting sensation where I'd been hit, the lady fir turned slowly to me, tipping her angular face. The resin in her eyes shifted color from amber to a slightly transparent golden as the cracks in the wood above them lowered. Whatever this wooden woman was, she had the capacity for anger and I could feel it burbling. I heard more cracking and creaking as she pulled completely away from the tree, leaving bare, smooth wood spanning the trunk, and took a single, heavy step toward me.

"That's the ticket," Kincade muttered, her emotions sparking with delight and excitement. I took a few steps back, tried unsuccessfully to tear my gaze away from the darkly lovely creature slowly crossing the forest floor toward me.

"What the hell is that thing?" I asked.

"Angry, I'd say."

"That's not what I meant!"

The creature paused and I noted the toes on her feet growing outward into the soil to take root while she stared at me. When frozen in place, only the needles of her hair looked alive, settling from being jostled as she'd moved. Kincade had started sidestepping around to her back, a hand slipping into the pocket of her puffy jacket.

"What are you doing? Oh god, don't make it mad—madder," I whispered, unable to make my voice carry. Kincade ignored me, choosing her steps carefully so as to not attract the creature's attention. Taking the creature's stillness as a sign from fate or the universe or President God Morgan Freeman, I took a few big steps back, my wrists jerking against the cuffs. My actions were mostly without my permission; I just wanted use of my arms to defend myself—or more likely to catch myself if I fell while running away screaming.

Kincade took one last step, producing a thin, gold chain from her pocket. She let the length of it drop to the ground, holding one end between her thumb and the second knuckle of her index finger. As her arm pulled back, the tree immediately to her right screamed. It was the sound of rage, the sound of mourning.

It was the sound of a rusty band saw and it shocked Kincade enough that she rolled defensively into the leaves, dropping her golden chain.

As the roots of the tree that was focused on me uncurled from within the earth and pulled back into proper toes again, she took another step, her resin eyes going completely clear. I yelped, tried to back up again. I only managed to keep from getting my own knuckles ground into my ass when I tripped and dropped backward, but it was a hollow victory. The lady tree was still pursuing me and the friend she'd called or teleported or just spontaneously created in the face of two stupid, human ladies was pulling free of her own paralysis.

She was shorter than the fir, bushier, with red and black moving along her trunk like a kid shaking a metal tray of marbles. As the branches that would become her arms twisted and thrashed, reaching for Kincade, I felt a pure menace shoot out of her. Kincade swore heavily, shoved her hands through the dead leaves and branches covering the forest floor. Her eyes darted rapidly between her moving hands and the swinging branches coming at her like the muscular arms of an angry body-builder. Swearing just before the second tree managed a swipe that would have hit her, she rolled out of the way.

"Do something!" I yelped, trying to figure out how to control my thudding heart and push myself to my feet to escape. My wrists were aching, possibly bleeding from the cuffs, and the tree approaching me did not seem distracted by the incredible, pure anger from the other tree creature behind her. She had her own outrage in her glimmering eyes and it was all for me.

"I am doing something," Kincade sniped, dodging another swipe aimed for her face. The crack of leafy wood on bark brought my gaze to the other lady tree and I saw her stand tall, her own thighs wide and adorned with more crawling red and black. As I heard the decidedly unpleasant sound of hundreds of papery, flapping wings, Kincade turned her eyes to me. Jerking her brows up once, she shrugged a shoulder.

"Sorry, lover. Gotta go."

"What?" I asked, sure I'd misheard her. Kincade turned on her heel and took off. The rippling red and black along the tree's body suddenly lifted, clouding around it before taking off after Kincade. I realized that, unlike the tree focused on me, this one was covered in bugs.

"Oh god," I yelped. "Oh g—" I cut off with a scream as the lady fir planted a foot firmly by my left shoe, bent over, and lifted me into the air by one leg. She held me high, her own branchy arm seeming to stretch to accommodate her desire to be eye level with my upside down face. I struggled as she tipped her head and looked into my eyes. I flailed my arms as the blood rushed to my head and the leg she wasn't holding struggled to stay upward instead of falling forward to knee me in the chest. I just don't have that much muscle control on a good day, let alone when getting beaten up by a tree.

I looked past her at the other creature, watched as she took slow, plodding steps after Kincade, who was long gone. This second tree, I noted, had a hollow back, as if she were just a shapely plate you snap over the front of the trunk to make it sexually attractive. Fear burbled through my throat in a laugh as I thought fondly of the Dolly Pops and their little snap on clothes that I had played with as a child.

The tree holding me tipped her head again, pulling me closer. I felt a tinge of confusion bleed into her psyche. I tried a smile.

"Please put me down?" I asked. She did not respond, barely seemed to understand me. The tree beyond her screamed again, more bugs lifting away from her to fly through the forest and disappear. I hoped, briefly, that Kincade would trip over a branch, break her leg, and fall face-first into a pile of poison oak. That would have been fair, I thought. Well, no, even that wouldn't have been comparable to leaving me to get murdered by foliage, but the idea of it at least generated another nervous, bubbling laugh.

Abruptly, the grip on my leg disappeared and I plummeted.

"Gwen?" I heard a voice in the soup of my consciousness but it went away shortly after. I was dreaming about trees shaped like Playboy Bunnies and giant bug-men.

"Hellooo!" A jaunty voice sang into my brain, a hand touching my cheek. The lady tree in my dream served me tea, but there wasn't enough sugar. I spat it out. She got angry and slapped me, the rough bark on her hand scraping my skin.

"We need to get her home," the lady tree said. I frowned at her across the wide stump. The bug man approached from the left, did a little twirl.

"I got it!"

"Can you carry her?"

"Oh sure," the bug man said, before leaning close. His wings spread away from his fat body and they were incredible, red and black with little eyeballs along the edges. The eyeballs were spinning madly, taking in every sight at once. As he leaned close to slide an arm under my back and another under my neck, all the eyeballs turned at once to focus on me. I whimpered.

Thirteen

"Gwen?"

I could hear crying.

"She's waking up," my father said. A loud crunch immediately to my left startled me into opening my eyes. I saw the ceiling of my brother's room, the puffy face of my anxiety-ridden mother in my peripheral vision. Then, Izzy's face slowly slid into view from the right, his nose nearly pressed to mine. He smelled like peppermint candies. When he poked a smooth, tiny orb against my closed lips, I realized it was because he was snacking on them.

I lifted a hand to shove at him, caught sight of dried blood on my wrist. Izzy smiled, ignoring my shove against his shoulder.

"What—" I croaked, wheezed over my own dry throat. "What happened?"

Izzy disappeared just as my mother let out a wail, threw herself against me. I felt my father's annoyance at my feet, a jagged bolt of lightning in the misty cloud of worry from everyone else.

"My baby! What happened? Are you okay? Where did you go?"

"Gwen?" Chloe said. I swallowed, tried to pat my mother's shoulder to ensure her I was alive and then turned my head. I found Chloe kneeling next to the bed, Natalie at her immediate left. Natalie gave me a small watery smile and I felt my eyes widen.

"Oh god," I mumbled as it all came back to me. My father was standing at the foot of the bed, watching me with an unhappy expression on his dour face. I swallowed, looked once around the whole room, and tried to sit up. Chloe put a hand on Natalie's shoulder.

"Is she okay?"

"Her head is okay. I made it stop bleeding," Natalie explained Robin's breath hitched behind her and I squeezed my eyes shut. I had a hell of a headache but I couldn't feel any actual wounds along my scalp. My wrists were sore, my body hurt like hell, and Izzy's peppermint breath was making me hungry and nauseated all at the same time.

"Okay," I said. "I need some space. I'm okay." My mother wailed again, tucked her arms under my body and hugged me to her. Izzy wisely pulled back, crunched into another solid mass of sugar. I gave my mother's back a light pat, tried not to absorb the sadness shoving out of her and into me like an invading army.

It took me a second before I realized that, compared to what it should have been, I could barely feel anything from anyone.

"Whoa," I said, shoving at the bed with my palms.

"It's okay," Chloe said, setting a hand on my arm. "Your father's got it handled."

"He what?" I asked. I glanced down, blinked over my mother's shoulder as I noticed my father wasn't just standing idly by, disapproving of my injuries; he had a hand on my ankle. I couldn't feel much from him but from the look on his face, that was probably for the best. Our eyes stayed glued to one another's for a moment, before I swallowed my pride.

"Thanks, dad." His mouth quirked up slightly at the side and his eyes flicked to my mother. I realized I hadn't answered her questions.

"Mom? I'm okay. I think," I amended. As my mother sat up, pulled me up to lean against her, I fought a head rush. She patted my cheek, slid her hand to touch a tender part of my scalp just behind my ear. Wincing, I looked over to Chloe, raised my brows. The phantom pain of whatever had been tossed at me by Kincade flashed above my eye, bridging itself to the pain behind my ear. Before I could speak, Robin stepped forward, leaning down to pick Natalie up.

"What happened to you?"

"She fell out of a tree," Natalie announced. My eyes went straight to her; next to me, Izzy giggled.

"You fell out of a tree?" Robin said, cynicism dripping.

"Uh," I grunted. Chloe gave me a nod so small I wasn't sure I even saw it. I decided to go with it, bobbed my head forward. It made sense that Natalie would think that, considering what had attacked me.

"And the blood on your wrists?" Robin asked, her voice slightly hollow.

I moved my gaze to Natalie, waiting to see what she'd seen for that. She didn't speak but her bottom lip started to quiver. It only took a second but soon she was bawling, fat tears sliding down her face as Robin, startled, holding her close

"What's wrong, sweetie?" Robin asked, fighting tears of her own.

"I can't help her anymore," Natalie wheezed out through sobs. "I tried, but I can't do anything else."

"Oh, baby," my mother said. "It's okay, she'll be fine." Mom reached a hand out toward Natalie, but Robin didn't close in. Curious, I lifted my hands, inspected my wrists. The skin was still raw, scabbed over. She hadn't been able to heal that, which made me wonder if her healing powers were very limited or if my head had been so bad that she'd exhausted everything she had making sure I didn't die from brain trauma.

"I don't remember," I lied. My mother just switched tactics, twisted to pull me into a hug. "I'm still pretty fuzzy on the whole tree thing."

"Next time you need to be alone," Chloe said, pitching her voice as if she was trying to make a joke but failing to get it right. I couldn't feel what she was feeling, thanks to my father sucking my emotions and, apparently those around me, right out of my brain. I recognized her tactic, though. I was sure my father did, too, but everyone else seemed convinced. "Stay out of the forest."

"Yeah," I said. "Sure."

"We should take her to a hospital," Robin announced, rubbing Nat's back. I wondered briefly where the rest of the family was, but figured maybe Thom and Jake were keeping the kids busy while everyone else fussed over me. "If she's having memory trouble, it might be something more serious than we thought. Natalie can't be expected to know. She's too young."

"No," my father said abruptly. He shifted, shook his head when mom took a breath to speak. "She's fine. It's actually common to have memory issues if you're supernaturally healed of a head wound."

"Really?" mom asked, relief in her voice. Izzy crunched loudly on another candy, pushed to his feet on the bed, and walked over my legs to drop to the floor. "You really believe she's okay?"

"I wouldn't put her in danger, Cora. Trust me." He eyed me for a second and I felt myself shrink back a little. Suddenly the memory of every moment that I'd been untruthful to my father came rushing back to me. Had he known every time that I was lying?

Shit.

"Sweetie, do you need anything? Are you hungry? Do you want a snack, or a bath?"

"I don't think I'm hungry—" Robin let out a shaky laugh and interrupted me.

"Maybe she *should* take her to the hospital."

"*But,*" I snapped. "I could use a shower. I don't know how long I was out there but I think I have leaves in—uh. Well, places they shouldn't be."

Next to me, Chloe chuckled, pushed to her feet. "We'll give you some time alone."

"Everyone out," my dad said. Chloe glanced at him and then back at me. Her expression said something that I couldn't read and she seemed to sense my cluelessness. On a sigh, she gave me one last disapproving look and then left, taking Natalie with her. Robin stepped forward to give me a hug and kiss the top of my head. Mom gave me one last giant hug and then headed out. I stared at the closed door as if I could just delude myself into believing I wasn't about to be in heaps of trouble.

Letting me pretend, at least for the moment, that he wasn't there, my father took his hand off my ankle, moved to sit next to me on the bed. I let out a defeated sigh. Pulling my knees up to my chest, I wrapped my arms around my shins, turned to look at him.

He watched me for a moment and then chuckled. My empathy eased back in slowly and I felt something like an echo of the amusement in my father.

"Why can I feel what you're feeling?" I asked. "I've met a few other empaths and I can never read them. I assumed it was a trick of the power, to keep us from falling into some endless loop of emotions."

"Never been good at shielding," dad said with a shrug. "I'm assuming you're the same. You practically scream your every feeling."

"Well, that's your fault. You should've passed on better genetics." I felt a stab of disapproval spike toward me on a wave of worry, but he didn't take the bait.

"What happened?"

"I ..." Trailing off, I lowered my forehead to my knees. I could smell dirt on my clothes. "I was attacked by a giant tree creature."

Dad was silent. He knew I was telling the truth; that was a given. But him believing me? I couldn't count on that. It took about thirty seconds for me to get up the courage to look up and meet his eyes. He was smiling, lips closed tight as if he was trying to stop himself from cracking up.

"What?" I asked. He shook his head.

"Tree monster?"

"Yes," I said, feeling defensive. My spine went a little straighter and I pressed on through clenched teeth. "It looked like a pretty sexy lady, in case you're curious."

"Gwen—" dad started, turning away from me slightly. I jumped in, unwilling to listen to a lecture when I'd just told him exactly the truth.

"Don't start calling me a liar—or crazy or telling me I'm seeing things. I was in the forest, and one of the trees just mutated into a woman ... shaped-thing and attacked me. She picked me up by the leg and then dropped me when I laughed at her. That's the truth, I swear."

"I believe you," he said quietly. "No need to get worked up."

"Why aren't you *more* worked up? I was attacked by an Ent, for chrissakes."

"Not an Ent," dad corrected, patting my foot. I was confused at how calm he was being; usually by this point in a conversation, at least one insult had been hurled and we'd both gone hoarse from yelling.

"It's called a Lofriska. They *are* basically tree monsters but it's not that simple."

"And how do *you* know about them?"

"Ah," dad said, apparently not expecting that question. I felt a bit of embarrassment puff out of him and my eyes narrowed. I suddenly wasn't sure I wanted an answer. "When I was younger, I was a big hiker. I used to spend a lot of time in the woods. Lofriska are generally pretty kind to humans, though not if they're crossed. One appeared to me."

His entire body language shifted as he pushed against the bed, moved subtly away from me.

"If you demonstrate a respect for their environment, for their kind, they reward you." I thought of the gold coin we'd gotten off Samuel. My brows shot up.

"It gave you gold?"

Shock arced out of my dad, but the embarrassment from earlier wasn't entirely gone.

"Among other things."

"Do I want to know the other things?" he watched me with pursed lips and I wondered for a second if he was going to pick a fight just to avoid the conversation. There was something in his brain he wasn't comfortable telling me, despite the fact that it seemed relevant.

"I don't want to tell you the other things, I know that."

"Then we'll stop there. As far as I'm concerned, you were given gold and that was the end of it.

"They don't just hand you gold. They're not just mystical ATMs. They provide, ah." He cleared his throat. "Aid, friendship, occasionally, uh, you could call it companionship—"

"Okay!" I nodded. "Got it."

"To lonely travelers," he spat out, moving on as quickly as he could. "And, like I said, reward those who show respect for the land. They're part of the forest. It's their home, but it's also their livelihood. If the forest dies, so do they. If you're good to them, they give you sticks and twigs, rocks, moss, something. If you cherish it enough to bring it home, it turns to gold."

"What if you're not good to them?" I asked, though I was pretty sure my head wound was the answer.

"I was never malicious; I don't know. That brings us back to the issue at hand: what did you do to piss of a Lofriska?"

"I wasn't the one who did anything." I held up my hands, showed my dad the wounds on my wrists. "I didn't exactly go there willingly."

Suddenly, the fact that Kincade had been the reason behind all of this came back to me. Not only had she left me to die at the rough hands of a forest fae, she'd stolen my phone and my keys.

"Shit!" I snapped. Dad, having sensed my emotions before my outburst, wasn't fazed. "Shit! Dammit! God damned asshole!" Pushing to my feet, I did a little turn in the room, flailed my arms. Dad watched me, let me be mad.

"What is it?" he asked when I'd stopped swearing and hissing out nonsense.

"The woman who dragged me out there has mom's keys and my cell phone."

"I don't think so."

I turned to him sharply, frustrated. "Oh, you don't?"

"Her car's parked outside. Your phone was in the middle console. It's how Chloe knew something was wrong, I'm guessing. She found it, gave some half-assed lie—she's a little too good at that, by the way—about promising to pick you up at a friend's place and then her and that boyfriend of hers disappeared. They showed up an hour later with you in tow." Irritation burbled up inside my father and he pointed a finger at me. "You better be sure you trust her enough to justify telling her about Natalie's power."

"Chloe loves me," I said, shaking my head. "I have literally trusted her with my life. She wouldn't do anything to hurt Nat."

My father let the line about my life being in danger pass but I could tell he wasn't pleased. After a few silent seconds, dad sighed, got to his feet. "So this person kidnapped you, dragged you to the forest. She tell you why?"

I swallowed. How many of my big secrets was I going to have to reveal on this trip?

"Ah. We have sort of a mutual … Um. Friend, that introduced us. She could tell I had some sort of power, apparently figured I'd be of use to her. She deals in the supernatural for a living. Evidently she wanted me as bait, I think for one of these creatures."

"You get a description? We can call the police. We can't exactly explain that you were attacked by sexy trees, but you have the cuff marks to prove she kidnapped you. She may have left fingerprints in the car, on the phone or keys."

"Sexy—?" I cut myself off, letting that go before we could dive deep into a pool of information I wanted nothing to do with. "I can't really do that." I shook my head. If the cops went tromping around in the woods, they may end up in worse shape than I was. "I know someone who can help, though. I was supposed to see him this evening, actually."

I glanced around, my eyes catching on the clock. I let out a slow oath again. Getting knocked unconscious for hours at a time was really starting to become an unpleasant habit for me.

"Dammit. You have my phone? I should probably call him."

"I wouldn't mention the 'him' part to your mother," dad said with a small smile. I returned his expression with an equally small smile, wary of the pleasantness but liking that, suddenly after thirty years, it was possible at all.

"Oh?"

"No. She's on the verge of setting you up in an arranged marriage; don't give her any ideas."

"Got it," I said. We stared at each other for a second before I thought about the conversation I'd had with my mother earlier. For the first time since I could remember, I was feeling affection for my father that wasn't being ruined by irritation or wariness. I thought about how life could have been for me as a teenager and what he'd done to protect me from things I hadn't even been aware existed.

I thought about how ungrateful and terrible I'd been and how he'd never once disowned me or strapped me to a rocket and shot me out into space like I probably deserved.

Letting out hitching breath, I pushed forward, wrapped my arms around his neck, pulled him into a hug. He sighed against my ear and squeezed me. I felt a hesitant sort of relief trying to surface within him. I ducked my head to rest it on his shoulder, doing my best to indicate without awkward words that I wasn't planning on picking a fight or screaming obscenities at him. His posture relaxed slightly.

"Thank you and I'm sorry," I said. He kissed my cheek and I felt the nostalgic sadness in me leak away, too rapidly to be my doing. I pulled back, lifted a brow at him. He gave me a small smile, eyes glittering, jaw tight.

"Get out before you see me cry," he grumbled, turning away slightly.

I laughed, gave a small nod. He turned around, lifting his hand to his eyes as I reached for my bag. I'd left it open on the chair by the bedroom door and my sore hips and ribs were pretty happy I didn't have to bend over to get it. Pretending I hadn't seen anything, I made my way to the bathroom.

Fourteen

I eased out of the shower realizing I'd missed lunch and possibly dinner. My stomach, having finally come out of the injury-induced hole in which it had been hiding, was crying out for satiation, growling like J.J. pretending to be a zombie dinosaur. Ignoring it, I swiped a towel over the mirror, took a look at my naked body.

It was a pretty miserable sight.

The bruises on my ribs and left breast were still present, having been joined by the scrapes along my wrists, a small lump under my right eyebrow where I'd been hit. The back of my neck felt raw, but I didn't have a second mirror to see what had happened there, so I could only guess it was similar to the scrapes along my cheek. As I swiped lotion over my legs, I found more bruises along my ankle and calf where the Lofriska had gripped me. I hadn't noticed it at the time, but her bark had managed to scrape the back of my ankle raw. I was not looking forward to trying to find shoes that wouldn't irritate that happy little wound. I took one last glance at myself in the mirror before pulling on my softest, no-underwire bra. I was purple and raw and pretty sure there were scabs on top of scabs.

Overall, I kind of looked like a piñata full of beet soup. I had to just hope nothing else tried to crack me open.

I dug through the pockets of my clothes before balling them up. I would have to wash them—or, more likely, my mother would—before I could wear them again and I didn't want anything going through the wash that shouldn't be wet. When I found the coin that Chloe had stolen from Samuel, I tucked it into my pocket absently, not thinking anything of it.

Chloe met me in Thomas' room, handed me my phone. As she frowned at my face, I felt pity roll out of her. I noted that Izzy and his holiday candies were nowhere to be found. Shutting the door, I moved to set my bag back on the chair by the door, dug around in it until I found some fat, fuzzy socks.

"So, what really happened?"

"This woman—did I tell you about Owen's … friend?"

Chloe lifted a brow, shook her head. "Not entirely. The ex?"

"Yeah. Apparently she knows—she does what he does, so they've crossed paths. Anyway." I dropped onto the bed next to her, winced a bit when my body reminded me not to treat it quite so roughly. "When he and I ran into her she must've caught some sort of scent off me. Figuratively: she's human. She showed up after I went to see Thomas, pulled a tiny knife on me, and dragged me out to the forest. She cuffed me, asked me what it was I did for Owen."

"And you told her what?" Chloe asked. There was a simmering anger inside her that seemed much too intense for stemming simply from worry over me.

"Initially I just told her we were fuck buddies and that was it. She said she knew better and threatened to shoot me in the kneecap if I didn't spill the beans. I *wanted* to point out that she sounded like a bad movie villain."

"Cheesy or not, it worked, didn't it? You told her?"

"Sort of. I told her part of what I could do, but I was too scared to tell her everything. I claimed I could sense supernatural creatures."

"Ah," Chloe said with a nod. The anger in her shifted slightly toward smugness, but she didn't elaborate. "Let me guess, she wanted you to point out some creature to her."

"I guess. She didn't tell me what she wanted, but I'm thinking it was what attacked us. I felt nothing for awhile, but then *bam!*" I smacked my knuckles against the palm of my other hand. "Tree lady."

"Tree *lady?*" Chloe asked. I was glad to feel a tinge of amusement seep in. "Are you sure you hadn't already been hit in the head?"

"I'm sure. This tree just … I—it separated from, you know, *itself.* It wasn't just a tree, anymore, it was a bare trunk that stayed put and a lady … thing. She was beautiful, I mean, for a piece of wood with moss and mushrooms all over it. One minute, there was a Douglas fir there and the next some pissed off—Lofriska, dad called it. Kincade threw something at me." I gestured to my lumpy eyebrow. "Probably as a distraction."

"She ran away?"

"Eventually, but not at first. She pulled a chain out of her pocket and it looked like she was going to throw it at—or around?—the lady tree, but another one showed up and attacked her with bugs."

"Another …" Chloe trailed off, squinting. It wasn't confusion I felt from her, but she was choosing her words carefully. "Another creature?"

"Yeah, Lofriska. Please don't ask how dad knows that."

"I know what those are," Chloe said with a nod. "I've heard—ah—*interesting* stories about them. I think I can guess how your father knew about them."

"Let us never speak of it again. It's bad enough knowing where babies come from and knowing that I was once a baby."

Chloe chuckled, shifted on the bed. Frowning at me as more pity rolled out, she reached over, pushed my hair away from my raw face. "That looks bad."

"It stings a little, but that's it. The bruises are worse." I jerked a chin at her. "How'd you know about Natalie?"

"Izzy told me. He bumped his head when they were playing and she offered to help."

"He couldn't take care of that himself?"

"He probably could, but he let her. It was his idea to bring you back here and not to a hospital."

"I'm better off here, anyway."

"Did you catch what Kincade threw at you?"

"No, I was kind of tied up."

"No—sorry. I meant, did you see what it was? Could you tell?"

"I have no idea. It hit me and then the tree got mad and here we are."

Chloe hummed thoughtfully and turned to look forward.

"So, we know that Kincade wanted you there to sense the Lofriska, possibly as bait. Whatever she threw at you was probably important. We should go find it."

"I'm not going back in those woods," I said, holding up my hands. "No way, no how. I've been beaten up enough for one day, thank you very much. I'm just lucky Natalie misunderstood what she was seeing and that no one took my shirt off. I can't explain away all my injuries—and I still haven't told my mother about my Mel scars."

I lowered my head into my hands, rested my elbows on my knees. I groaned a little bit. Chloe patted my back.

"Izzy and I will go check out the forest, see what we come up with. I think I can find the place where you were again." I sat up, turned to her.

"How did you find me? How did you know where to look?" Chloe bit her lip and I felt a nervous discomfort shimmer inside her. I pointed a finger at her face. "Don't clam up on me. Don't lie to me again and tell me it was Merrin."

Shock and embarrassment propelled out of her and I winced like I'd been shoved. Chloe sighed, pushed to her feet. She rubbed her hands over her eyes, paused facing away from me, and then turned to me.

"I used to have a job that required me to …" She swallowed, blinked rapidly. "Augment my natural abilities with tricks and gadgets. One of those gadgets allowed me to find you."

"And?" I asked. Chloe lifted her hands, palms toward the ceiling.

"And now you're safe."

I stared up at her, frowning. She dropped her hands to her side, stayed silent as we kept uncomfortable eye contact. Finally, I sighed, shook my head.

"Okay." I love Chloe and I trust her to know what's good for me better than I know for myself. I wasn't going to press the issue if it wasn't something she was comfortable discussing. I felt relief seep out of her and she stepped forward, bent to pull me into a hug. My stomach rumbled, reminding us both of my body's priorities.

"Your mother made you a plate, said you should come down when you're feeling up to it." She pulled away, smiled down at me. "Call Owen, if you're feeling up to that."

"I don't think I can have sex in my condition."

"Probably true." Chloe reached down to grab my hand, pull me to my feet. "But I meant, you know, for talking and stuff. Bet he'd wanna know what happened today, don't you think?"

"True," I agreed, though I wondered honestly what he might do to Kincade upon hearing what she'd done to me.

"Did you ever find your brother, talk to him about Owen?"

"Ah, yeah. I'd just seen him when Kincade showed up," I said, wondering briefly if I'd thought to tell Chloe Kincade's name the first time we'd talked. I couldn't recall, but she'd known about it, so I must've.

"Did he have any idea what Izzy was talking about?"

"Does Izzy even have any idea what he's talking about?" Chloe just shrugged, but I could tell she secretly found my dig funny. "Thom doesn't even know my Owen. He knows another one, though. He's the brother of the sick—of the hiker? The one Owen's here dealing with. Ah, shit, I was gonna call him and talk to him about all this."

"I'm sure you still can."

"Has he called me at all? Where's my phone?"

"I've been keeping it safe and no, he hasn't called. I'm sure he won't mind if you call him."

"Okay. If he's not calling, he's probably busy, though, and I'm starving, so I'm gonna hold off, at least until after I eat."

"Forgoing saving the town to stuff your gullet: that's the Gwen I know."

I rolled my eyes but didn't fight her when she led me downstairs to do just that.

Mom probably made my bruises worse with the hugging and kissing and general displays of showing how glad she was that I hadn't died. Dad and I went with the story that I had no memory of what happened and Chloe claimed Izzy had found me. This, of course, got Izzy extra servings of dessert, which he declined to share with me.

After my mother had doled out everyone's dishes of ice cream and cookies, and Chloe and Izzy excused themselves to secretly check out the forest, I'd moved to the living room, parking myself in front of the fireplace. I tried Owen's phone twice, but got no answer either time.

"You okay?" I heard. I looked over, found Jake standing next to the couch, frowning down at me. I lifted my brows, felt the regret in him. "I would have been there when you woke up, but I wanted to keep the little ones out of it."

"It's okay," I said, turning to face him.

He took a few steps, considered the couch that was still bare of cushions and settled down on the carpet, crossing his long legs at the ankles. I smiled, spoke before he could.

"I should probably apologize to you. It's one thing to marry into a family of super humans. It's another entirely to be forced to share a meal with a magical creature who eats all your waffles and a sister-in-law who makes your daughter cry." I shook my head. "I really thought I was just coming home to eat cake and have a big Thanksgiving dinner and eventually go into a tryptophan coma. I didn't know any of this weird, wacky stuff would happen."

"Is it rude if I ask what Izzy is, exactly?"

"It might be; that's why I've never asked."

"So you just hang out with this guy without knowing anything about him?"

"I know enough about him to know he won't hurt anyone. He'll steal your candy and show no respect for your personal space, but he's … harmless."

"You're sure?"

"I've never felt any malice in him and he's helped me out with strange problems a time or two. Plus, Chloe trusts him and I trust her."

"Hmm," Jake grunted, turning to look down at his feet for a moment. I felt the discomfort in him ease away and he lifted a brow. A smile formed and I met his pretty eyes when he looked back at me. "You look like shit."

"I feel like shit."

"You really can't remember what happened to you?"

"I remember leaving the tea shop after seeing Thomas and now I'm here." I shrugged; strictly, I had not just lied to my brother-in-law. "I wish someone had gotten the plate number of the whatever hit me though."

"Well, Natalie's devastated that she can't do more to help you."

"No," I said, waving a hand. "Please tell her she's done enough. It's not her fault. She—shit." I sighed, feeling my heart try to crawl up into my throat.

"I told her," Jake said. He scooted forward enough to pat my knee.

"I can't stand that I made her feel bad. I can't even imagine—no, I can exactly imagine what it's like for her having to feel me in pain and not be able to do anything about it. I've been there and it's miserable. Can I buy her something?" I offered desperately in an attempt to stave off crying. "What will make it better? Candy? Ice cream? A pony."

"I don't think we have room for a pony, but she's managed to get herself an Amazon wishlist full of dolls and robotics that I'm sure would ease her pain."

"Robotics, eh?" I asked.

"Yeah, she's already taking apart anything we'll let her get her hands on. Sometimes she puts it back together and sometimes it even works after. I'm hoping she's going to be an engineer and create giant mechanical men who will take over the world."

"Not giant mechanical women to take over the world?"

"I prefer my dreams for my children to be realistic, thank you very much."

I snorted. After a moment, I considered my other tiny relatives. "Has J.J. shown any sign of having any powers?"

"No," Jake shook his head. Running his hands through his hair, he met my gaze halfway, head still tilted down. "I'm not sure if I want Stella to be like me or like her mother. Like you guys."

"Understandable." I nodded. "It's not all fun and games being an X-Man."

Jake let out a laugh and sighed. He glanced up and I felt Robin enter the room, worry swamping her.

"Don't you start," I said, looking up as she walked over to stand next to me. "I'm fine."

"Do I have to *make* you tell me the truth?" she asked. I glowered up at her, tugged my sleeves over my hands, shook my head.

"No ma'am."

"Then how are you really?"

"Sick of being asked how I am. But!" I yelped when she reached a hand toward my face. "I'm hurting! I'll be okay!" She paused, a hair's width from my skin and then looked over at her husband. He shook his head. Robin sighed, pulled back.

"Fine. Then I'll leave you alone. Come on, sweetie." She stepped around me, reached a hand down to Jake. Before he touched her, he glanced at me.

"I guess it's bedtime."

"You guess right. Come on." Robin wiggled her fingers, helped pull him to his feet when he put his hand in hers. I looked up at them, felt my eyes well up at the love in the room. Robin sighed and leaned down to kiss me on the forehead.

"Get some rest. We'll see you in the morning. We can start planning your birthday properly."

"Ooh," I agreed. She laughed.

"Once it's about you, you're all over it. Night, chipmunk."

Jake chuckled and they moved through the living room, disappearing into the dark kitchen. I turned back to the fire, let out a sigh. My phone buzzed. It was a text from Owen, letting me know he'd be back at the hotel in thirty and that he'd call me from there. I considered my options, deciding I had slept enough and wanted to talk to him in person.

Olivia R. Burton

Fifteen

I sat on a fat, squishy couch in the lobby of the hotel waiting for Owen to show up. The girl behind the counter wasn't happy to have me invading her solitude, but I did my best to ignore her and let her know I expected nothing from her. It was mutually assured displeasure, though hers was tinged with curiosity, possibly about the wounds on my face and body. She'd seen me healthy and whole just a few days ago and now, here I was, scraped up and bruised.

I was sure she suspected foul play, but I didn't have the energy to worry about it too much.

I felt him before I saw him, a sort of frustrated discomfort that he was trying to fight off. I looked over at the doors, saw them part as he walked through. I half-smiled as I considered that my brain went straight to sex while my body protested heavily. He looked damned good in his charcoal gray coat and black slacks. His hands were bare, his hair a little mussed like he'd run his fingers through it without realizing it was damp outside. His nose was tinged red and I wondered if it had gotten colder outside since I'd come in or if I was in too much pain from my injuries to take proper stock of the temperature.

Confusion swept through him when he saw me, and his gaze fell to the scrapes on my cheek. His jaw tightened and he closed the distance between us, looking down at me. I smiled up at him, noted that, once again, he'd come to me with scraped knuckles.

"I was going to call," he said, his voice thick.

"I know, but I wanted to see you."

"Come on," he said, jerking his head toward the elevator. We passed the desk and I felt that curiosity from the agent wound and tighten. Perhaps she assumed his knuckles and my bruises were related.

When we got into the room, he unbuttoned his coat, tossed it over the suitcase and turned to me. I took off my jacket, draped it over one of the chairs at the table. When I met his gaze, he jerked his chin toward me, his gaze on my wrists. I felt an irritation in him, bordering on anger.

"Kincade paid me a little visit and I've maybe learned what your creature is. Which would you like to hear about first?"

He sighed, brought a hand to his face to rub his forehead. It was an uncharacteristic gesture for him and I cocked my head, stepped close. I could feel discomfort in him still and his voice sounded funny.

"What's the matter?" I asked. He looked up at me, sniffled a bit.

"I spoke with a lot of people today, a few of them sick. I think—"

"Sick?" I interrupted. "Who did you speak to who was sick?"

Owen squinted at me, lifted his hands to his hips. "Why?"

"Shit." I said, took a half-step back. "I went to see my brother today and Thom has a friend of his who's sick. Carter caught it down the line from that amnesiac who was in the forest. Apparently he was patient zero, spreading it all over town. I knew things here felt different, but I'll admit, I've been mostly focused on my own shit—and on you—so it was sort of a background worry. But if you're getting sick like everyone el—shit! You didn't see a Troy or an Owen Mathers, did you?"

Owen sighed, gesturing loosely before speaking. "Go back to what led you to Kincade."

"Why?"

The look he gave me was pointed and I relented, backing up to sit on the edge of the bed as I told him about my day, from running into Samuel and his fancy gold coin all the way up to talking to my dad about what had creamed me.

"Surprisingly, he knew exactly what had attacked me."

"I know what it is, too, and you should probably go."

"Because you're gonna head out now and slay it?" Owen laughed at the suggestion, the edge of it turning into a cough.

"Everything going on stems from the Lofriska—perhaps the same one Kincade pissed off, for all we know—and whatever I've caught, you do not want to get. If we don't figure out a way to make them happy again, things could go south fast."

"For you?"

"For everyone."

I grimaced, getting to my feet again and closing in to cup his cheeks. He smiled, but wouldn't meet my eyes, and I didn't feel the usual lust or pleasure at my touch swirl up inside him. Telling myself it was just because he felt awful, I stayed put.

"How?"

"These creatures have been known to kill entire villages just because one or two people pissed them off, insulted them, or hurt them. They can cause disease when they're mad and I'm pretty sure they're pissed." Owen leaned back, out of my grip, and took a seat at the little table where we'd eaten dinner. "I'd guess that's why they let one person free. The rest are likely dead, but they let one come back to civilization to spread whatever this is."

"What pissed them off?"

"Fuck if I know," he said, shaking his head. "But I caught something from one of the people I spoke with today and it hit me hard and fast."

"Well, I've been around two sick people today and I feel—well, I don't feel fine, but I don't feel sick. I'm sure it's safe for me to stay." I closed in, running a hand through his hair.

He looked up at me, very serious, and then looked down as he brought my hands up so he could look at my wrists. An echo of the malice I'd felt in him when we'd run into Kincade flashed but he was too weak or tired for it to be as damaging to my psyche as it would have been any other time. His thumb edged one of my scabs and I felt the pressure in his other hand increase slightly.

"Did she say what she wanted at all?"

"Nope, just that she wanted me to tell her if I felt anything. Then, when the Lofriska popped up, she got giddy and produced some gold chain, like she might whip it or tie it up."

Owen shook his head, sniffled again. I rubbed his cheek as he pressed on.

"She wouldn't have gone in unprepared and just wandering. She knew exactly what was out there and she wanted it. You were bait, or a distraction, or an unwilling guide. I don't know." His eyes still on my wrists, he leaned back against the chair. "I don't know what the chain she used was exactly, but I'm guessing it's enchanted or forged by fae. It would have given her the edge she needed to do whatever it is she went in there to do."

"What do you think that would have been?"

"I have no damn clue. Kincade is …" He looked up at me, but his eyes were unfocused. "She doesn't play by the same rules as I do, doesn't work for the same rewards. She's a lot like—" He cut himself off and I felt a sudden shock and embarrassment rattle us both. I lifted a brow.

"She's like what?"

"I …" He trailed off, shook his head. "I was going to mention someone, but you wouldn't know what I was talking about." It wasn't exactly a lie, but I nodded and didn't press the issue.

"Ah."

"I'm off my game, need some rest." His expression folded, disappointment evident across his features.

"I'm not here for sex if that's what you're worried about."

He grinned. "Why would I worry about that?"

"Because we both feel like shit?"

"Ah," he murmured. "That."

"Believe me, normally I would be all over you. Not a single bit of you would be safe from a single bit of me. But," I dragged the word out, leaning down to eye level, cupping his face in my hands. "Raincheck?"

"Raincheck," Owen agreed.

"At least let me help?" I suggested. I wasn't entirely sure what I could do, but I'd spotted a room service menu set out on top of the dresser with a bunch of other hotel guides.

"I could be persuaded," he said, his voice sleepy. I pulled back, went to grab the menu. I flipped through it, held it up.

"I'll be company while you eat hot soup."

"That's very noble of you, but you don't have to stay. You're here to be with family; you should go do that." I laughed, shaking my head.

"No thanks, I'd rather be here nursing you back to health, trust me. We can eat, talk this through some more, figure out what might make sexy tree ladies angry and brainstorm ways to make it better."

Owen considered me and I felt a spike of lust try to light him up; it was no match for the fatigue from whatever flu or cold he'd caught, however. After a moment, he gave a nod.

"As long as you don't try to pay for anything."

"Oh no." I snorted, gave an exaggerated roll of my eyes. "You're definitely paying and I am *definitely* ordering more of that cheesecake."

I woke propped up in bed a few hours later, head lolled back on a pile of pillows. Owen lay at my hip, one arm tucked under my knee and wrapped around it, hand resting on his chest. I didn't remember either of us making a conscious effort to fall asleep, but there we were. I felt him wake up as I yawned, felt the tension in his body that followed the emotional shift. As he moved to stretch a bit and catch his bearings, I glanced at the clock. I felt touch of shock flow out of him.

"Yowza," I said. "It's four in the morning. I hope no one at my house is up, or they're probably worried sick."

"Can you blame them?" he asked through a yawn. "You're appallingly bad at keeping yourself out of danger." I rolled my eyes, tensed the fingers I'd brushed into his hair to shake his head slightly.

"Quiet, you."

He laughed, pulled his hand out from under my leg, and pushed himself up to sit next to me. "What were we talking about?"

"Movies, I think."

"Hmm," he mumbled, shaking his head when he yawned again. His throat had gone raw and I could feel how warm he was next to me. I pressed a hand to his cheek. After a moment, I moved my hand to his, figured I'd ask what I'd been wondering since well before we'd fallen asleep.

"You're sure this thing won't kill you?"

"I'm never sure I won't die, but I do the job anyway."

"But you made it sound like you knew how to be cured."

"Tuesday, Wednesday, stay in bed."

"Hunh?" I asked, lost, feeling a teeny prick of mischief in him but not sure what it could mean. He laughed and shook his head.

"It's a song, by The Cure."

I smacked him lightly, which seemed to make his laugh gurgle into a cough. He cleared his throat, got up to move into the bathroom. I heard the water running, the sound of gargling and spitting. When he came back out, I could see the way his body had hunched slightly with fever and fatigue. Normally he was long and lean, narrow at the waist with a slim face and a confidence you wanted to slurp away from his skin. In the light of the dim hotel room, though, he looked exhausted, beaten.

He must've caught my assessment of him in my expression.

"The Lofriska can cause as well as cure sickness. While I'm not sure that what they crafted is deadly, I'm guessing it could be if they wanted. Whatever they did to the fine people of Balanis, Montana should be curable, assuming we make amends for whatever they've found offensive. I'm choosing to believe I can make it all better."

"If it helps, I don't think it's deadly. My brother was talking about this thing hitting his friends a few weeks ago at least. Carter—his buddy—sounds awful and looks like he was hit by a train, but he isn't dead."

"Well, if it's only as bad as being hit by a train, why try to cure it at all?"

I rolled my eyes and pressed on through a laugh. "Assuming I want you back in fighting shape, what sort of things would make it all better?"

"We're going to have to ask them," he said simply, as if it were the most natural answer. My brows shot up.

"You mean we should give them a phone call, or write them a happy letter on some cute, little stationary, right? You're not suggesting we go back into the woods?" He nodded once and I went rigid, shaking my head, panicked at the idea. "I don't think that's a good idea. Last time I walked into those woods, they got pretty angry pretty fast. I think going back there might only make them reconsider their decision not to break my neck."

Wincing—or maybe frowning, it was hard to tell—Owen came forward to sit on the foot of the bed. Something was brewing in him, a frustrated curiosity. His eyes narrowed after a moment and he met my gaze.

"We went into those woods before and nothing happened. Can you tell if whatever you sensed the first time was the same thing?"

I thought about it, tried to bring back the sensations in my head of coming across the invisible creature and compare them to the anger I'd felt from the Lofriska.

"Maybe? The first time was so faint that I didn't really get a sense of anything specific. I think that—or something similar—is what I felt the second time, but I got my bell rung pretty hard so I could be mixing it up."

"I'm going to assume that it was the same thing, which leads me to assume that, since they didn't attack us the first time we were in their territory, that you were not what they were angry at. I'm thinking it was Kincade."

"That makes sense, though not enough to make me think I want to go prancing into the forest all yippy-skippy. That second Lofriska couldn't have given a fig about me, but it seemed to want her pretty bad. The first one—the one that dropped me like a sack of trash—was pissed, but I guess if it had really had a problem with me I wouldn't be here now."

"Thus, I'm betting it's Kincade they're after; you were just in the wrong place at the wrong time."

"Dammit," I swore. "Goddamned asshole bitch."

"Now you want to punch her in the face too, don't you?"

"Kind of," I admitted. I felt a spurt of amusement from Owen and I narrowed my eyes. "What?"

"Just thinking about the one time you tried to punch me. It was pretty pathetic."

"Hey," I protested. "I've never had reason to punch anyone before, not for real. I don't have the practice you do."

"Fair enough," he agreed.

"Although, considering how easy it's been for me to get beaten up lately, maybe I should learn some self defense tactics."

"Once I'm feeling better, I'll teach you a few moves."

"Can we roll around naked and sweaty like the Greeks of old?"

"We can, but I don't know if it'll be much of a learning experience."

I grinned, wagged my brows. "Let's just try it and see."

Sixteen

I got home around five in the morning, pleased to find that no one was awake yet. I went straight upstairs, stretched out in bed with my clothes still on and fell back to sleep. Robin woke me up a couple hours later, dropping into bed and wiggling her finger along my ear like a roaming fly until I grunted, slapping at her.

"Wake up, chipmunk."

"Hrrrmph," I responded, grabbing for the blanket. I felt a mischievous tickle of friskiness dance over my empathy before her warm hand fell full on my cheek.

"Wake up, Gwen."

My eyes snapped open, consciousness rushing in. I jerked up, tensed, and looked around. Robin smiled at me, pulling her hand away and tucked it under her cheek with her other.

"Whoa," I said. "Morning. Did you just whammy me?"

Robin shrugged. "Only slightly."

"Well don't. That's … Wow. I feel … I don't think I've ever woken up that fast before."

"It's great when the kids won't quite heed their alarms."

"God, how does Jake put up with you?" I asked, stretching my shoulders and cracking my neck. She laughed, shook her head.

"I don't only make him do unpleasant things."

"Nope," I argued, holding up a hand. "Don't go there. Not listening."

Robin's emotions were fuzzy for a second, amusement and love swirling with the hesitant curiosity she'd come in holding onto. Unfortunately, as I stretched my arm upward, my droopy sleeve slid down and she caught sight of the scars Mel had given me.

"What's on your arm?" she asked, sliding my sleeve back before I could stop her. Immediately, shock took over as she grabbed my wrist, baring my arm completely and gasping. "Oh my god! Are these scars?"

"Uhhh," I improvised desperately, trying to pull away. Robin jerked her gaze to my face, her expression going tight, real true anger like I hadn't felt from her more than a handful of times rumbling through my chest, before she sat up and spoke.

"Tell me the *truth*."

I opened my mouth, slammed it shut. There was enough of me that didn't want to tell her that I considered just staying silent. Honesty won out, however, and that tipped the scales in favor of her compulsion.

"I was attacked by a werewolf; he thought I was a giant spider. I've had them about four months."

Robin bowed back like I'd socked her in the stomach, but her wide eyes stayed locked to mine. I felt her hand on my arm shake a bit before her gaze dropped to my scars again. I swallowed, trying gently to pull my arm away as if that would end the conversation and everything would be fine. She squeezed harder.

"No," she said. "Tell me the whole story. What—" She cut off, shifting as if to get into a position more conducive to hearing your crazy sister spout nonsense. We sat on the bed facing each other, legs crossed, knees touching as though we were children playing paddy-cake as she held my arm in her lap and looked over the skin. After awhile, she lifted her gaze, her brow knit, her lips tight.

"There are werewolves?" she asked, surprising me.

I only gaped at her for a bit, felt my jaw move as if I would speak, even though no sound came out. Then, unable to control myself and wondering if being whammied into waking up before I was properly rested had anything to do with it, I let out a short giggle. The giggle turned into a fit, making my scraped cheek feel raw and dry, but I couldn't seem to stop.

When I finally got myself under control, I nodded. "Yes."

"Is that why you haven't been calling as much? You didn't want to tell me about werewolves?"

I felt no compulsion this time; Robin was just asking. I could lie, though I guess I didn't have to, not completely.

"Mostly, yeah."

"Mostly?" she asked, her grip on my wrist—and my freewill—tightening again. "What else is there?"

"Vampires," I babbled. "Demons. Fairies. Izzy. There's a tree monster out there right now. It dropped me on my head. Dad fooled around with it."

Robin was frozen, mouth open in disbelief, eyes narrowed, grip on my wrist loose enough that I was finally able to extract myself from her grip. Time passed, leaving me sitting in a soup of her concern, with the occasional burst of glee from one of the kids or rumble of grumpy affection from my dad downstairs.

"I think," she said carefully, as her concern deepened into a shard pressing against my chest, "that you were hit too hard. I think—I'm *sure* you need to go to a hospital."

"No," I said, not sure if I should be as genuinely insulted by her reaction as I was. I hadn't habitually been a liar, at least not about anything that wasn't related to my poor diet. Dad had promised everyone I was fine, and she'd believed him. That should have been the end of it, but here she was, questioning my painstaking revelations. "I'm not crazy and I'm not lying."

"I'm not saying you're lying!" Robin assured me, grabbing for my hands again. I flailed, evading her repeated grasps, but she pressed on, likely having had this same sort of fight with the kids here and there. "I'm saying you're hurt! Look at you, you're in awful shape, full of bruises. You said yourself you were dropped on your head. Let's just—"

"No," I argued, still doing my best to make sure she couldn't touch bare skin. She was getting frustrated with me, but it was mild compared with the worry settled in her chest that threatened to explode and shove me off the bed like being hit with a cannonball. I didn't like it, I didn't want it, and I hated that I'd made her feel it. She had gotten our mother's compassionate nature, while I had gotten dad's damned empathy. My constant absorption of emotions good and bad often make it hard to be as selflessly worried for the state of others as she could so easily be. Still, I also knew what it felt like to be drenched in concern over the well being of a loved one.

I flashed on the time when I'd thought I'd seen Chloe get shot and it briefly paralyzed me, letting Robin get her hands on my bare skin again.

"Come on," she began, her compulsion soaking into my skin. "I'll get mom and we'll all go to the—"

I don't know what made me do it, or even how I was able to do it. I couldn't tell you why I'd never done it before, or why this moment was so different from every other time I'd seen someone I cared about having a hard time. Regardless of the how or the why, I pulled a trick out of my hat that had apparently been sitting there gathering dust my whole life.

Grasping for her worry, her anguish over the state of me, I let Robin's emotions flow out of her and into me. Like experiencing feelings from the outside, it was a physical sensation; her worry had been thick, hot, pressing against me like viscous, boiling syrup. When I made the conscious effort to calm her, it didn't stop at my flesh. I shivered when it sucked in through my pores, settled inside me in a well in my gut.

Robin sighed as if in slow-motion, her wide eyes drooping, her posture slumping. I let out a shocked, wavering moan as if I'd stepped with bare feet onto icy tile. I could feel her worry sitting in me, waiting for something. Was I supposed to release it back into her? Should I have been using it on someone else? How long would it stay there?

"Wow," Robin said, blinking at me. "It's been a long time since I felt that."

"Felt what?" I asked, feeling panicked and desperate. I was full, sick, like my insides were threatening to slosh out through my mouth. My body was quivering, my voice shaking. "What just happened? Oh god, I need to get up. I need—What do I need? I think I want ice cream. I think I want candy. I think—Are you okay? Where's Natalie? Is she okay? Is Jake still mad at me? Is Stella okay? The kids are—god, how *much* does dad *hate* me? Holy shit, what is—this is *awful*."

Fighting off her loose grip as if it were an angry tiger, I pushed up, compelled to get out of there. I needed to leave the room, check on those I loved. I was feeling panicked and stressed as I crossed the room twice, rapidly. Confusion was overtaking me, making me unsettled and paranoid.

"Gwen," Robin said, her voice light. She wasn't worried anymore; she was exceedingly calm, actually. When I twisted, took two steps back toward her, I could see the calm in her, feel it like standing next to a small fire in a wintery nightscape.

"What? Jesus, what did I do? I'm cold. Or hot. I'm—Are you okay?"

Robin laughed, pushing off the bed so she could pull me close.

"Come here. Come *here*," she repeated when I stood there shaking. Without waiting for me to actually move, she pulled me into her arms, pressed a hand against the back of my neck. "Calm down."

The worry dissipated. The tension in my body ran out in a sigh through my lips and I was fine.

"Jeez," I grumbled. Robin ran a hand over the back of my head and then pushed away, holding my cheeks in her hands while she looked into my eyes.

"Are you okay?"

"I think so?" I shook out of her hands, took stock of myself. "I've never done that before."

"Done what?"

"Taken emotions. I've ... uh, taken them *on* and experienced them at a distance before, but nothing like that. I didn't—is this was dad was talking about?" She smiled at me, dropped her hands to her sides.

"I would imagine so. He's better at it than you, though. We should start this conversation over."

"Okay," I said warily. "What part do you want to hear again?"

"Start at the beginning. What's been happening in your life?"

"That's a long story. It's a confusing, strange, and unbelievable long story."

"I've got time. Jake took the kids to see a friend of ours from high school for breakfast."

"Even Stella?"

"No, she's with Mom. What do you say we have some hot chocolate and you tell me about your unbelievable, long story?"

I considered her offer. I wasn't sure how long my emotional drain would last on her, or how much time it would take for her to go into panic mode again. I didn't want her to have some sort of freak out and go running off to tell the police to toss me in a loony bin.

Hot chocolate was a good bribe, though.

It took quite awhile to get through everything I had to say, but I told my mother and sister almost everything. They knew about Mel, Dirk the vampire, Stan being kidnapped by a succubus—even about Owen and the arrangement he and I shared. I had to make it very clear to my mother that Owen and I were not dating, that there wasn't a future there.

Of course, she moved on to Mel, asking if I was sure he wasn't a viable option. His family sounded so nice, she insisted. Shouldn't I at least give him a chance? Couldn't that magical necklace that blocked his emotions from me fix the problem? I didn't explain to her that we'd slept together, but I did push hard on the point that he was physically painful to be around and the necklace was only a part-time solution. Eventually, she dropped the subject, but she wasn't happy about it.

By the time Owen called, Robin and mom seemed to have accepted what I had to say to them and moved on to questioning my sanity and lack of steady male companionship.

"Hey," I answered, stepping outside to avoid sappy glances from my family members.

"Are you ready?" he sounded worse than he had twelve hours before. I winced.

"To catch the plague? Because that's what it sounds like you're offering."

"I can go without you," he said. I sighed. It seemed cruel to make him go out into the woods by himself in his state.

"No, I'll go. I may insist on driving, too, if you look as bad as you sound."

The front door opened and life exploded back into the house. J.J. shot by, followed by Jake and finally Natalie. My brows shot up. "Hold up— Owen, hold on a second."

Stepping back in through the sliding glass door, I reached out to Natalie, gave her a small smile when she looked up at me.

"Nat? Could I ask you a favor?"

Jake frowned over at me, but Robin put a hand on his arm, mumbled, and I felt the emotions within in transform rapidly from wary unhappiness to calm.

"I can't heal you anymore." Her lip quivered and I shook my head rapidly, dropped down to pull her into a hug.

"No, it's okay. Not me. I'm okay. It's a friend of mine. He's sick with a cold. Can you help?"

"Maybe," she said. I pulled away, looked into her eyes. "I dunno."

"Owen?" I said into the phone. "How soon can you be at my place?"

"Not long," he said, paused to cough. "Why?"

"Come pick me up. My niece might be able to help." In answer, he blew his nose, coughed again. I took that as an affirmative, said goodbye and hung up. "Kid, I'm going to buy you so many robots."

Seventeen

"I feel pretty good. Not completely better, but good."

"That's about where I am," I said, glancing away from the passing scenery at Owen. "She's not very powerful, but she's still pretty handy. I did take a painkiller before we left, though."

"Legal?"

"Well, it wasn't prescribed to me, so probably not, but it's helping to numb the soreness so I'm not terribly concerned."

Owen hummed an agreement and took the last turn on the narrow road leading out to what was rapidly becoming my least favorite part of Balanis. I shifted uncomfortably in my seat, shook my head.

"You really think we'll be safe?"

"I believe they'll refrain from hurting us if we're respectful."

"And how are you going to get their attention? The Lofriska didn't seem interested in talking to us the first time we went out there, not even after you yelled at them for no reason."

Owen smirked as the car slowed, yanking up the parking break when we halted. After turning off the car, he reached into the back, pulled out a bag I hadn't known was there; it held more fresh produce.

"Oh, come on," I groaned. He smiled at me, still close, and then kissed my mouth.

"Come on," he said, twisting to climb out of the car with his sack. He didn't come around to my side to open the car for me; he just waited several steps away, watching. Realizing he was probably expecting me to be his bigfoot compass again, I sighed, climbed out after him. He jerked his head to the side, took a step.

"Let's go. I'm going to assume you understand the sasquatch rules of conduct this time."

"Don't get punched in the boob, yeah I got it."

We walked in silence for a while, Owen glancing around, still unbothered by the situation. I watched his profile, smiled a little when I considered how different he felt from when I'd left him that morning.

"You're looking pretty good, Reid," I told him, leaning into him for a step. He grinned and I felt delight in him.

"You still look pretty bad, Arthur, but I wouldn't kick you out of bed."

"Damn straight you wouldn't," I asserted as smugly as I could manage.

"Feel anything?"

"A little self-conscious," I joked, pressing a hand to my heart. "But that's about it." He turned to lift a brow at me over a smirk and I laughed, shaking my head as I answered seriously, this time. "Nope. It's just us so far. Do you know where the bigfoots are?"

"They're somewhat nomadic. I was able to get a rough idea of their location, but my ..." He paused, choosing his words; when he spoke, there was the barest hint of deception there. "Methods aren't so specific that I could walk right over and expect to bump up against them."

"What would you do without me here?"

"This would take longer, that's for sure."

I let out a pleased little sound, pushed a bit harder with my empathy to see if I could pick up any itchy sasquatch feelings about. While I probed, I jerked my chin to catch his attention again. He regarded me mildly, that small smile still tugging at his great mouth. I considered that maybe part of his draw had always been how mellow he managed to stay in any situation. I love even Chloe and her random outbursts of excitable eagerness, but it was nice to be with someone who didn't exasperate my empathy or make me feel wired when I hadn't been prepared to be.

"You never told me what they told you last time we saw them."

"Ah," he said, as if it had just occurred to him. "They didn't know what was happening, but they were able to tell me about the campers. Apparently the kids who went missing were assholes."

"So I heard," I said, thinking of Troy.

"They were loud, obnoxious, leaving garbage and cigarette butts everywhere. The bigfoots weren't exactly sorry to see them disappear."

"But they don't know why they disappeared?"

"Nope. They mainly stick in their own groups. Outside of mating, they don't even cross into each others' territories."

"You think the Lofriska were pissed at these kids because of the garbage and stuff? Would that be enough?"

"Unlikely; if every camper who was a disrespectful dick went missing, there wouldn't be too many left in the world. Especially since the Lofriska have somewhat more of a," he quirked his fingers in air quotes, "*Fairy* idea of what respect is than humans."

"That's slightly terrifying," I said. Owen patted my back.

"Don't worry, they rarely make a habit of attacking humans these days. Humans kill them in droves for agriculture land and strip malls. They don't particularly want to draw attention to themselves, make themselves targets. They're not stupid creatures."

"Why don't they just wipe us all out with some ebola-Zika concoction?" I asked. Owen considered it for a moment, before giving me a look that said he didn't know. We didn't speak for a bit, though I did find myself considering the revelation as we walked.

I sort of felt sorry for these creatures—for all forest creatures, really, having to bump up next to us greedy, asshole humans and not being able to do anything about it. The more I thought about it, the less I blamed them for trying to break my neck.

The itching started shortly after and I whined when I felt it really take hold. Owen turned to watch me rake my nails over my skin, squinting with sympathetic discomfort when I'd hit a bruise or a scab. He let me go at myself for a few seconds before gesturing widely to nothing.

"Which way?"

I grunted unhappily instead of speaking, trying to figure out which part of me was the most irritated. Before I could use my words, the bigfoots appeared to our left. Owen turned, gave a small bow, and then held out the bag. The bigfoot who had hit me before looked me over with its mouth open in what might have been an attempt at a smile. The itching driving me mad seemed to indicate that he found my discomfort funny, which I can't say I appreciated with any sort of grace and poise, despite my guilt at being an asshole member of forest-burning human race myself.

Signing something quickly, Owen took a few tentative steps forward, set the bag down and then backed up. The non-smiley bigfoot reached out to grab it, handed it back to the little ones and then closed ranks with its mate again. It and Owen signed back and forth while I took a few giant steps back. It didn't help the itching as much as I would have preferred, but at least I was less worried about being knocked around like a pool ball.

After a few minutes, in which the little sasquatch kids grunted and growled and tore into raw onions and snapped apart carrots, the bigger sasquatch grunted at its mate and then stepped toward Owen. The others disappeared and Owen turned to look back at me.

"She's going to lead us to the Lofriska that attacked you and be our intermediary if necessary."

"Well, this will be ridiculous," I said, digging my finger into my ear to decimate the line of wiggly irritation there. "She'll be translating for you and you'll be translating for me."

Owen smiled, turned back to the bigfoot, and gestured a go ahead. The bigfoot grunted toward me twice and then signed something that seemed to delight Owen. I was pretty sure they were making fun of me.

The bigfoot led us in silence and Owen made no move to get it to chat with him, either in grunts or hand gestures. I just followed along, trying to avoid pulling open scabs or deepening my bruises. I felt it when we came upon the Lofriska and it made me let out a small sound of panic.

Owen stopped and looked to me, still facing the direction we'd been walking. The bigfoot sensed or saw something too and stopped dead, staring at a Douglas fir tree that looked vaguely familiar. I turned to my right a bit, searching to see if I could find the other tree that had chased after Kincade. I spotted the writhing blanket of black and red and let out another sound of panic.

"What is it?" Owen asked.

"That one, the one with the bugs. It—*She* tried to chase down Kincade, and I'm just a little scared she'll remember me."

Abruptly, the bigfoot let out a long grunt that sounded vaguely like a belch. I jumped back, my eyes darting even as the rest of my body settled into a leporine stillness. Moments passed in silence before the fir started bending, creaking, groaning. Still absolutely still, I considered the war going on in my body and mind: half of me wanted to cry and maybe scream, but the other half wanted to stay as silent as possible and perhaps tiptoe away into deep thicket or even wedge myself into a hole in the ground.

When the Lofriska laid amber eyes on me, I felt a slow, oozing confusion in her. She recognized me, but seemed uncertain what I was doing there—or possibly what I was doing there *alive*. Owen stepped into her field of view, bowed low. Her eyes rolled to him before she pulled away from her trunk, the needles in her hair shaking wildly with the effort. When she was a separate entity, toes once again rooting themselves into the ground, she opened her mouth and a surprisingly civilized voice came out of her.

"Humans."

The bigfoot grunted four times in rapid succession, turned away, and disappeared as it passed behind a narrow tree.

"He left us," I whimpered. "He left us!"

"She," Owen corrected mildly, standing up tall. He held out a hand toward the tree creature and spoke, keeping his voice quiet and respectful. "I'm Owen. How shall I address you?"

The Lofriska tipped her head, her gaze dipping to the ground. I felt the curiosity meet up with confusion, before her eyes went slightly more amber and she looked up toward Owen again.

"You may address me as Evergreen."

"Evergreen, we humbly ask for your help. We understand that several of our kind have caused you great offense. We would like to know how we can make amends between our peoples."

Evergreen turned to look at me, the amber in her eyes leaking away once again. I whimpered, remembering what had happened the last time her eyes had gone transparent. Annoyance lashed out of Owen, though he showed no sign of it as he shifted to place himself between us.

"Please," he said. "My companion means you no harm. When you last met, she was here unwillingly. Any offense she has caused you is the fault of another. She begs your forgiveness."

"I do!" I agreed, though my voice was barely a whimper. The bigoot had gotten far enough away that I wasn't itching anymore. My skin felt cold, though, and I couldn't stop shivering. I didn't want to be dropped on my head again. "Please forgive me. I will totally beg."

Owen tipped his head down to hide the amusement that burbled gently out of him and then looked back up to Evergreen.

"Will you help us? Is there anything we may offer you in return?"

"We want only the return of our sister."

"Your sister?" Owen asked, surprise washing out across us both.

"Your companion walked with the one we wish vengeance upon. Bring her to us, or deliver our sister back to the forest."

"Kincade?" I asked. "Is that who she means?"

Evergreen turned back to me, took a giant step toward me as malice broiled inside her. I held up my hands, too scared to even cry out, and shrank back.

"The woman who was here with my companion before, is she the one who took your sister? Is that who you mean?" Owen asked, trying to draw her attention away from me again. I felt worry ruffle him a bit as she approached, but to his credit he didn't back down or piss himself like I would have done if she'd gotten that close to me again. Evergreen stayed in his personal space for a moment before looking down to meet Owen's gaze, a snarl cracking the bark of her lips.

"Come." Abruptly, she turned and started plodding through the forest away from us. Her back, like that of the other Lofriska, was concave. Owen stepped close, reached out a hand for me.

"We should follow her," he said.

"I don't know if I can move," I admitted shakily.

"I can't carry you," he said grabbing my hand. "So you walk, I drag you, or I leave you here with the other Lofriska."

"I'm coming!" I said, feeling adrenaline flood through me. Owen nodded and we followed Evergreen through the forest. As we passed by the other creature, I caught a flash of irritation in it, saw the swarm of black and red bugs lift rapidly away from a face that was terrifying in its own right, bugs and scratchy bark aside. Nothing reached out and grabbed me or chased us into the woods, however, so I just hugged close to Owen, did my best to keep my pants dry, and let her lead us.

We came to a stop near a dying tree ravaged by what felt like despair. Before that moment, I hadn't been aware trees could feel despair, but I couldn't deny what I was experiencing: this poor creature sent echoes of pain and loss through my ribcage, like someone had set the bell of a tuba next to my chest and then banged it really hard with a hammer.

Without really knowing what I was doing, I closed in, bleeding with empathy for the creature, on the verge of tears. The Lofriska watched me silently as I stepped forward, pressed a hand to the bare bark, and shuttered with a sob.

"What happened to her?" I asked quietly. Evergreen moved up and matched me, pressing her own rough hand to the tree.

"Our sister was taken. She offered aid to one of your own and was betrayed. She is dying."

"Your sister, or the tree?" I asked, unsure how I could feel something from a creature that was no longer present, but still human in my assumption that a simple tree could feel anything at all. Disgust flashed inside Evergreen, swamping me and filling that hollowness of despair with viscous acidity that burned.

"They are one."

"Ah," I said, swallowing to keep from screaming.

"How long do we have to bring your sister back before she dies?" Owen asked, still back where he'd stopped. I wondered if he had any inkling of what I was experiencing, or if he was curious about my perception of things. Unlikely, I realized, considering that he was not only just a human, but not prone to emotional flights of fancy, regardless of the grimness of any given situation.

"Not long," the Lofriska said, shifting her stance. She looked upon Owen with her chin up, confidence filling her, brimming out like sunshine and warming me a little. It wasn't enough to fill the pit the missing Lofriska had carved in me, but I liked the distraction, either way. After a moment, bark crackled as she smiled. "You have been infected."

"Yes," he said. "This is not exactly a selfless endeavor."

Evergreen turned to me, looked me over. "You are not infected."

"Just lucky I guess."

"No," Evergreen said, lifted a hollow brow. "You are fae spawn; our sickness does not touch your kind."

There was that phrase again, leveled my way like I should find it somewhat insulting, even though I could only just guess at the meaning of it. I had powers, Owen didn't: seemed to me that Evergreen seemed to think my abilities had come from some sort of fae creature in my lineage, but I didn't see how that could have been possible. I'd met grandparents on both sides of my family and none of them had sported horns or a tail, so I could assume we were all just human.

Evergreen smiled again, warmth glowing out of her, before she turned to address Owen as if they were behind schedule.

"You agree to bring us what we seek before the second sunrise?"

"We do," Owen said, casually, as if finding the missing tree creature—or Kincade—would be as easy as typing them into a search engine.

"The contagion will halt until you have proven yourself one way or the other. In revenge or restoration, the sickness will dissipate. Your failure, however, will result in dire consequences for your kind."

"Agreed." Owen gave a steep bow making me think I should do the same. Evergreen found my clumsy act of respect amusing, which relieved me rather than insulted me because, honestly, fae spawn or not, she could still kick my ass without even trying too hard.

"Come on Gwen," Owen said, reaching out a hand to lead me back the way we'd come.

Olivia R. Burton

Eighteen

"I hope we're headed to the car," I said after enough time had passed that I was tired, and starting to worry we were lost.

"We're almost there."

"How are you feeling?" I asked. Owen shrugged.

"Still okay. It's gone from full on flu to feeling like I'm about to get full on flu."

"I thought she said the—uh, the thing would, what'd she say? Halt? Shouldn't you be feeling right as rain?"

"My guess is she put the kibosh on it spreading any further, rather than ending the symptoms all together. It would be pretty suspicious if every person who felt like shit felt better in the blink of an eye—only to drop dead in two days if we fail. You?"

"Uhhhh," I said in lieu of answering, picturing everyone in town collapsing to the ground, still and dead like in the climactic scene of *Surrogates*.

"Still bruised and sore?"

"Yeah, though I didn't pee myself in terror back there, so I'm better than I expected to be once we found Evergreen and her pissy pal." Snorting softly at my assessment of my own bravery, Owen pulled out his cell phone, annoyance spiking within when the screen lit up. "What's wrong?"

"No signal out here."

"Were you gonna call the psychic hotline, ask for advice?"

"Do those even still exist?" Owen asked, thoughtfully, putting away his phone. "I thought they went the way of brick-sized cell phones and Ginsu knives."

"Maybe they did," I admitted. "This is probably the first time I've even thought about them in, I don't know, ten years?"

"Well, way to be topical. Very contemporary references you've got there," Owen teased as the car seemed to appear out of nowhere past a line of trees that looked familiar in that way that all trees generally do. I'd had no idea we'd made it back to the clearing, but it pleased me that we didn't have to walk anymore.

"You think Kincade actually got away?" I asked as he unlocked the car, grabbing his arm gently.

"From the Lofriska? Most likely. They would know if one of them took her out."

"Any one of them?" I asked, hand still on his jacket.

"Perhaps not one in another forest or another state, but they wouldn't know she was an enemy to them in the first place. It's unlikely she'd be in any danger from a creature who couldn't communicate to these that she'd been nabbed. Besides, you said that your car and phone showed up back at your parents' house. That didn't happen by magic."

"Oh yeah," I agreed, having forgotten about that little tidbit.

"She's out there; we just need to find her. I was going to call around, see if I can find anyone willing to help me locate her, but it'll have to wait until we're closer to some cell phone towers."

"Yeah, Balanis isn't exactly known for high-speed in any capacity. I think the speed limit on the nearby highway is still forty." Owen smiled softly, reaching for the passenger door handle. A thought occurred to me in the silence, as my gaze dropped to the rectangular bulge of his phone in his pocket. Barely holding back a happy dance, I tugged at his jacket until he looked my way.

"So here we are, alone in the woods and you with no cell phone?"

"Are you threatening me?" he asked, favoring me with a snarl as if trying to scare me off from attacking him. Still grinning like an idiot, I admired the lines of his lean face. The man even had good teeth, my god.

I slid my hand up his arm, tucked my fingers around the back of his neck.

"I had considered jumping you," I said before pulling him down into a kiss. Delight and surprise puffed out of him to crackle against my skin like PopRocks. Lust followed shortly after, warm along my skin. His hands came around my waist to slide up my back and press me close. I hissed into his lips as the motion irritated the bruises along my spine, but he didn't stop. Moving my hands up into his hair, I gripped, forcefully turned his head away so I could kiss along his jaw, nibble his ear.

He made a small sound when I bit his neck and it riled me up.

"Thank god for painkillers," I mumbled, scrabbling with my free hand for the door handle. Apparently my technique or focus suffered, however, because Owen pulled away, watching me as lust curled delicately through him.

"How're we doing this?" he asked, his voice enticingly deep and drunk on desire. I didn't have an answer; I hadn't really considered the logistics past, *Take Pants Off, Enjoy Self.*

"Ah," I said, unsure. "I hadn't really thought that deeply about it."

"Which is often what I enjoy about you, actually," he said, before leaning in to kiss me. His hands moved to my waist as he guided me to press my back against the car. He was gentle, but I could feel that he didn't want to be. There was a tension along his body, a restraint that I knew was related to my injuries.

I wrapped both arms around his neck, moaned when his palms slid up the front of my body to cradle my neck. I could barely feel his fingers through the thick jacket when they slowed on my breasts and it was frustrating. Despite his chilly hands on my neck making me tingle, it wasn't what I wanted; my brain was too fuzzy to pinpoint exactly where I needed his fingers to move, but I did know we were wearing too many clothes.

"Not enough," I mumbled against this mouth as I attempted to shove up his coat and pull his shirt out of his pants. "Touch me—I want more."

Abruptly, his grip slid back down my body, mirroring my actions, though more aggressively as he yanked my undershirt out of my jeans. I yelped against his tongue when his cold fingers touched my bruised, heated skin, but he ignored the distress and pressed on. I felt him scrape teeth along my neck and then bite hard just behind my ear. When I cried out at the pressure, he dropped down in front of me, his lips surprisingly gentle as they moved along my exposed belly. Feeling a little drunk, I blinked down at him, realized he was unbuttoning my jeans. He kept up the kissing, breath hot against my skin as we fogged in the chilly air.

"Come," he ordered and my brows shot up.

"You're good, but not that good," I murmured, relishing the cocktail of slightly frustrated need and raw anticipation splashing out of him to sting my wounded skin. He rolled his gaze up to me and I felt his teeth against my skin as he smiled.

"No," he said, delight at my joke warming my skin. Grabbing my hips roughly, he ordered, "*Come.*"

Yanking me upright and away from the car, he switched his grip to hook his thumbs over both my pants and underwear and strip them down. The chill that hit my legs was a shock and, even though I squeezed my eyes shut and let out a thrilled little squeal, Owen stayed crouched, his gaze catching mine when I opened my eyes again. My heart started pounding against my ribcage when his warm palms gripped my hips again.

Every one of my erogenous zones lit up to say, "yes, please!"

Sliding one hand behind me to lay it against my butt, he nudged me back to lean against the car, keeping his hand between my exposed skin and the cold metal. He met my eyes again through his pale lashes, lips pressing gently just below my belly.

"Smart boy," I purred. Without answering, he tucked his other hand between my legs, hooked it under my thigh and lifted my knee over his shoulder. His eyes drooped shut as he leaned in and I felt the warmth of his tongue in a quick tease. As he pressed harder, angling his face slightly upward, I felt his free hand slide up my body. His fingers tucked under my jacket, moved gently over my bruises to find my left nipple through my bra.

Suddenly the cold air didn't matter so much. I could feel his arousal, his lust and his excitement pulsing against me, adding to the motions of his fingers and his tongue. I dropped my head back, my legs fighting a brutal war between tensing up and going boneless. My breath was coming quicker and, when I felt his fingertips dig in to grip my ass, I let out a high moan. One hand trying frantically to grip the car, as if I could squeeze the metal between my fingers like silk sheets, I reached my other hand down to the top of his head. I felt his pain when my fingers fisted, pulling his hair and then lost myself in the rush of his excitement and my own as I came.

He leaned away slightly, but my hand was still gripping pretty tightly, so he couldn't go far. He was patient, giving me a moment to revel as he slid his hand free of my jacket.

"Brace yourself," he murmured, before tugging his hand out from between me and the car, leaving me to suffer the frozen metal as he righted me back to both feet. I didn't squeal this time, my shivering mainly the result of the orgasm, rather than the cold. Still somewhat brainless, a total mess of stupidity and affection really, I considered him. He stood there, hair tousled, one brow up, watching me as if I was a masterpiece he'd just created. Finally, sensing I wasn't in any shape to make decisions or, really, do more than stand there pantsless, he chuckled.

"We should get back."

"What?" I asked, sure, despite being fuzzy-headed and distracted, that he had misspoken. He laughed, leaning in to kiss my forehead and then dropped out of sight again. I felt him tug my pants partway up my legs, before continuing with just my underwear.

"It'll work better if you do the rest."

"I assumed we weren't done," I realized aloud. He winked, as if flirting, but checked his watch instead of removing his own pants.

"We do have a time limit. We should get back, try to locate Kincade, and possibly kick the shit out of her."

Frowning at him, I bent to pull my pants up, wiggling my hips to settle my underwear into place. He stood as I did, his eyes on my face.

"Are you sure that's the best course of action?" I asked, both because I wasn't a fan of the idea of beating anyone up, and because I had certain expectations of a man who had so eagerly stripped me half-bare.

"I didn't bring a condom," he said, though there wasn't the disappointment behind it I felt there should have been.

"So, let me return the favor." Waggling my brows at him, I grabbed for his groin, giving him a gentle—and hopefully enticing—squeeze. I didn't need the tactile proof to tell he was ready to go, but I wanted it anyway. He danced back, lifted a hand to shake one finger at me.

"Raincheck, remember?"

"But—"

"Don't worry about it." He grabbed the zipper on my fly and yanked it up before stepping to the side and moving around the car.

"Really?" I asked, still sure this was some sort of hard-to-get tactic.

"You can return the favor later," he said casually, before climbing in and shutting the door.

"Dammit," I sighed, following suit and cranking the heater all the way up as soon as I did. His arousal was still there but it was quickly being forced out by a fat, happy contentment.

"I'm not blowing you off," he assured me, as he started the car. "Really, that was more for me, not for you."

"Oh?" I asked, laughing at the idea. "I think I got more out of that than you, pal."

"Well, I needed to make sure you weren't spending the next 24 hours trying to jump my bones. Now I'll be able to work without distraction. I'm a professional, you see."

I laughed, shaking my head as gravel pinged the car and dirt crunched beneath the tires.

I knew the second we hit civilization; my phone beeped to let me know I had several text messages and a voicemail. Chloe had sent the texts and my mother had left the voicemail, making sure I was okay. I was certain she was joking, but her suggestion that she was worried I'd been attacked by a Minotaur or something made me somewhat nervous and I couldn't figure why. I called her back just long enough to assure her that I was safe and that we were well on our way to solving the town's problems.

When we pulled up in front of the hotel, Owen pushed out of the car with his phone already pressed to his ear. He didn't speak until he was out of earshot, so I figured it was business, and texted Chloe back to ask where she was. She called as I was about to hit SEND.

"Hey, we're at your hotel," I said.

"What a coincidence, so are we!" Chloe sang, before going serious. "Owen looks mad, what's up?"

"We figured out what's going on and we have a day to make things better with the Lofriska."

"What's the plan?"

"According to Owen, we'll need to find Kincade and beat her up."

"Just for being an asshole?" Chloe said, in a way that made me think she knew something I didn't.

"No, she took one of the creatures, I guess."

"Shit," Chloe spat, and I heard Izzy mumble something in the background. I wondered in the silence if he'd broken something and she'd lost track of what I'd been saying.

"Did you two end up making it out to the woods?" I asked after a bit, realizing that, if she had, Owen and I might have just missed her.

"Eventually. Izzy took me on the longest nature hike ever, we met a bear, he talked to some bees, and finally we got back to where you were attacked."

"Met a … No," I said, dismissing that line of questioning, knowing it would take us off on a tangent. "Did you find anything useful?"

"A chunk of gold, like the coin we found, but not coin-shaped."

"Coincidence?" I asked.

"I doubt it. You said Kincade threw something at you and we know this sort of thing means a lot to the Lofriska."

"Yeah," I said, though my gaze had drifted to Owen across the parking lot. He was tense in a way I rarely saw from him, though I could feel that the strain there was only a small part of what he was keeping inside. I wondered briefly if I should be worried.

"Are you staring at Owen's ass?" Chloe asked after a bit. I frowned, considering then that she could probably see him from her window. I leaned forward, peering upward and poking outward with my empathy trying to spot her in the building. "You must be; you're struck dumb."

"Well, can you blame me?" I asked when I spotted her and Izzy. He was staring directly at me, his psyche a gelatinous ooze of worry. "What's wrong with Izzy?"

"From you, that question could mean so many things," Chloe said, before handing the phone over. Izzy was quiet, breathing into the phone like a creep, before he made a thoughtful grunting sound and handed it back to Chloe.

"What was that?"

"He's having a moment."

"Meaning?"

"He gets this way sometimes, like the future is perplexing him."

"I think we *all* get that sometimes. Look, I'm not sure what Owen's plan is, but I'll keep you updated once I know—"

"She's coming up, right? You have your bag?" Izzy asked from out of my view.

"Oh yeah," Chloe said to him, before getting back to me. "I may be in the game soon."

"If Owen lets you," I said, watching him. He'd taken a few steps closer, but stopped abruptly, his jaw set as he listened to whatever was being said to him. "I'll ask."

"You do that," Chloe said, a laugh in her tone, before she hung up. I pushed out of the car, moved around to stand near Owen. He glanced at me, his expression fixed in a way I'd never seen, his emotions matching the intensity. Immediately, I regretted standing so close to that fire raging within.

"No, that's *not* good enough," he said, his tone calm, despite the anger crackling. Time hopped forward, his temper broiled, and then he let out a derisive snort. "Do you know what *I* could do to you?"

By some trick of my empathy or practiced avoidance or maybe even my own self-preservation, I felt panic light me up, drowning out the malice he was projecting. Deciding I didn't need to hear this conversation, I jerked my thumb toward the side door of the hotel. His gaze never wavered from the spot of concrete as he dipped a hand into his pocket, produced a key, and handed it over. Without hesitation, I spun and marched myself toward the hotel until I was far enough away that his mood couldn't affect me one way or the other. I stayed in the warmth of the building, watching him from a safe distance, considering our brief history together and what it had taught me about him, before my mind jerked in a different direction and contemplated when the painkiller I'd taken would wear off.

Izzy approached as I realized that it already was, and I sighed as he stepped up next to me.

"I think I can find Kincade."

"You can?" I asked, suddenly alert, wondering if his brand of crazy was going to come in helpful once again.

"I mean, I already have at least eight times. Though, I guess it might not be one of those times," he reconsidered, making me sigh. I felt Owen's annoyance as he closed in, but kept my gaze on Izzy's lovely face even as he leaned well into my personal space to push the door open to let the other man in.

"Thanks," Owen said, his expression a mask of pleasant calmness, despite the fact that his insides were still curdled. He didn't ask why Izzy and I were together or what we were talking about, but I figured if there was a chance Izzy could be of help, I should at least introduce them.

"Owen, meet Chloe's boyfriend Izzy. Izzy, this is Owen."

"We met in Cairo," Izzy said.

Owen jerked his head a smidge, before looking Izzy over with a fresh interest and asking point blank, "Fairy?"

"I just look good in a skirt," Izzy said, as if that cleared it up. Owen didn't press, turning to me as if Izzy had ceased to exist.

"No one is willing to tell me if they know where she is," Owen said with a sigh.

"Isn't she here?" I asked. Owen shook his head minutely, moving to the staircase.

"We know she was the other day, but you failed to net her what she wanted. She could have moved on to something else."

"You think?" I asked, though I could tell he didn't.

"I strongly doubt it, but there are … circumstances that could have sort of forced her hand."

"Like you being here?"

"Like Chloe being here," Izzy said, trailing us up the stairs as if we'd invited him along.

"Why would she care about that?" Perplexed, I turned to eyeball him, wondering if he was having another one of his weird time flux fits where he thought things had happened that hadn't really, or hadn't yet, or should have but didn't—his explanations never really made sense to me, so I'd stopped asking when it became clear that was the case.

"They had a thing."

"Izzy, was it?" Owen asked curtly as he paused on the third floor landing. He opened the door and pointed down the hallway. "Why don't you go ask your girlfriend if she thinks that's what it is?"

It sounded like a suggestion but I sensed it was really more of an order. Without hesitation, Izzy headed through the door and down the hallway, presumably toward Chloe's room, without saying goodbye.

"What was he talking about?" I asked, turning to Owen, though I have no idea why I thought he would know. He sighed, his irritation worming its way across my throat in a way that made me shiver nervously, and then shook his head.

"I just don't have time for Fairy bullshit."

"How the hell do you keep housekeeping from finding all those guns?" I asked, once we were up in his room and he'd gotten himself all kitted out.

"Same way I got a *free*," he gave air quotes, "bottle of wine: I paid them a lot more than this room and the rooms to each side are worth."

"Wow, money talks."

"It doesn't just talk," Owen corrected, settling the leg of his pants over his ankle holster. "It sings, dances, and seduces."

"Well, it's got me beat."

Owen smiled as he turned to look himself over in the mirror. I was assuming it wasn't just vanity, but he looked really good. The painkiller had continued wearing off, making me more aware of my sore muscles, scraped face, and purple skin. He lifted a brow, turned to me.

"Any noticeable bulges?" he twisted to the side then back. I knew he was asking if I would have noticed any of the weapons on him, but I grinned lasciviously.

"No, but I could help with that," I offered as I pushed away from the bed.

"I know exactly what that look means and I think I have the solution," he said as I closed in.

"I do, too." Grabbing the front of his shirt, I yanked him down into a deep kiss. He let me and I felt lust in him again. He held it at bay, however, and gently moved my hands away from his shirt.

"Not enough time for that, but I've something almost as good." Stepping around me, he moved to the little counter along the wall outside the bathroom. It held a small coffee pot, a box of tissue, and loomed over a mini-fridge. Owen pulled open the door to the fridge, reached into the little half-freezer compartment and pulled out a fist-sized tub of ice cream. Almost as eager as I'd been to help with his bulges, I watched him cross to me, gasping with glee when he pressed the icy treat into my hand.

"Satisfied?" he asked.

"I kind of just want to fuck you more, actually."

He laughed and there was a rare and genuine joy in it that made me happy. Sliding his grip from my hand to my shoulder, he leaned in in to plant a quick and crooked kiss on my mouth.

"We don't have time, but later I'll collect for all these favors I'm doing you."

I peeled the top off the ice cream, found a thumb-sized plastic spoon inside.

"You are the best friend with benefits," I said, before stuffing my face with as much ice cream as I could balance on the useless, paper-thin threat to the world's oceans and fish.

"That's because half the benefits are ice cream."

Nineteen

We met Chloe and Izzy down in the lobby, though I wasn't sure that had been any sort of plan or if Izzy had just managed to orchestrate it that way. Owen didn't miss a beat, gesturing for us all to head out to the parking lot, opening the car door for me as we got to his rental. Chloe stopped short of the car, hanging back a few feet, but Izzy skipped around to the other side, climbing into the back seat next to me as I settled in.

"You two stay here. We'll be right back," Owen said.

"You're going off and leaving me in the van again?" I asked, letting a little tantrum slip into my voice.

"I beg your pardon," Owen said. "This is a sensible, little *sedan*. Be good."

Before I could question or argue with that order, he shut the door and moved off to where Chloe stood, putting his back to me and keeping himself between she and I as if worried I might glean something from her expression that I couldn't from her emotions. I turned to Izzy, intending to joke about reading lips or spontaneously gaining super-hearing and eavesdropping, but never managed to get any actual sound through my lips.

He licked me.

It wasn't sexual; there was nothing in his mind indicating he was doing this for the carnal thrill of it. There was a wobbly sort of giddiness but the pleasure he got from sliming his tongue over my chin was nothing like the thrill Owen would've gotten from the same action. This was like turning to find that a Corgi had suddenly shown up to kiss you hello.

"Um?"

Rather than explaining or addressing my confusion, Izzy grabbed my chin, shoving my head up and turning it side to side, inspecting me. After a bit, he sighed and disappointment jiggled madly at me like an overenthusiastic exotic danger trying real hard to earn a tip.

"No more," he grumbled.

"No more what?"

"Ice cream. You dribbled. I wanted it."

"Eugh," I grumbled, not interested in addressing that any further. Izzy let me go, settling into the middle seat as if it were comfortable to be folded up with his knees practically infused into his eyebrows and I turned my attention back to Owen and Chloe.

The set of his shoulders had relaxed and I could see Chloe gesturing loosely beyond, but I still didn't know what was going on or why they were teamed up like this was a normal, every day problem.

"Chloe's kind of a mystery, huh?" I asked idly, not sure Izzy would know what I was talking about, but figuring he was just as good a sounding board as any.

"Only to you, despite all the clues."

"What clues?" I asked, offended, though not entirely sure why.

Izzy rolled his eyes and shook his head, snorting like he was sure I was joking, and then turned back to the front of the car, whistling idly.

"What the hell?" I asked, frustrated, though not really more so than I usually got with the candy-thieving weirdo who had waltzed into my life and left it a sugarless mess.

The driver's side door opened shortly before the passenger's, and then Owen and Chloe slid in respectively, buckling up and addressing Izzy and me as Chloe tucked her red backpack between her feet.

"We've got a line on Kincade, but it could take a bit for her to take the bait."

"We?" I asked, wondering why, once again, Chloe and Owen had paired up like it was the most natural thing in the world.

"She's got a number you can call if you want to give her money, so I called it," Chloe explained. "As far as she'll know, she's got someone interested in buying something from her. We've set up a time and place to meet, so as soon as she gets the message, she'll call, give us a different time and place, and we'll go grab her."

"Wait," I said, holding my hands up, lost and confused. "You called?"

"She's likely got feelers out to tell her if *Owen* were to call, so it had to be someone she wouldn't expect to be trying to trap her."

"And you think she's just going to fall for some random person wanting to buy something from her in the exact small town she happens to be hanging out in now?"

"Not at all," Owen said, before I felt a jolt of satisfaction dart through him. "She was surprisingly prompt." Starting the car, he pulled his phone out, tapping in the unlock code, and handing it to Chloe. She took it, frowning, before turning back to me.

"Isn't Stripped Teas where your brother's been working?"

Alarm screamed through me, memories of Kincade's veiled threat against my brother lighting up my nerve-endings like each one had individually been set on fire.

"Why? What's up? Is she there?"

"She will be in thirty minutes."

"Shit," I swore, digging my phone out of my pocket as Izzy patted my shoulder gently.

"It'll be okay," he said. I snarled his way, especially not interested in his nonsense as worry for my brother clawed at my insides.

"She knows he works there, made some threat about getting to him to get me to go with her when she nabbed me. I have to call and warn him."

"He's got that luck, you know," Izzy said, avoiding the swipe I aimed his way, and managed to pat my thigh when I settled back into my seat to call Thom. Each of my vertebrae tensed and ached as it rang. Finally, skipping like a record, Thomas' voice cracked out half a confused hello, before the line cleared up.

"—lo? Gwen? Can you hear me?"

"Crisply! Where are you? Are you okay?"

"I'm fine, I guess. I'm lost and my phone—Jesus, are you sure you can hear me? I can't believe you got through. I've been trying to call Carter and mom and dad for, like, an hour. No one can hear me, when I even get through."

"You're not at the shop?"

"No, I went out this morning for a jog and … I do this all the time, I don't know what happened, but my usual path was flooded, so I had to go another way and I just got lost. I'm supposed to be helping Carter but I'm not sure where I am."

"He's okay?" Chloe asked.

"Tell him to take a left at the tree that looks like Robert DeNiro," Izzy offered.

Frowning, bothered by the imagery for several reasons, I glared at Izzy, and then got back to Thomas.

"Can you tell dad to come get me? He's out here all the time, he knows the area better than me, even when it floods—did it even rain last night?" Thomas asked, suddenly confused and thoughtful.

"I'll call—"

"DeNiro!" Izzy insisted, poking me.

"Dammit!" I growled, wincing with each jab of his bony finger. "Find the tree that looks Robert DeNiro, take a left."

Thomas laughed. "What? Gwen are you—whoa, it really does look like … how did you know?"

"Never mind that. Just … Look, I think your luck's done exactly its job, whether it seems that way or not. I'll call dad and send him after you."

"Now the bush that looks like a chocolate chip cookie," Izzy interrupted, grabbing for the phone. "Lemme talk to him."

Without asking, he grabbed the phone, greeting Thomas eagerly and leaving me sighing. Chloe reached out to pat my knee.

"Let him, he'll have your brother home before you know it. We're going to need you once we're in there, so get your game face on."

"I have a game face?" I asked, distracted by Izzy's babbling.

"Just think about how Kincade got you beaten up by a tree," Owen said, catching my eye in the rearview mirror. At my ensuing expression, he snorted. "Yeah, that works."

"You go in first, do your best to maneuver her so she can't see the door," Owen said as we approached the building. Izzy and Chloe had gotten out of the car two blocks down, though Izzy had split from her nearly immediately. I didn't like that she was involved, but I wasn't willing to brandish a weapon and run two blocks, so that left me out of the loop. Well, almost.

"She's just going to fall for that?"

Owen flashed me a grin. "Nope."

"You two are a pain in the ass," I sighed. Owen chuckled, pausing one store down and grabbing my arm. Turning me to face him, he leaned in to give me a soft kiss and then stood up tall. "After this, you and Chloe will have some things to talk about, I think."

"Yeah, I think so too," I said, dropping my gaze as I sighed.

"Buck up, soldier," Owen said, standing tall and regarding me like a judgmental drill instructor. "Your brother's fine, Kincade's one step behind, and the sooner we get this done, the sooner you can take my pants off."

Despite my dour mood, I laughed, shaking my head but glad for his ability to cheer me up. Winking, he gave a small nod and then jerked his chin toward the shop. I sighed, turned on my heel, and walked up to the door.

With a deep breath to calm my nerves, I pushed it open and glanced around the tiny shop. I shoved my empathy in ahead of me so I would know exactly where the people in the building would be before I saw them. Carter was behind the sample display, looking much worse than he had just the day before. Kincade was next to him, leaning against the very edge of the counter, a pretty, delicate, pink mug in her hand. She took a sip as her eyes roamed to me and a smug sort of joy twisted around my throat. I got the impression she'd been expecting me and I'd walked into a trap. Setting down the mug, she lifted her hand to catch my attention, as if she hadn't already.

"Lover, welcome. Come, drink some tea with us. I was just telling your friend here about my trip to Italy last year."

I swallowed thickly, my eyes darting as I considered that, even more than I hadn't wanted to go back into the forest, I really didn't want to go any deeper into the store. Carter and I weren't the only people in there she could hurt. A young woman was in the back corner, curled up reading a book in a fat, torn easy chair. An older man who looked no better than Carter was sitting near the front, a mug of steaming tea held close to his wheezing mouth as if the steam was all that was keeping him breathing. I was worried for them all and really wanted them to leave.

Hell, I really wanted to leave.

Instead, I pushed forward, tried to look angry and powerful. She snorted at my display and it faltered a little

"Which way is Owen coming from?" she asked, crossing her arms over her chest so she could point both left and right with opposite hands. "Front? Back? Is he finally getting creative and dropping in from some crawl-space in the ceiling?"

"I don't know what you mean," I said. Carter looked between us, his puffy face full of the confusion I could feel trying its level best to triumph over the exhaustion that was weighing him down.

"You're not friends?" he asked. Kincade turned to him, gave a condescending little smile.

"We have a history, but I wouldn't say it was *friendly*," she said, matching the tone Owen had used when we'd met.

I glowered at her, walking wide around her as if I had business near the rack of teas behind her and hoped she would turn to face me. Amused, she watched me for a beat, before turning back to face the front of the shop. Frustrated she hadn't even pretended to fall for my maneuver, I watched as she moved her arm to drape along the bar. Her fingers tucked into her jacket as she took a sip from her teacup with the other hand.

"You know who else wasn't friendly?" I accused, trying to get her to turn toward me. "That Lofriska you left me with."

"She seemed delightful," Kincade said, still watching the doorway.

"Is something going on?" Carter asked, before coughing and grumbling to himself. Owen pushed open the door, confident and armed, while Kincade shifted like water.

Her hand at her breast shoved into her jacket as the other splashed the steaming tea into Carter's face. He yelped, jumped back, and she darted behind him, wrapping an arm around his neck and holding a gun against the side of his head. Backing up until she was sure I couldn't reach her and Owen couldn't see enough of her to aim, she jerked her head toward me.

"She must be a good lay for you to trust her this much," she said, one eye watching Owen over Carter's shoulder. Owen glanced at the old man in the chair, at the woman reading her book and then pulled his right hand away from the gun to gesture toward the door.

"Get out."

They did not hesitate, which made Kincade giggle with glee. Having forgotten to shield, I echoed her immediately, though my giggle had the higher pitch of anxiety.

"I take it you spoke to the trees," she said. Carter let out a snot-choked whimper and I frowned, eased away. It occurred to me that, while she seemed pretty content with sticking a gun in Carter's face, I was still just a wide-open target. Kincade rolled her gaze to me as I felt smugness bump out of her to ease against me like waves lapping a shore.

"What did you do with the Lofriska?" Owen asked. Kincade sighed and the smug tide became poisoned slightly with an acidic irritation.

"You're here on a job, I appreciate that. Believe me, I respect the profit motive as much as the next gal, but your job interferes with mine. So, what do you say you take your bird, tell your employer to screw off, and I give you a third—"

"Set the gun down on the counter."

Frustration, explosive and raw, crackled out of Kincade as Chloe melted out of the shadows, pressed her gun to the back of Kincade's head, and gave her order. The smugness faded away and Kincade's eyes narrowed. She stayed exactly as she was for a moment, before I saw the finger pressed to the trigger squeeze ever so slightly.

"I could kill him out of spite."

"But then you'd die," Chloe said, matter-of-factly. "Don't bullshit me, Kincade. I know exactly what you value most and it isn't your pretty tits."

Carter whimpered and I watched one of his hands come up to pry at Kincade's wrist, desperation slipping out of him and slapping at me like eels writhing in my chest. I let out a low, wavering cry at the feeling, my whole body shuddering, but Kincade completely ignored him.

I glanced between Chloe and Kincade, wondering where the hostility slinging around the room was coming from. There was no way this was fresh, no way it was based on the fact that Kincade had kidnapped me and left me for dead. Even the fact that Chloe had a gun to Kincade's head didn't seem like enough to justify this level of rage.

"I'm touched you remember my tits, Gavel," Kincade said, after a long, considering pause. Before she could continue, though, Carter let out a massive sneeze. His entire body jerked with it and, next thing I knew, he and Kincade had toppled to the floor.

Exasperation sparked out of Owen as he rapidly crossed the shop, kicking the gun away from Kincade's limp hand. I gaped down at them, wondering what the hell had just happened. Owen sighed, gun still aimed at Kincade.

"Chloe," he scolded, disappointment lacing his voice. Chloe, gun held at an awkward angle in her hand looked up at him. A grim was trying to take over her mouth, but she was fighting it.

"Sorry," she lied. "I though she shot him."

"No you didn't," Owen said.

On the floor, Carter wheezed and groaned, "What happened?"

"You're fine," Owen said.

"I am?"

The bell on the door jangled and Izzy entered, completely casual as if this were any other store and not one filled with armed lunatics. I glanced over, found him peering over shelves, mouth wide open, hair mussed.

"Oh my," he said, crossing the store. "Dumpling Cheeks, you shouldn't be in here."

"Hmm?" Chloe asked, crouched over Kincade. She yanked the other girl's arms behind her back, being just as rough as the anger in her demanded. Still distracted, she dug around on Kincade, collecting an amount of weapons that honestly surprised me.

"They're sick," Izzy said, watching her work. "You're gonna catch it."

"Oh, dear," Chloe said, pushing to her feet. I felt a bit of distress flag through her as she met his eyes over the pile of weapons she'd left next to the pretty pots of tea. "Can you help?"

A grin split Izzy's lips and he gave one nod. "I'm on it."

The lust started building before he even reached Chloe. When he touched her, though, it was like a swamp. Her arousal, his excitement, and the love between them sucked me in, coated me in a thick, gooey, inescapable morass.

I caught a small smile on Chloe's face as Izzy hooked an arm around her back, slid one hand into her hair, and yanked her against him in a manful fashion. Despite his slight build and delicate features, he kissed her like men kissed women in old movies. The intensity pushed her head back, his mouth on hers like a bruise. Her arms came around him, held him against her as he pressed his groin to her pelvis and moved the hand on her back to grope her ass.

I took two steps forward, my body throbbing with the need to rip clothes and taste flesh, before I realized what had happened. I caught Owen's look, his brow up, amused curiosity welling inside. I stared at him, breathing heavily, honestly considering yanking him into one of the storage closets and returning the favor he'd done me earlier. He pointed his free hand at me, the other still aiming his weapon at Kincade.

"Don't make me buy you more ice cream."

Izzy pulled away and left Chloe heavy-lidded and swollen with need, catching her bearings. They looked at each other for a moment and, though the lust wasn't dissipating, it took a back seat to the love on their faces. Owen let them have a moment before he cleared his throat. Below them, Carter let out a little groan.

"What happened? Can I get up? Is she dead?"

"You're fine, my friend." Izzy reached down to grab Carter under the shoulder, heaving him up like he was a rag doll and not a portly twenty-something laden with sickness and mucus. Then, he turned to Owen, lifted a brow. "You're sick, too. You want the same treatment?"

One hand up in surrender, Owen only shook his head. Izzy nodded, turned back to Carter, and slapped him once on the back.

"Go throw up that gack. You'll feel a bit less sick until they finish this."

Carter's confusion warped rapidly to panicked disgust before he made a gurgling sound and I saw his cheeks puff up. Abruptly he turned, dashed into the dark storeroom Chloe had come from. I heard a door slam shortly after, Chloe glancing back at the sound as she holstered her weapon under her coat. Izzy turned to look over Owen and me, a half-smile on his face.

"What's up, guys?"

"Your girlfriend just concussed our only source."

"Hunh?" Izzy grunted, looking around the shop until his eyes fell on Kincade, as if he hadn't noticed her before. "Oh, hey."

Annoyance sparked out of Owen again and he caught Chloe's eye. "This is what you're doing?"

"I'm also a secretary," Chloe said, infusing her voice with a breathy, childlike pride that would have perfectly matched her blonde hair and pixie features had I not known her so well. Izzy bent down, poked Kincade in the back of the skull and then hopped to the side immediately as Kincade flipped, kicked out a leg, aiming straight for Chloe's knee. With barely any effort, Izzy cupped his hand outward, blocking her attack.

Despite the power in her kick, he caught her boot in his hand like it was nothing more than a stuffed animal tossed by a young child. His woozy psyche floundered for a second and I felt the sudden giddy glide of glee along my empathy as he knelt there, one hand gripping her boot so tightly it looked like he was denting the thick, reinforced leather. I swallowed and then coughed dryly, feeling like I'd been drinking hot chocolate and someone had dumped in a heap of cayenne pepper. The sweetness was still there but it was briefly transformed, made into a spicy shock to the system.

"Don't," Izzy whispered, his expression pleading and serious, his eyes a touch too wide.

The room was silent for a moment before Izzy dropped Kincade's foot to the floor and stood up straight. His gaze fell on a pink pot of tea at the end of the counter and I felt his psyche settle bit by bit. Stepping over Kincade's legs, he grabbed a shaker of sugar from the counter, a mug from the back wall, and paused at the teapot. I inspected his expression, found it calm and a little bored as he poured some tea and then upended the shaker over the cup. Kincade's eyes were on him, worry and interest pulsing out of her. After he'd dumped nearly a quarter of the little bottle into the cup, he looked over at each of us in turn.

"Oh, did you guys want some?"

Owen caught my gaze, then Chloe's, before looking down at Kincade.

"Spill it," he said simply, knowing she didn't need further explanation. She sighed, the tension running out of her body. Her gaze darted once to Izzy, before she rolled over onto her back, propping herself up on her elbows and crossing her ankles as if we were all just having a friendly conversation.

"I sold it," she said, simply.

"The Lofriska?" I asked. "Why?"

"Look at what's going on in town. Hell, look at what's happening to your boyfriend here. They're a bio-weapons gold mine. You have no idea how much I got paid just to bring *one* in." She rolled her gaze to Owen, opened her palms above the floor to show she meant no harm. When he nodded, she got to her feet, noticing Chloe's look as she did. They locked eyes for a moment, before Kincade sighed, turning to present her wrists to Chloe behind her butt. Chloe didn't hesitate, locking Kincade's wrists together with thick, plastic cuffs, and then moved carefully past her to Izzy. Kincade turned to face us all again as Chloe took a sip of the tea Izzy had offered.

Owen still had his gun trained on Kincade and I wondered how his arm hadn't fallen off yet.

"Last chance to make a buck, my friends," Kincade said with a grin. Eyeballing Owen, she lifted a brow. "Sick sounds good on you, Reid. Gives your already sexy voice a real nice gruffness. Really gets the motor revving."

Owen sighed, irritation at her naked in the tired roll of his eyes, but he didn't speak. Carter cleared his throat from behind Kincade and it sounded better than it had before. We all turned our attention to him.

"I called the police," he announced. Kincade laughed derisively and Carter looked to her like a defiant child standing tall in the face of a rule-breaking adult. I was beginning to think of Kincade as someone who didn't have too many friends.

"I'm sure you're not the first," Owen said, catching Chloe's eye. Chloe gripped Kincade by the cuffs and steered her toward the back door.

Izzy held up a hand, waving at Carter eagerly. "I'll help you out, man. Thomas is at home for the afternoon and you're about to have a rush."

"Who are you?" Carter asked. Izzy set down his cup, crossed the room to pump Carter's hand genially. Carter's alarm was palpable and probably not just to me.

"He's harmless," I said. Izzy snorted, pulled back, and pointed to the far corner.

"So, I was thinking we need to move some stuff around, starting with that shelf. It really messes with the flow."

Olivia R. Burton

Twenty

Owen didn't want to bring Kincade out to the forest, even a different forest than the one in which we'd been spending so much time. While Chloe and I were borderline-okay with bringing her to the Lofriska so they could take their revenge, Owen was not. He didn't explain why, but it wasn't about love or lust or any emotion I could discern into a clear reasoning.

Owen asked me to point out some place quiet, preferably abandoned, where we could talk to her for a bit. The only thing that came to mind was the old high school. Most of it had burned down shortly before I'd gone off to college and my mother was always complaining that they needed to rebuild it and get it running again.

Kincade glanced over at me from her seat at the uncomfortable metal desk that really should have been much dirtier than it was. Chloe was off to the side, leaning against a wall watching Kincade. We were pretty confident she wouldn't make a break for it with both her hands cuffed to the desk, but Chloe wasn't about to leave anything to chance. Owen grabbed my arm, pulled on me slightly.

"I need to talk to you for a moment."

"Sure," I said, wondering why they hadn't actually started asking her questions or choosing who got to be the bad cop. I was betting Owen would assume it would be him, but I've seen Chloe's face when I try to weasel out of going to the gym; she was definitely a better fit for the role.

We stepped outside the classroom into a crusty hallway that looked fine if you only faced one direction. Past Owen, I could see debris under the scorched and open ceiling. He led me down the intact side of the hall, leaned against a wall that was weather worn, but otherwise in decent shape.

"You remember what we did on our first date?"

"I certainly do." I wagged my eyebrows up at him and he smiled, but no lust came.

"I meant right after the shooting stopped."

"Ah," I grumbled, nodded. "Yeah. You want a repeat performance?"

"I do, but I do not want Kincade knowing what you can do. It's bad enough she knows you have any power at all."

"Yeah, okay." I gave a nod, crossed my arms across my breasts. "So how do we do this?"

"Very similarly. I'll ask her questions; you let me know if she's lying. Stay behind her, nod or shake your head. Try not to speak, which I know will be hard for you."

I stuck my tongue out, but said nothing, figuring I could be a brat and get a jump on his orders. He reached out, grabbed an invisible zipper at the left of my mouth, dragged it to the right, and then mimed putting a key in his pocket. Fighting the urge to gasp at my throat and pantomime not being able to breathe, I only stepped to the side. He watched me briefly, probably sensing my mischievous thoughts, and then walked back toward the classroom. I entered the room a few steps after him, found him standing in front of Kincade. She was looking up at him, unbothered by his intimidation tactic.

"Have you two considered just asking nicely?" Kincade rolled her gaze to Chloe, winking and kissing the air. "Or are you going to smack me around a bit, just the way I like it?"

I moved down the line of crooked desks, eyed a grouping of them that had been pressed together to form one large table; I was pretty sure there were several used condoms on the ground around them. Wrinkling my nose, I looked back to Kincade, then up to Owen. I glanced at Chloe, realizing it was only me who was at all nervous or uncomfortable. No one was speaking but it seemed I was also the only one with any interest in breaking the silence. Finally, I felt a curiosity in Chloe and she gestured vaguely with her right hand at Kincade.

"You're wearing my rings."

"They fit me better."

"For now," Chloe said. I couldn't see Kincade's face from my position, but irritation was beginning to simmer, stemming from a judgmental derision that I didn't understand.

"These beauties don't deserve to be locked up in some closet safe. They were designed for action, and you're out of game now."

"Am I?" Chloe asked, her voice quiet, the barest hint of threat running like lightning through her tone. Eager surprise wriggled within Kincade and she gasped.

"Are you off your leash, Gavel?"

Chloe's lip quirked up and I felt an explosion of humor in her. She didn't say anything further for a moment, but she did look back to Owen. When he remained silent as well, she gestured vaguely, stepping back. "Go ahead."

"Where's the tree?" Owen asked.

"I sold it. I told you that." Kincade sounding annoyed at the question, but it was a show. I nodded at Owen, but he wasn't watching me and I wasn't sure he noticed.

"To whom?"

"That you don't get for free."

Before I could even nod to let him know she was telling the truth, Owen darted forward, shot his fist out in one quick jab. I felt an eruption of pain, anger, and outrage from Kincade as her right arm jerked against the cuff. Owen wiped the blood from his knuckles down the front of her shirt and then stepped back, waiting Kincade out.

"Asshole," Kincade spat, blood all down her face.

"Just one?" Chloe asked. Owen turned to her, blinked as if he didn't understand what she meant for a moment. Shaking his head over a laugh, he looked back to Kincade.

"No, that was for the other day. She kept touching me in the bar and I just remembered I hate that."

"You love that," Kincade said, but her bravado was false, covering that sharp and burning hate I remembered from our first meeting. Something in Owen was plump and happy, pulsing in a way I thought I recognized from the sweaty moments when he and I were alone, but I didn't want to acknowledge what I was feeling. I focused entirely on Kincade, using her raw rage to distract me.

Owen kneeled down so he could see her while her nose bled all over the desk.

"I'm not going to pay you for anything. I have done you too many favors—"

"You call Detroit a *favor*?" she asked, spitting blood onto the ground. Amusement lit Chloe up, but she remained calm and still on the outside, as if she didn't have any opinion on Kincade's comment. Feeling entirely lost, like a fourth wheel on a tricycle, I crossed my arms over my chest, deciding that Chloe and I really needed to have a conversation at the end of all this.

Owen didn't argue or agree, just reached into his pocket and produced a handkerchief. He held it against Kincade's nose, making her hiss.

"Baldachin Corporation," Kincade finally said, her voice thick and muffled by the kerchief. "They have a—ha ha—branch about two hours from here, medical research mainly."

I gave a nod, but Owen's eyes were still on Kincade as he helped stop her bleeding. Chloe caught my nod, leaning down as if she needed to look into Kincade's eyes to be sure of something.

"She's telling the truth," Chloe said after a bit.

"Your mistress tell you that?" Kincade asked. Something in me jumped to attention, a memory that wanted to crest the surface of my mind and overwhelm my consciousness. I held it back, feeling as threatened by it as I had by the feeling in Owen just moments before.

"Good," Owen said. "You need medical attention, Kincade."

"Shit," Kincade said, quietly, though I didn't understand why.

"You're taking her to the hospital?" I asked.

"Of a sort," Chloe said, dipping a hand into her red bag, which she'd left open on a nearby desk. She slid out a syringe that made me think of the last time she and Owen had paired up to be gun-toting badasses. Kincade swore, lifting her head right out of Owen's grip.

"Just leave me here, I'll find my own way."

"Emergency bourbon?" Owen asked. Chloe laughed as if the joke made perfect sense, and I felt a small swirl of nostalgia curl in her as she approached Kincade and jabbed the needle into her arm.

With Kincade tucked securely in a decimated classroom at the abandoned high school, Chloe, Owen and I all drove out toward another sleepy forest town, at the edge of which was a medical research lab for The Baldachin Corporation. At about the ninety-minute mark, wherein Chloe and Owen had been chatting nonstop about books, movies, and occasionally politics, I threw up my hands.

"You guys have to stop pretending there's nothing strange going on here. Tree people are killing people-people, Chloe and Kincade have some sort of weird, kinky history, and we're about to break into a lab that might have naked zombies wandering around deep inside its bowels. And what if Kincade wakes up and gets out of the room you locked her in? Come on. Let's all freak out a little."

"We didn't date," Chloe said twisting in the passenger seat to face me as best she could. "It's a long story, but I was in a weird relationship when she and I crossed paths." Chloe waved a hand as if that should explain it all.

"Go on," I insisted, frustrated by her skirting of the truth.

"I did a lot of traveling when I was younger," she said carefully, as if wanting to make sure that the exact words she used weren't a lie, but, for the first time in my life, I didn't trust her. "You know, the specifics don't matter." That was definitely a lie.

"A woman from your past shows up threatening my life and wearing your ring, and it doesn't matter?" I asked. Owen let out a small snort but didn't intervene. Chloe flicked her gaze to his profile briefly, but wasn't bothered by his amusement.

"Does it really surprise you that someone like Kincade stole from me?" Chloe asked after a long moment. I couldn't argue with that; it was clear Kincade was a bad apple.

"No, that doesn't surprise me, but there's a lot here you're not telling me—either of you," I said, wanting Owen to know he wasn't getting off scot-free either.

"Hey, you know my history with her," Owen said. "Don't rope me into this."

"Traitor," Chloe mumbled, making Owen laugh again.

The car went quiet, Chloe still twisted in her seat, watching me quietly. I had so many uncomfortable questions, too many to really articulate.

"Let's just focus on the now, okay?" Chloe asked, pleading with me softly. Nervous energy had started brewing in her guts, replicating madly, growing desperately and threatening to flood the car. Unwilling to take on that responsibility—either by making it worse asking for details or in the way I'd taken it on with Robin—I nodded.

"Fine. But later we need to talk."

"Yeah," she said simply, the nerves dissipating slightly.

"So, where are we going and why am I going?" I asked, hoping to change the subject and ease her completely.

"The fit you threw last time we tried not to include you made me think it would save time to bring you along," Owen said.

"Hey, I'm supposed to be the one of us with a monopoly on bad decisions. Stop horning in on my schtick."

"My apologies. I'll make sure once we get there you do and say nothing. No matter what."

"Hey now," I said, not liking the thought of that, even though I knew he wasn't serious.

"We're headed to Baldachin, where hopefully we'll be able to find the tree and bring her back to where she belongs."

"In this sensible sedan?" I asked, hoping Owen caught the snark. "Won't her branches and needles make us all feel a little crowded?"

"Moon roof," Owen said simply, as if that was the solution to the world's problems. I thought about that for a moment, giggled at the image of a Lofriska stuck up through the roof like a drunken bachelorette speeding through Vegas, and nodded.

"Okay. Well, what about before that? Are we gonna knock and ask politely to get back our tree lady? Or—wait, do they even know what she is? Can we just replace her with a ficus and be on our way?"

"We didn't bring a ficus, so it'll be some mix of the two," Owen said as he pulled the car to off to the side of the road. "Now, remember that game face? You're going in with us."

"Oh no," I argued, opposed, though I wasn't entirely sure why. "I don't know how to break and enter into anything that isn't a Kit-Kat. I'm staying here." Chloe pushed out of the car, coming to open my door and reach a hand out.

"I'll protect you," she said, wiggling her fingers insistently. She wasn't lying, had every intention of making sure I stayed okay, but I knew from personal experience that I have an abnormal talent for getting into trouble. This seemed the perfect place for me to get shot up by friendly fire or beaten up by another tree. I did not want to get out of the car.

Sighing, feeling guilty for making her feel bad and for somehow being the reason she was here in the first place, I let her pull me out and followed her around to the trunk, where Owen was digging for supplies.

Chloe hefted her red bag, dug inside until she found two leather cords with tiny copper circles hanging from each one. I couldn't see the little disks clearly in the dark but, when Owen shone a tiny flashlight on his wrist so Chloe would tie one on, I caught the edges of something carved into it.

"Do I get one? What are those?"

Neither one of them answered me as they strapped on weapons and stiff vests that I could only assume were Kevlar. The fact that I wasn't getting either made my stomach drop into my butt.

"Are we sure I'm not waiting in the car this time? I should wait in the car," I said, edging back toward the passenger door. Chloe let me go as Owen stuck the flashlight between his teeth, tying the second cord onto Chloe's wrist.

"We need you to locate the Lofriska," she said as I opened the door.

"So where's my vest and gun?" I asked, standing there, tantalizingly close to what I had decided was safety. Owen snorted, laughed. I couldn't help but glare.

"I barely trust you with a stapler," Chloe said. "I'm not giving you a gun."

"Then let me stay here!"

"We're not actually going to make you go inside," Chloe insisted. "The building isn't very big; we just need you to walk the perimeter, poke around until you find the tree, and give us a rough location. We'll be with you every step and then you can go hide in the bushes while we go in."

"You know what hides in bushes?" I griped, pointing at them. I was scared and it was making me mouthy. "Stray bullets fired at you two, that's what. You assholes are going to get me killed."

"Here," Owen said, sighing. Before I could argue, he was coming at me with a shadow of something stiff. He yanked it over my head, Velcro'd it around my sides. "Now stop complaining."

Before I could do exactly the opposite, he grabbed my chin, tipped my head up, and kissed me. I was momentarily too distracted by the feel of his tongue to consider complaining anymore. When he pulled away, though, I glared up at him, pushed him back a step.

"Put out or shut up, buddy."

"Later," he whispered, giving my ass a quick squeeze, and then moving back to Chloe's side. She pulled a few things out of her red bag as I tried to adjust the uncomfortable vest. When snug, it felt secure but caused the bruises along my ribs to complain; when loose, there was no pain, but it made me feel vulnerable. By the time they shut the trunk and started moving, I'd found an unhappy medium, but at least I was fairly certain I wasn't going to get killed accidentally.

It didn't take us more than twenty-five minutes to clear the tree line behind the building. Chloe had to cut through a perimeter fence and we had to do a lot more hiking through the woods than I would have preferred, but I kept my huffing and puffing to a minimum.

"What if I can't feel the thing?" I asked, thinking of when Owen and I had initially come across the Lofriska.

"You seemed to feel her fine when Evergreen showed you her trunk," Owen pointed out. I couldn't argue, so I just sort of grunted in agreement, frustrated my one shot at getting out of my given task had missed.

We stood at the edge of the parking lot, hugging the trees, and Chloe pulled out a small pair of binoculars. Owen produced some little gadget that looked like it belonged in an episode of Star Trek, swept it back and forth in front of him. After a moment, they switched. I tried to peer to see what the machine showed them, but they were too quick.

Chloe turned to me as she tucked the binoculars into a pouch at her hip. "I'll be right back."

She took off at a light sprint, hit the edge of the building, and stuck close to it as she disappeared around the other side. I looked up at Owen, found him watching me.

"This isn't as intimidating as it looks," he said.

"What do you mean?"

"This place does have security, but it's nothing we can't handle."

"Well, sure, with your Tricorder there, you're all set."

Owen smiled. "Just think, within—oh—" He checked his watch. "Three hours max, we'll be in my hotel room, naked."

"If you don't turn your phone off before we even get there, I'm throwing it in a lake."

"Scout's honor," Owen said, a skinny streak of lust curling through him.

"I bet you were a cute Boy Scout," I mused, picturing a young blond Owen in a brown uniform, aggressively out-scouting all the other kids. Chloe was jogging back, a bit of worry clouding around her.

"We have about thirty minutes, so we need to get moving."

"Thirty minutes until what?" I asked, and was promptly ignored. Owen nodded, pressing a hand gently to my back to get me moving. We all took off at a jog toward the building, hugging the wall as we got close.

"Do your thing," Chloe ordered briskly, making me wonder about all the moving parts of this possibly doomed operation and why it seemed Chloe was in charge of so many of them. Shoving it all away, I took a deep breath, doing my best to control my empathy and not let my nerves take over. Eyes drooping, I searched as much of the building as I could from where we were. Without knowing the layout, it was like reaching a hand into a barrel of black tea and trying to locate one single teabag.

In what I felt was lucky for us, I sensed very few humans. Most of them seemed pretty chill, if not outright bored. I couldn't tell what they were doing, but the two ambling slowly through my field of empathy seemed like security guards more comfortable with their jobs that our presence warranted.

There were, however, distressed, sad, pained, and confused animals all through the section I was exploring. I controlled the crying that wanted to come, though I couldn't stop all the tears from spurting. Chloe rubbed my back as a sob forced its way through my lips, and I found my empathy reaching for her pity as if it wanted to wrestle it inside me and add to the dystopia of distress and sorrow thrashing about. I fought the urge, walling myself up as best as I was able, and kept moving.

When several minutes had passed and it was clear I hadn't found anything useful, Chloe gripped my shoulders, squeezing gently until I opened my eyes.

"Is it too big for you to feel the whole building?"

I sniffled, wishing I had a tissue, or at least that I could get to my shirt under my jacket and Kevlar. I swiped my hand over my nose, wiped it on my jeans.

"No, I can get a sense of the whole thing, unfortunately."

"Let's move a little faster, okay?" Chloe asked, rubbing my shoulder encouragingly. I nodded and started moving again. Owen had his back to us, but he kept up as we moved further along the line. I could still feel the animals at the edge of my empathic range, but it was more bearable in this section. There were no people, no animals and, unfortunately, no Lofriska.

"Nothing," I said once we'd reached the spot where we'd started. Chloe nodded, stepping away from the building, checking something on her watch, and then moving further out into the open. I followed, curious what she was looking for, eyeballing the building from a new vantage point. It looked like every other office, boring and bland, with a covered seating area we'd moved through in our initial pass.

"This is their only location in the area," Chloe said, shaking her head and pacing away from me, frustration pulsing like a raw wound. "If she lied, I swear—"

"She didn't," I insisted, closing in on her, intending to ease her discomfort. "What if—whoa." I paused, my empathy picking something up to my right that everything in me hoped mightily was an awful hallucination.

"You find it?"

"Maybe," I mumbled. Staring out into the forest past the edge of the parking lot, I took a step forward. "But it's not in the building."

"Excellent," Chloe said and I felt a spark of relief in her. "As long as you're sure it's what we're looking for."

"It is, but it's not alone." Four more steps and I was sure I knew exactly what I was feeling and what a pain in the ass it was going to be. "The Lofriska is in the woods, but there are four—five guards. At least."

"We can handle that," Chloe said. The edges of my empathy charred from proximity and I swore, pulling back.

"Not all the guards are human."

Olivia R. Burton

Twenty-One

"I can't believe you're making me do this," I whined. "Do you understand what kind of message this sends to children?" Chloe looked around, made a show of it.

"What children? We're all adults here." She landed her gaze on me, lifted a brow. "Mostly."

"You should come up with another plan; it's freezing out here."

"Take off your clothes or I'll take them off for you." Chloe reached out, swatted away my attempts to stop her, and unzipped my jacket. "Come on."

"You look smug," I said to Owen, pointing as Chloe shoved my jacket over one shoulder; she'd already rid me of the kevlar. "You come up with better idea?"

"No, I'm just picturing you both naked while she undresses you."

Chloe snorted and I felt a giddy dance of mischief wiggle out of her at his joke. I let her pull my jacket all the way off, hand it back to Owen. As his hand touched the fabric, she wagged her brows at him before she looked back to me.

"If it makes you feel better, we can both picture him naked, too."

I rolled my eyes, but couldn't resist smiling at the idea. Crappy situation or not, Owen looks pretty good in the buff. Chloe just kept working on my clothes, tugging my shirt up until she couldn't go any further.

"Up," she ordered. I sighed, lifted my arms.

"Why do I have to be bait? Why do I always have to be bait?"

"It's your only skill," Owen told me, still leaning against a nearby tree, my jacket in hand.

"Not my *only* skill," I said, despite the fact that I couldn't, in that moment, think of any outside my empathy and the fact that I was a pretty okay driver.

"Making fun of Mel and eating cakes is not going to help. Distracting the werewolf while we take out the others is."

"But why do I have to be naked? Why can't I just sashay up, jiggle my boobs and go, 'Hey Sailor?' That works in movies."

"No it doesn't," Chloe argued, dropping down to untie my sneakers.

"Whoa!" I said. "I don't get to keep my shoes?"

"You can't take your jeans off with shoes on."

"Oh," I relented with a nod.

"But, no, you can't keep your shoes. No one will believe you've been held captive and beaten up if you're wearing sneakers."

"Dammit," I grumbled. "Okay, stop. Wait. One more thing, why can't you guys just pull out some sniper rifle and drug them all from thirty paces?"

"I left my rifle in my other pants," Owen said, looking around idly as if keeping watch, but just for, like, interloper bunnies or something that couldn't actually hurt us.

"The guards are spread out far enough—most of them, two are having a smoke and chatting, which probably wouldn't get them fired if we weren't about to steal what they're supposed to protect—that we could probably knock them out without them hearing what was going on, but the werewolf's gonna know. He'd—"

"So take him out first," I suggested, sure I had her.

"He'd hear us coming," she said, before pressing on. *Dammit.* "If we start with the others, he'd still hear the shots or the struggle, then he'd call to the others or, worse, call backup from inside. Those naked zombies you were worried about? What if they have a whole army just slavering over the idea of eating a pretty empath brain?"

"Zombies don't have ideas," I grumbled, though I couldn't argue with the rest of her logic. Guns were out and none of us were willing to just outright kill anyone, so that left only me in my skivvies, fooling a werewolf into being so distracted he couldn't do his job.

Sighing dramatically, I yanked off my shirt, procrastinating in the chilly air by bitching some more.

"I'm not happy about this, I'd like that on record."

"What record?" Chloe asked.

"Shh. I'd just like to say ... to karma or the world or ... whatever is out there listening, that I'm not happy to strip down and prance around the frozen woods to save a *tree*."

"You're doing it to save the town."

I unzipped my pants, hopped and grumbled as I took them off.

"I still don't see why you can't do this," I said to Chloe as I fought with my aching limbs, which refused to bend enough for me to get proper hold of my sock. "You're probably a much better actress."

"Two reasons," Chloe said and poked my side just hard enough that I grunted. "One, you come with bruises pre-installed. Two, you can't take out a guard using just your wits and thumbs."

"You can do that?" I asked, momentarily forgetting the icy air. Chloe laughed, dropped down to pull off my sock and toss it back at Owen.

"I guess you'll never know, will you?" Chloe asked, before standing tall again and tapping the side of my breast. "Now hoist'em up, make yourself look pathetic and sexy."

"Like the hottest victim in a horror movie," Owen offered, making me wish I still had a shoe on to kick him with.

I'd been instructed to circle the guards and come up behind the werewolf. Supposedly, freezing my pretty ass off would help convince the werewolf that I'd been kidnapped—not completely a lie, considering the day before—and held hostage. He wasn't mated, so he'd be more than happy to take me in his manful arms, offering comforting words, and then be distracted by my boobs until Chloe could conk him on the head or jab him with a needle.

Come to think of it, she was much too good at knocking people unconscious; maybe I needed to watch out.

I felt like an idiot, hobbling in nothing but my underthings, trying not to cut my feet open—or off—on twigs and rocks as I traversed the dark terrain of the forest. I sensed no otherworldly life except the werewolf and the Lofriska, which was locked in an impressive metal cage in the middle of a large clearing. It seemed the corporation had assumed that she could live just fine if she had access to the outdoors. It was clear from her hunched posture that being able to root into the bare ground was not going to outweigh the fact that she was being held hostage and probably experimented upon.

I kept a bead on them as I moved, making sure I stayed far enough away that they wouldn't know I was there without expressly looking for me, and fought the urge to mumble to myself about how moronic this was.

I felt it when the werewolf got a whiff of me. Confusion, a bit of worry, and a heavy dose of arousal swamped his brain, making me uncomfortable and slightly dizzy, even from my position. Taking a deep breath, I dropped my shoulders, did my best to look beaten and depressed. I stumbled against a tree, which was an accident but it helped the act anyway, and fought my first instinct to cry out several rude words.

I let my pain out in a low groan, took a few more anguished steps toward the wolf. I heard underbrush being crunched, the beep of a radio and then a light flashed into my eyes, making me cry out again. I threw my arm up, stumbled back.

"Stand by," said an unexpectedly high, male voice. I whimpered, trying to see him through the light.

"Help," I whispered, stumbling a step forward. "Can you help me?"

"Stop where you are, ma—" He cleared his throat, embarrassed excitement crackling through him, though the typical werewolf hungers were still there too. The whole cocktail made me want to peel off my skin. "Miss? Stop right there."

"Please?" I asked, still trying to get an eyeful of him through the glare; I couldn't see anything except blinding white. "I was kidnapped. I escaped. Please."

The radio beeped again, a voice crackled through. "Report."

"It's a woman. She's nak—er, she's hurt pretty bad."

"Bring her in."

"Roger." A hand covered the light, dulling the brightness to a peach hue. I squinted watery eyes at him, moved another step forward, my arm still held out.

"Can you help me?"

"Where did you come from?"

"Please," I let my voice hitch, felt my skin jump and twitch in reaction to his emotions. The only good part of being so close to him was that my brain no longer perceived the cold air. My goosebumps had settled, but my skin was jerking like I was shoving every individual nerve ending directly into a light socket. It was exhausting in a way that even being around Mel hadn't ever been. Dizziness swamped me and, before I knew it, the pathetic act became a tumbling reality as I began to topple forward.

Immediately his feelings—all six hundred thousand of them, it seemed—warped into a sticky flood of pity, worry floating along the surface like an oil spill. The light lowered, aimed at the ground and I heard him dive to catch me. I craned my neck, expecting to look up into piercing eyes and a strong jaw. I hadn't met many werewolves, but they'd all been pretty fucking fantastic to look at.

My eyes met with the top of a mop of unruly, curly hair lit partly by the crooked flashlight. I lowered my gaze to his face and had to stop myself from asking what the hell was going on and who was playing a joke on me.

"Miss?" he asked. I continued to stare, too shocked to answer, draped bonelessly over his arm like every fainting leading lady from the nineteen-forties. He waved pudgy fingers in front of my face, pulled back to look me over once more. "You're hurt—" His voice cracked and he cleared his throat, embarrassment berating me stabbily once again. I hated this man and I'd only known him ninety seconds.

166

"You're injured," he repeated, doing his best to make his voice sound manly and impressive; it was like listening to a fifteen-year-old try to fool a bartender into selling him a beer. "Are you bleeding?"

"I—I don't know," I said, not really sure. It wouldn't have surprised me if his emotions were so desperate that they'd managed to actually slice me open. All I could feel in his presence was pain and heat, which wasn't conducive to being able to tell if my own blood was leaking from my inside to my outside.

"I'm going to pick you up, is that okay?" Cupping an arm behind my knees, he pressed his angry flesh directly against me, making me whimper. The sound made him tense, his gaze darting to my legs as if he was worried he'd badly mangled me with the contact. "Miss?"

I couldn't answer. I couldn't stop staring at his face.

He wasn't really ugly; there wasn't anything specifically wrong with his features. He was just … unfortunate. His forehead was too big, his nose too short. Chubby of neck and round of cheeks, he kind of reminded me of that last pumpkin in the patch in which no one can quite envision a design. Maybe someone would see something in him one day or take him home out of pity.

Maybe he was really fucking charming and I was just being a shallow asshole because I'd expected to find Mel and I'd run across Paul Giamatti instead.

"Please, answer me," he begged, his hand moving from my knees to his radio again, as if he might need to call for help because he didn't know how to deal with the deranged, half-naked mute who'd dropped literally into his arms.

God, he was sort of adorable in all his horny, awkward discomfort. I wanted to pat him on the head and shove him down a flight of stairs all at the same time. Even though I knew it was probably going to be physically painful—I really should have been used to that by now—I grabbed his hand before he could call for help and blow the whole operation.

"I hurt," I moaned, not really sure what else to say. It was the truth, at least.

"Oh!" he said, surprise and relief flooding out. "I was worried you were in shock. Yes, I—" He made a terrified squeaking sound, tried to make his voice impressive once again. "I'll carry you."

He was a perfect gentleman, finally lifting me under my legs, pressing his plump forearm to my back and turning to carry me back toward the office building. His eyes drifted to my boobs as he walked and, awkwardness aside, I wasn't really surprised. I'd worn a boring bra meant for comfort rather than temptation, but he was squeezing me against him pretty tight and they were sort of on display.

Owen stepped out from behind a tree, a gun pointing at the both of us.

"I see you found my girl," Owen said, barely visible in the shadows. The wolf's arms tightened, bravado lighting him up even brighter than before. I whimpered desperately, which he took entirely the wrong way.

"Don't worry, miss, I won't let him have you."

"What about me?" Chloe asked from behind, drawing my gaze to her. She'd pressed a knife against the wolf's neck just hard enough to let him know that, unlike most blades, this one was meant specifically to cut werewolf skin. "Set the girl down carefully, and we can talk."

"I'm not alone out here," the wolf asserted, and I could feel something dangerous growing.

"Chloe," I squeaked, not really sure what his emotions were building toward, but recognizing them from the few times I'd seen Mel about to pull out some crazy feat of strength. She only sighed, shifting slightly behind the wolf just before he yelped, pushing briefly up to his tiptoes, and then dropped me unceremoniously on my ass in the dirt.

Twenty-Two

As I yanked my shoe on and then pulled my leg in to tie the laces, I stared up at the werewolf, trying to ignore the pulsing, jagged anger shooting out from his psyche. He was glaring at Chloe, who seemed oblivious to his rage. Owen was standing off to the side keeping an eye on the cage in the center of the clearing.

The Lofriska was a heap of brown leaves and bare branches. It was hunched over, hollow back looking scarred in the faint moonlight. I could feel its despair from where I was, but it wasn't enough to overcome the werewolf's rage.

"Hold tight, Romeo," Chloe said, glancing over at him when he jerked against the thin silver chain she'd used to bind him to the tree. "We're just here for the tree and then we'll be on our way."

He grunted, tried once again to get free.

"You don't think he'll just rip out of there and tear our throats out?" I asked as I pushed to my feet. Chloe shook her head.

"Nah, that chain's unbreakable. Little fairy gift I got from an old friend."

"That looks like the one Kincade has," I said, before reassessing wondering if they were one in the same. "Had?"

"Come on," Chloe said, rather than answer one way or another. Taking my arm, she led me down the little slope into the clearing, stopping outside the cage. I attempted to push forward further, but Chloe grabbed my arm, exasperation and panic arcing within her.

"They might have booby traps around. We have to make sure we can get through without getting a leg snapped off in a bear trap."

"Your plan for that?"

"A big stick," Owen said. I turned, lifted a brow at him.

"You have a very high opinion of yourself, don't you?"

Chloe snorted but Owen just gave me a look of mild admonishment and then moved to grab a giant branch he'd apparently set out when I'd been getting dressed. He tossed it forward, turned his head to the side slightly as if he expected repercussions. The Lofriska lifted her head to look us over. Her face was desiccated, the left half torn away so that the wide-open hole that might have been her mouth formed more of a backward C. I felt hope try to spring up within her but she didn't have the energy.

She lowered her gaze back to the earth and I heard a wooden snap crack loudly through the air before she drooped to the side.

"We have to help her," I said.

"That's the plan," Owen said, crouching down to grab the stick. Apparently satisfied that his initial toss had thwarted the worst of the danger, he moved in careful circles, closing in on the cage incrementally, poking the ground at equidistant intervals, before tossing the stick against the metal. Nothing happened over the ten or fifteen minutes he worked, and Chloe stuck by my side, rubbing my arm gently.

"You're up," he said to Chloe once he was done. She just shrugged.

"It's fine." Owen lifted a brow, doubt flitting through him. Chloe pointed to the sky. "We're outside. Soon as it rains, most magical alarms would be neutralized. No point in setting them up."

"You're sure?"

"Think about it," Chloe said, shifting into presentation mode. I caught something in her that relished the moment, the opportunity to shine and it made me wonder ever more about her history. "Baldachin clearly has magical aspirations, but if they had any real talent on their side they'd know you can't hold a Lofriska captive separated from her trunk, especially not in this monstrosity." Pointing to the cage as if it were offensive for reasons beyond being a tool of enslavement, Chloe sneered, the disgust in her running deep, echoing like it had roots of steel.

"Ah right," Owen nodded, shook his head. "This flu is still kicking my ass." Hunkering down, he pulled a slim tool set out of his pocket, got to work on the cage lock. Chloe and I stayed back, watching in silence, but the Lofriska's pain was like a beacon, calling me in closer in a way that I wasn't used to. It even drowned out the werewolf's still festering outrage. Normally I run from pain, or try to mask it desperately with things that give me pleasure like cake or candy or Owen's abs. This time, though, I wanted to reach in, to touch the creature, to pull in her sadness like I'd done with Robin's anxiety.

I could, I knew, though I still wasn't entirely sure the mechanism behind how I'd done it.

Owen flicked his gaze to me as I moved closer. Chloe didn't follow or ask what I was up to when I crouched down, leaning close to the bars. The Lofriska didn't look my way or acknowledge my presence until I moved to wrap my fingers around the bars of the cage and instantly felt my skin sear.

"Shit!" I yelped, calling everyone's attention. Owen swore lightly at the jolt of alarm my cry sent through him, but his muscles remained trained and still. "What the hell is on these bars?"

"Iron," Owen said mildly, before jerking his chin to my reddened palms. "Pure, from the looks of it."

"Iron?" I asked, frowning. "Like, a hot iron? That didn't feel hot."

"No," Chloe corrected, crouching down next to me. "Your fae blood, it's allergic. My guess is they beefed the metal up with something to make it more caustic to fae, but this can't be the first time you've gotten hurt on metal?"

"Uh," was all I could say. I'd never really liked the stuff, but not for any conscious reason I could remember. I'd tried getting my ears pierced as a kid, but it hadn't stuck. Past that, I couldn't recall any real interaction with a bannister or dog bowl that had bothered me all that much.

"We'll come back to that," was all I could say, before I leaned in, carefully sliding my hand between the bars and reaching in to press my fingers against the Lofriska.

Her bark was dry, splitting and cracked, unpleasant to touch, and not just because of my sensitive palms, but the outside of her was nothing compared to what lay inside. Much like when I'd touched her trunk, despair flowed outward, icy and rough, like being engulfed by frigid salt water. I gasped, twitching at first, most everything in me wanting to pull back, to turn tail and run back to the car. The goodness in me, the guilty part of me that knew she wouldn't have been in this awful position if it wasn't for humans, made me stick it out, however, and I found myself gripping her loosely.

"I'm sorry," I murmured, turning to catch her cratered gaze. She moaned, the sound hollow, and I echoed her pain as I took it into myself.

This went no more smoothly than it had with Robin, my empathy grasping and tugging, losing grip here and there as I struggled to pull it all inside. My capacity for sadness astounded me, my guts a deep, bottomless well that couldn't seem to fill, no matter how much I pulled from her. Despair waned as I slurped, turning to nostalgia, and finally thinning down to a wistful version of the blues, like a kid whose weekend campout is ruined by heavy rain.

I was crying when I felt my grip loosen and my hand drop into the dirt, sobbing like I'd lost a loved one, and Chloe had wrapped herself over my back, squeezing my shoulders and murmuring that things were going to be okay.

Owen swore quietly, pausing in his efforts to look up and consider me in my useless grief.

"Hey!" I heard a familiar voice say from our left, drawing everyone's attention. I pulled back, careful not to brush the metal with bare skin, watching Izzy move closer, my weeping tapering off as I tried to figure out if I was really seeing him or if the depression I'd taken on had made me crazy. I wiped away tears and noted, with confused shock, that my hands were healed, all traces of burnt flesh gone.

"Apple-butt!" Chloe cried, rubbing my back once before getting to her feet and moving in to give him a light squeeze. "We found the girl."

"Yeah, she looks pretty okay. Good job, Gwen."

"What?" I asked, wiping my face on my puffy sleeves, knowing the smoothness of the fabric would just smear, rather than absorb, but not having much choice. Izzy took a sip from the little china cup he held and I felt a wobble of tottering love force its way to the front of his psyche as Chloe kissed his cheek gently and whispered something in his ear.

After a moment, Izzy moved closer, leaning down to look the Lofriska over. He spoke low, in words that weren't really words, and then hooked an arm under my armpit and yanked me to my feet. Tugging me back, well out of the sunken pit in the center of the clearing, he called to Owen.

"Hey, Bond, you can stop." Izzy tipped his head back, downed the rest of the tea, making a come-here gesture with his free hand. "Quick, come on."

Getting to his feet, Owen surveyed the scene again for a moment, taking one step to the left as if he'd come around to our side. Then, pausing, he lifted a brow at Izzy.

"Are you going to open it?"

"No, but it's no use at this point. Come on, before—Oh, there she goes."

I jolted as I felt a torrent of emotions flow forward, threatening to drown me. Perhaps because of the fact that I could feel her every negative emotion in my gut, still sloshing about and making me feel heavy, only good rushed out of her. Relief, eager glee, joy, and finally an almost orgasmic delight pushed against my body, nearly taking my legs out from under me. I stumbled, felt Chloe wrap her arms around my middle and hold me up before I could acquire yet another bruise by crashing to the ground.

Greenery appeared, rolled out from the dry bark in all directions. It ran up Owen's body before he could react, coating one side of him in a bright emerald moss. Tiny flowers bloomed up his leg, along his arm, even along the bare skin of his neck.

Confusion and unhappiness bobbed about within him for a moment as he surveyed the damage done by the death of the tree lady. After a moment, he swore again, doing his best to peel the flora away from his clothing. It had sunk in, grabbed hold of the cloth and made it its own. He sighed and Izzy pointed his way, letting out a snorting laugh.

"Told you."

Chloe helped me get my feet steady before she turned back to the tree. "She's dead?"

"I think so," I said, though the idea didn't make me as sad as I knew it should have. Something about the way she'd gone off into the ether hadn't seemed too unpleasant. If that was what I'd feel when I kicked the bucket, I wasn't all that worried about the prospect.

Izzy shook his head, moved around to Owen's side of the cage and yanked open the door as if it had never been locked in the first place.

"No, no," he said, crouching down next to the dead, twisted bark. I moved forward, my feet nearly sinking fully into the mossy ground. My empathy whispered gently as I tiptoed closer, calling me toward the tree in an entirely different way than it had before. There was something there, but it was different, familiar in a way I couldn't peg.

Izzy reached his teacup into the gnarled branches wrapped around the curving stump. Arm wiggling, he grunted once before pulling back. In his cup was a hunk of dirt, a lanky stalk no thicker than a cocktail straw and five leaves that even the tiniest herbivore would have found lacking as a meal. The whole thing was barely taller than the teacup, and as I leaned in to get a better look in the dark, I felt an adorable sense of excited pride, like a child standing up for the first time. I laughed, the last of the Lofriska's sadness dissipating out of my gut in an instant.

"Hey little one," Izzy said. Turning back to Chloe, he wandered over, taking his time. I followed, though I waited to make sure Owen wasn't permanently affixed to the ground before doing so. Reluctantly, he followed, trying again to free himself of the foliage once Chloe and I were hovering over the teacup.

"Do we leave her—the other her, I mean?" Chloe asked. Izzy nodded.

"Yep, that's not her anymore. We're almost out of time, though!" Izzy turned, headed back into the forest the way we'd come. Chloe followed, but Owen stepped up next to me, his emotions warring between embarrassment and frustration. I fought the urge for a few seconds before giving in and speaking.

"It's not easy being green."

"Hello!" Izzy called out. "We're back!"

We hadn't even spotted Evergreen yet, but he was already running excitedly ahead of us. One hand still held the sapling, while the other lifted in a spastic wave toward a tree that had, so far, refused to show any signs of life.

As I managed to pick Evergreen out of the bunch, Izzy tripped on his own foot, nearly went sprawling face first into the dirt. He let out an embarrassed squeak, managed to catch himself before he lost the sapling, and kept moving.

"We are here!" he announced as he came to a stop next to Evergreen. Strangely, she stayed silent. Chloe, Owen, and I caught up, though I kept my distance. While we'd just brought her what Izzy promised on the ride over would solve our problems, I was still wary of the creature who could toss me around like kibble.

"Why didn't he just *bamf* us all back here? Why did we have to drive?" I asked as Izzy continued to hoot at Evergreen, trying to get her attention. I was getting sleepy and cranky. Chloe shrugged a shoulder.

"He doesn't always end up where he means to," she explained. "We could have all ended up in the middle of the ocean."

"Probably the closest thing he gets to a bath," I said, wondering sometimes on the state of Izzy's hygiene. Chloe made a low sound, catching my eye and winking.

"I get him to shower often enough."

"Oh jeez," I grumbled, which made her laugh.

As Izzy knocked a knuckle against the trunk of the tree, I saw the resin of Evergreen's eyes shift. She took in each of us, before her gaze moved to Izzy. I felt a tiny seed of what might have been annoyance before the crackling sounds of her breaking away from her trunk took over. When she was completely separate, Izzy grinned at her, held out the cup.

"Here you go."

She lowered her head, inspected the sapling. I felt a flash of anger in her, before she looked back to us.

"This is not what I asked for."

"It's all we can deliver. Here," Izzy thrust the teacup into her hand. "Say hello."

The Lofriska shifted slightly as Izzy pressed the cup into the curves of her wooden fingers. Tipping her head, she frowned at it; when she brought her other hand across to touch the leaves, they strained toward her. I felt hope, excitement and even possibly love from both of them. Evergreen smiled, her gaze going to me. Initially I tensed, but almost immediately realized this wasn't her usual disdain. It felt familiar—familial, even, like she could see me as something more dear than just some idiot who'd wandered into her territory and pissed her off. I'd pissed her off, sure, but there was forgiveness there, affection for my existence.

"You eased her passage," she said, as the leaf of the sapling curled as much as it was able around one of her fingers. "She felt only joy in the end. For that, you have my gratitude."

"Oh," I said, realizing she meant what I'd done with my empathy. "Of course, yeah. I didn't want … She was so sad."

"She will be at peace now," Evergreen said, before chuckling, and turning to move through the forest once again. "Though, she will need to grow into her own again."

Izzy bounced like an excited child, gesturing wildly for us to follow, as if Evergreen's glacial pace might leave us in the dust. We followed dutifully, but Izzy reached the dying tree before any of us, throwing his arms around it in a hug that squished his cheek and left bark imprints on his forehead. Evergreen approached next, set the cup down next to the trunk. Izzy plopped down on his butt, tucked his fingers into the cup and scooped out the little sapling. He dug a small hole at the base of the tree, which looked tough with bare, blunt fingers, and tucked the sapling in, before making sure the hole was filled around her.

I felt a snap of something all around us. It startled me but it didn't scare me. This wasn't a Lofriska waking up and deciding I would look better without a spine; this was something else, something beautiful. It was as if the entire forest gasped in surprised gratification. I glanced at Chloe, wondered if she knew something had just happened. She looked touched, a little teary, and I could feel a small pit inside her, sucking at her happiness in a way I recognized as wistful regret.

Before I could as if she was okay, the sapling moved, leaning its tiny leaves toward her trunk minutely. Evergreen's smile widened, her arms lengthening to caress the sapling delicately, as she turned back to me.

"Consider your debt repaid."

"The disease?" Owen asked. Evergreen didn't look to him as she spoke, her eyes still on me as if trying to communicate more than I could understand.

"Banished soon enough, at a reasonable pace. Your hikers, as well."

"They're alive?" Owen asked. "I wouldn't have figured."

"We are not as blood-thirsty as your kind would believe," Evergreen said, turning to Owen, her carved brows drawing down in disappointment. "They will be free in due time, though perhaps not together."

"No further action is needed?" Owen asked.

"You have done enough," Evergreen said, before making a shooing gesture with her free hand. Without hesitating, Owen jerked his head, suggesting we all make our way back to the car.

Olivia R. Burton

Twenty-Three

Sometime around two, I was half-asleep, stretched sideways along the bed, when Owen stepped out of the shower. I opened my eyes, looked him over, and smiled. He'd dried himself off, wrapped a towel around his waist, and brushed his damp hair back. He smiled at me and I felt lust curl within him. I wasn't sure I had the energy to match it but I appreciated the feeling.

We'd come back to the hotel, separated from Chloe and Izzy on the elevator and, before I'd even gotten the door to his room shut, he'd stripped and gone straight to the shower. I was sure he was going to have to get rid of the clothes but he was sure he knew a dry cleaner that could handle the problem. Somewhere along the way, possibly when I'd been dropped on my ass, my underwear had picked up a spur and a fair amount of mud. Knowing Owen wouldn't mind, I'd stripped out of my clothes, left them in a pile with his, and stolen one of his shirts to wear.

My initial plan had been not to wear it for very long before he pulled it off of me but the bed was comfortable and I was suddenly so very tired.

"This will be the second time we've slept together with neither one of us getting lucky," Owen observed, sitting on the edge of the bed next to my head. I looked up at him, gave a sleepy smile.

"I'm sorry. I've had sort of a rough few days."

"I wasn't complaining," he said. After a moment, he leaned over, pulled open the drawer of the nightstand, and pulled out a small box. "Happy birthday."

I stared up at him, my brows shooting into my hair. I didn't remember reminding him it was my birthday—hell, I hadn't even realized that it was officially the big day myself—and I didn't think ours was the type of relationship that required the exchange of gifts. He smiled, set it on the bed next to me, and then crossed the room to his suitcase. Despite the fact that he was stripping off the towel right in full view of me, I stared at the gift.

I was worried it was jewelry. I pushed into a sitting position, picked up the box. Owen came back to the bed wearing sleep pants, sat down next to me.

"It's not jewelry," he said. I gave him a cynical smile, pulling the lid off.

"It's my cell phone." I frowned down at it, confused. He breathed out a laugh and nodded.

"Yep."

"You're giving me my own cell phone for my birthday?" I picked it up and he set the box aside. I turned it over, expected to find some fancy spy modification or maybe a new case. It was exactly as I'd left it.

"I put a permanent contact number for me in your address book."

"Oh," I said, looking up to meet his gaze. I gave a half-smile, lowered the phone into my lap. He'd given me his number before, but it had never worked longer than he'd been in town. "I thought you said you didn't do that."

"I figure you've earned it."

"Not on this trip," I sighed. He laughed, though I knew he hadn't meant sex. "So I can just call you whenever? We can talk about movies or I can order you to bring me pizza?"

"I'd rather you only use it for important situations."

"Pizza can be a very important issue. If I don't eat I get delirious, dizzy. I could lose consciousness and—" He leaned in, pressed his lips to mine. I lifted a hand, cupped his cheek, kissed him back. The kiss remained gentle, even as he pressed a hand to my bruised side, slid it to my back.

"Are we—is this getting serious?" I asked after a moment, leaning my forehead on his. He met my eyes before pulling away, shaking his head.

"Not terribly."

"Okay," I said. He cocked his head.

"Is that a problem?"

"No. I just like to know where we stand. As long as you're honest with me about what we're doing, I'm game."

"Good." He kissed me again, pressing against me until I was on my back, my arms around him. He kept our contact chaste, despite the fact that I knew he'd noticed that I wasn't wearing anything under his shirt. As he broke the kiss and moved to lie down next to me, I looked him over. I spoke as I grabbed my phone from between my legs and stretched to set it on the far nightstand. We rested in silence for a bit, his breathing slow but alert enough that I knew even staring at the ceiling he hadn't drifted off. After a bit, I took a breath of my own, diving in.

"How long have you known Chloe?"

When I met his eyes again, he was watching me with a slight quirk to his lips, studying me. He dropped his gaze, lifted a hand to prop his head on his elbow.

"Wasn't sure you caught that."

"There was a lot being thrown around, today; even I was gonna catch some of it."

Owen sighed, his gaze on my chest as he considered his words. After a minute or so, he met my eyes again.

"When I showed up at your office and saw her there, I was … surprised. That was the absolute last place I expected to run into *Chloe Warren*. We talked before she let me talk to you. She explained you knew nothing about … this world, and asked that I keep it on the down-low."

"She said I knew nothing?" I asked, a little insulted. "I knew stuff. I'd been attacked by a vampire and sexually harassed by Mel. I wasn't exactly Pollyanna."

"*Nothing* being a relative term," Owen assured me. "Comparatively, you knew nothing."

"Fine," I agreed, shaking my head, still somewhat annoyed at her former assessment of me. "But I still can't believe I didn't notice you guys were lying to me."

"We didn't lie to you," he corrected. "We just danced around the issue."

"Hmm," I said, considering that he was telling the truth about being dishonest. Shaking my head, wondering if them running around with guns and killing murderous fae had been a regular occurrence, I pressed on. "How do you know each other?"

"Now that's not my story to tell." He reached out, took my hand, linking our fingers. The lust was still there, lazing about in whirls and twists like smoke, but not quite ready to take over.

"I'm not sure it's one she'll tell me."

"Do you need to know?"

I thought about it, considering the facts. Even not knowing Chloe's history, I still trusted her with my life. Even if I never found out what she'd done before we'd met each other, I knew I could count on her to be there, even when I was doing something stupid.

"I probably don't."

"We good?" Owen asked, before a yawn split his lips.

I ran through the day in my mind, tried to think of anything else that had snagged on the folds of my brain and left me curious. I snorted, laughing suddenly at what did.

"Did you guys leave that poor werewolf out there tied to that tree? You think he's still there?"

"No, Chloe wouldn't have left that chain. It's not something you can just buy at a corner store."

"I hope he's not too mad at me."

"Really?" Owen demanded, a thorn of irritation jabbing into my side. I laughed again.

"He seemed so awkward! I'm pretty sure my boobs were the only ones he'd ever seen up close."

"So?"

"So I just feel bad making him think he was going to be the hero and then turning around and tying him to a tree. What'd you guys do to the other guards?"

Owen got a serious look on his face, but I felt the humor in him.

"Vulcan nerve pinch, every one."

"I didn't know you were a nerd!" I exclaimed, yanking my hand away as if he were suddenly offensive to touch. He rolled his eyes, reaching over to flip off the light. "I may not be able to sleep with you anymore."

"I think I can persuade you," he murmured though I could hear the sleep in his voice already and knew he didn't mean quite yet.

I woke up to almost pitch darkness, Owen's breathing calm and measured beside me. We'd never made it under the covers, but the room was toasty so I wasn't bothered. Taking a deep breath, I rolled onto my un-bruised side, reached a hand out so I could rest it on his chest. I felt it when he woke up, a spark of shock, a bit of worry. His body tensed, his hand coming up to mine. He realized nearly instantaneously that I wasn't there to harm him, but it took him some time to let the tension bleed out.

I could smell him, the soap from his shower, his shampoo, just the way his skin smelled. Moving closer, I laid a kiss on his shoulder, moved my hand up to cup his cheek. He tucked his arm under me, pulled me until I understood that he wanted me on top.

Glad to oblige, I brought my knees up to kneel at either side of him as I kissed his lips, ran my fingers through his soft hair. His hands were gentle as they moved along under the shirt to rub my back in lazy circles. Lust came slowly, arousal on its heels. I ground myself into him through his sleep pants; he answered by moving his hands to cup my breasts.

On a sigh, I sat up, pulled the shirt off; he left his hands in place as I did, shifting to rub a thumb roughly over my nipple and make me let out a moan of pleasure. He lifted to meet me halfway when I bent to kiss him again. I felt his hands leave my breasts as he pushed off the bed, forcing me upward. Once he was sitting up, he wrapped both arms around my back, pressing me hard against his naked chest.

I hissed along his lips, my ribs aching their displeasure at the tightness. The sound made him groan and he kissed, open-mouthed, down to my throat. He bit me hard and I cried out, fisted my hands in his hair. I felt both the pain and the spark of pleasure it brought him as I yanked. Pulling back so that I could see the rough shape of his face in the dark, I caught his attention.

"Too rough," I said.

"That's a surprise, coming from you," he murmured, a smile in his voice.

"Give me a break," I said. "I look like the Grimace."

He laughed, full and hearty, before loosening his grip. Gentle and slow, he slid a hand from my back to run his fingers through my hair.

"Fair enough." Leaning in to kiss me again, he petted a hand down my spine, his fingers feather-light on my skin. For awhile, we just touched each other, just felt the way it was to hold each other and enjoy the warmth of skin to skin. Eventually, though, I realized that between work, injury, and sickness, I'd been waiting too damn long.

I tucked one thumb under the waistband of his pants, pressed the palm of my other hand against his chest. He let me shove him down to the bed and lifted his hips so I could pull his pants off. As I stripped him I felt him stretch, heard the drawer next to the bed open, heard the crinkle of a condom wrapper. By the time his pants were in a pile on the floor and I'd crawled back up the bed, I found him dressed and ready to go.

I felt his hands grip my hips as I grabbed the base of him, angled my hips to glide him in. He held on to my waist at first and I laid my hands over his, keeping my pace slow. As my body started to feel full and tight, I gripped his hand, moved it along my belly. He took the hint, brought his hand to his mouth before bringing his damp thumb back to tease me. On a moan, I squeezed his hips with my knees, quickened my pace.

His other hand left my hip, moved up to rub over my chest. He avoided my bruised breast, was torturously gentle as he pinched my nipple, squeezed it. I let out a frustrated, uneven cry before dropping my hands to his belly, steadying myself as I started to lose my rhythm. Just as I felt the orgasm threaten to burst within me, he let out a breath that was almost a growl and gripped my hips. I felt him try to control my movement, try to force me to match the pace he wanted.

I smiled up at the ceiling, opening my eyes for a moment as I felt his frantic determination. I did my best to conform to what he wanted, moved my hand between my thighs to tease myself as he'd done, while I sucked up his excitement and pleasure, realizing distantly that stealing emotions was a trick my empathy had been pulling for years—just never outside the bedroom. I let my mind go fuzzy, glad for the brainless pleasure of orgasm when it hit.

His thumbs dug into my pelvis when he came. He tried to hold me still, arching against me, and I moved my fingers to his wrists, squeezing him as he did me. After a moment, I slid a hand down to rest on his heart, felt it pounding. He let his breath out slowly and his grip on me loosened. I bent down to kiss him, ran my fingers through his hair again.

"You may have just given me more bruises," I murmured against his mouth. He smiled.

"Hey, you started it," he said, making me laugh.

An hour later, cleaned up and dressed in some of Owen's extra clothes, I snuck in through the front door, hoping my family was asleep and no one would notice that I hadn't been home or talked to any of them since Thomas the day before.

"Were you off having sex with your cute friend?" Robin asked, startling me out of my smug satisfaction over having been perfectly quiet and successful in my sneaking.

Breath hitching, I spun around to find her settled into the sitting room, Stella asleep on her chest. Grinning, knowing she'd startled me in a way she'd so rarely been able to do through her life, she patted the couch next to her with her free hand. Rolling my eyes, I pulled my coat off, draped it over the newel post, and headed in.

I dropped down next to her, felt my heart melt a little at Stella's sleepy little face, and then met my sister's eyes.

"Yes. I was," I said finally. "Not that it's any of your business."

Robin reached a hand up, touched my jaw next to the scrapes and frowned. "You look terrible. And those aren't your clothes."

"I feel okay. Partly because these aren't my clothes."

Robin laughed and we both looked down, watching Stella snooze. Mouth wide open, body hunched like a tiny bell-ringer, she was out cold.

"How're things here? Thom made it home?"

"Oh yeah. He won't stop talking about how *weird it is* that he got lost— as if he's the first person to make a wrong turn—" Robin rolled her eyes and I felt a bump of sisterly affection. "—and dad took his sweet time getting out there, but they made it home. Mom worried about you all afternoon, but dad insisted you were okay, that you were with good people."

"He did?" I asked, shocked, thinking of his assessment of Chloe and her easy dishonesty. Robin nodded, considering for a bit, before her brows shot up.

"Oh, Natalie's still feeling bad that she can't heal you completely." I sighed, shaking off the idea.

"I wish she wouldn't be. The fact that she probably saved my life is more than enough."

"I know. That's what I told her, but she won't let it go. In fact, she's decided that, instead of wanting to take apart radios and expensive electronics that her father bought her to *play with* and not *destroy*, she now wants to be a doctor."

"Uh oh. Does Jake hate me?"

"For making his daughter want to go to a hundred-and-ninety years of medical school that's going to break us financially?" I winced and Robin laughed. "Maybe, but if he kills you, Natalie would probably be able to bring you back to life."

We shared a small laugh and Robin shifted, sliding Stella a little further down her chest so the baby wasn't drooling on bare skin anymore.

"Why aren't you upstairs with Super Dad?"

"Stella was fussy, so I had her whine it out and then let her sleep out here."

"Let her, or made her?"

Robin bristled slightly, before insisting, "I wouldn't—"

"Ah!" I interrupted, pointing at her. "You're *lying*."

Jaw set, she glared at me for a moment, eyes hard. Swallowing thickly, she rolled her eyes to the ceiling. I laughed, much too giddy to be able to catch my perfect sister in an admission of using her powers for selfishness rather than good.

"I *didn't*."

"That's the truth."

"I'm always so worried it might hurt the babies somehow," she said, a little flutter of panic flapping. "So, I just try to put them to sleep like a normal mother."

"But?" I drew the word out, wiggling my finger in her face. "Keep going."

"But!" She slapped my hand out of the way. "I'm not saying I haven't forced the issue. Once. Maybe twice."

"Yeah, *maybe* twice," I mused with a smile. After a second, my eyes fell to Stella again and my grin softened as I considered the future. "I wonder how I'll be as a mom, especially now that I know what being an empath parent involves."

"You thinking about finding out soon?"

"No," I said, despite the warm fuzzy feeling sparked by Owen trusting me enough to let me contact him whenever I wanted. "Not with Owen, not now. That's not how our relationship works."

"That's too bad."

"No," I repeated, shaking my head. "I don't think it is. I'm not ready for marriage and kids and your whole perfect life package. I tried it before and sucked at it. I'll stick to random hook-ups and long-distance friendships with benefits."

"Well, don't tell mom that."

"I try not to tell mom anything."

"Yet you bring your not-boyfriend over and rub his nice ass right in her face."

I laughed, happy Robin being happy with Jake and *his* perfect ass hadn't turned her into a nun.

"I was desperate," I admitted after a bit. "And Natalie is so very handy."

"But you're sure—" she began. I held up a hand, giving my sternest glare.

"Don't say it!"

"I wasn't!" she lied. "I was going to … I was just going to ask if you've read any of Stan's books."

"No," I wrinkled my nose. "But I guess he has another one coming out soon."

"Today, actually."

"Well, that's a coincidence." I considered, wondering for the first time in over a decade if Stan might call and wish me happy birthday now that we'd gotten back on speaking terms. "What's it about?"

"It's about pirates."

"Really?" I laughed, astounded and amused by the idea. "Stan? Wrote about pirates?" I couldn't imagine it. They seemed the furthest thing from what he would create—dirty and rude and willing to steal the shirt off your back even if it was all you had left.

"They're not what you'd think," Robin said. "It's got kind of a Steampunk vibe, so they aren't just sailing the high seas. Everything takes place in cities in the sky and aboard high-flying airships. Apparently there's one merry band that travel to other pirate ships and—" Robin gave a pleased little snort. "—and organize their loot for them, clean them up. They help the other pirates to be their best, teach them to read and such. It's its own genre, now. Sneedpunk."

"You are kidding me."

"I am. A little. About the new genre."

"I don't know if that makes them pirates, specifically," I said after a moment.

"Well, I haven't read it, but I'll let you know more when I do. It's probably on my Kindle right now, actually."

I made another non-committal sound, kicked off my shoes, and pulled my feet up onto the couch. Robin reached her free hand over and patted my knee.

"You never told us what you want to do for your birthday."

"Stay home. I want to stay here with my family, eat cake, and not move. I don't want to see any weird creatures—except Izzy—or sick people. I don't want to feel any emotions that don't belong to you guys. And Izzy."

"You need to talk to dad, by the way."

"Why?" I asked, feeling a little bit of the old panic flare inside of me; we'd been fighting for twenty years and getting along with him was going to take some getting used to.

"When you slurped my panic, I felt it. I haven't felt it from dad in … Well, I was little. You're bad at it."

"I just started!" I protested. Then, after curiosity got hold, I lifted a brow. "What did it feel like?"

"Um," Robin mumbled, her eyes going distant. "Kind of like getting my arm stuck in a vacuum hose."

"Weird," I said.

"You're going to have to practice."

"I don't see how."

"You'll figure it out."

I grunted, glanced at the clock on the wall. My eyes lit up.

"It's almost breakfast time! Birthday breakfast time." I let out a happy sound at the thought and Robin snorted.

"You can't have cake for breakfast."

"Aww, come on," I begged. "I look terrible, remember? It's comfort food. Besides, a stack of pancakes covered in frosting and sprinkles isn't cake."

"Yeah, you tell mom that. I'll watch."

Olivia R. Burton

Twenty-Four

Chloe and I sat alone in the sitting room, backed up to the fireplace. Izzy had led the kids on a parade through the house, each of them wearing paper crowns and blanket capes; it was a game only children and Izzy could understand. My dad had hung around, surprisingly, sitting in the living room with the rest of the family, possibly so high on the cake he'd eaten—homemade and vegan thanks to my mom and Chloe—that he was immune to Izzy's shenanigans.

I'd eaten a lot of cake trying to achieve that state of euphoria, but had yet to get that lucky. Dad really was better at empathy than me, from the look of it, so maybe he really did have a few tricks I needed to learn. I tried to get eager about learning, but it was going to take some time.

"So, how's thirty feel?" Chloe asked as Izzy and the kids made a second pass. Stella trailed behind them this time, but I could see her energy was flagging and she probably wouldn't make it back across the house.

"Like twenty-nine," I decided, before wiggling my shoulders uncomfortably. "But more achy."

"Aww," Chloe said, patting my back. "I've got more pills, if you want."

"Nah, Owen had to head out of town to another job. I'm fine for now. He said he might be back in Seattle soon, though. I might hit you up if it's real soon."

"Gotcha," Chloe said, leaning back to pull her knees to her chest. After more time passed and Jake and Thomas erupted with laughter, my empathy grasping at their happiness and making me giggle, Chloe leaned in to bump her shoulder against mine. "Did you two talk?"

"About you?" I asked, turning to face her, seeing the trepidation purring in her like a nervous cat. "Yeah. Though, he didn't tell me much. He's pretty good at that."

"The best," she said with a grin and a laugh. "I think you need natural talent to be that smoothly avoidant."

"He's got a lot of natural talents, that man," I agreed, unable to keep the purr out of my tone. Chloe chuckled and we went quiet for a moment, before she cleared her throat.

"Did you have any—" She cleared her throat. "—questions?"

"Um." I considered, going over what Owen had said in his hotel room, the things I'd wondered about Chloe in the past, and what Kincade had spat at her, intending to cause trouble. She didn't really want to talk about this, but she was offering, and I had the feeling she'd be relieved if I dropped it, but she wouldn't be overall happier. I could tell she wanted me to ask, to force her to tell me the truth she'd been tucking away since we'd met. It wasn't my empathy I was reading, but years of experience counseling people who'd spent too long avoiding the truth. "So many," I said finally, with a laugh.

"Should we start with where babies come from?" she offered. I snorted, glad when the tension snapped and crumbled around us.

"What about just ... what's a Gavel? Are you a Gavel? Is it important?"

"I was, though some consider it a life-long appointment, but I'm ... not anymore. And yes, it's very important. It's, um." She took a deep breath, like she was about to dive off a tall cliff into an angry tide. "I was an emissary of sorts, to a Fairy—that's capital-F—and I ran ... in an interesting crowd."

"With Kincade? And Owen? Is Kincade a Gavel?"

Chloe laughed at the idea, but it was bitter, like the suggestion was beyond ludicrous. "No one would trust her enough to give her that much power. No, you need to have integrity, which she does not. She'd sell her own grandmother to a rabid cannibal if she thought the payment was shiny enough."

"I doubt Kincade has grandparents," I mused. "I think she just burbled up from a pile of horse shit one day."

"Wouldn't surprise me," Chloe said. Izzy marched through again, though without Stella, his pace slowed to accommodate J.J.'s sleepy gait. I wondered how far past his bedtime it was, and if I could gorge myself on more cake after the kids weren't around to beg me to share.

"Is that how you know all the stuff you know?" I asked after they'd left. "How you got Evadne to help with the kids?" I gasped. "Were you Evadne's emissary?"

"No, no, she doesn't take Gavels. It's too ... um, complicated to go into, but it's not something just any Fairy can have. I still have favors to call in here and there," Chloe said, though she wasn't being entirely honest, "and I called one in back then. Truth is, I should have just come clean when Sy—er, Laurel and Hardy showed up, sent them packing, but I was … Honestly, I didn't expect her…" Chloe went silent for a long moment, her eyes distant, frustrated curiosity thudding against me like an angry heartbeat.

"I'd been out of the game, completely out of the world—except for you and Mel, really, and it threw me. Then you … My god." Chloe started laughing, leaning her head against her knees as if the thought was too funny to bear.

"You just started … *dealing* with them like you knew what you were doing. And by god, you tried your best. I got Mel to help, fed him information where he needed it, tried to stay on the sidelines, but you … you were so inept—I'm sorry—" Cutting off when she saw my expression, Chloe reached out, pulled me into a hug. "But you were. I had no choice but to help for real. It was fun, though. I can't argue that. It's why I jumped so easily into hunting Norma when Owen came around."

She smiled, her gaze unfocused, like she was remembering the good ol' times, and I found myself grinning too, caught up in her fuzzy nostalgia.

"Why'd you quit?" I asked after a bit. "You—I can feel you, you *loved* what you were doing. Right? Why'd you stop? Why are you sitting in my cramped office putting up with my bullshit?"

Chloe seemed to shake herself out of it, taking a deep breath. The nostalgia warped, skewed from fuzzy and pleasant to unsure and uncomfortable. Some rumble of a memory threatened to grow within me, a moment I'd repressed from after Chloe and Owen had killed the succubus they'd been hunting. It wanted to declare a truth, a bit of Chloe's history I'd gained through nasty means, and I took a shaky breath, shoving it down again.

"That's a long story," she said finally. I nodded, understanding that this she really didn't want to get into—and feeling my own panic at the idea, as well. "But rest assured, I'm happy. You're a pain in the ass but I love you and wouldn't wanna be anywhere but your cramped office."

"Really?" I asked, though I knew she was telling the truth—even about me being a pain in the ass.

"Really," she said, squeezing me tightly.

Thanksgiving felt the same at thirty as it did at twenty-nine, although I appreciated not getting into a screaming match with my father. I even appreciated all the vegan sides that Chloe brought to the table, especially since three of them had the word, "candied" in the name.

Chloe and I flew home together, but Izzy disappeared the day before we left. She explained that Izzy doesn't fly on planes but that we'd probably run into him back in Seattle at some point. Business was back to normal almost immediately, both at work and in my personal life. Standing in line at The Internets, I glanced over, noticed a plump, shapely girl with short dark hair and pretty eyes exit the bathroom area. Pleasure swamped her as she realized halfway across the restaurant that she'd forgotten to button her fly.

I watched her leave, winced when Mel stepped out after her. Snarling at him from my place in line, I felt when he caught sight of me; the swirling, scalding heat I'd felt since walking in was slightly dimmer, but still there. Lifting a brow over a smug smirk, he sidled up, easing like a greedy lover into my personal space, though he knew better than to touch me.

Mel is a very good-looking werewolf, the exact opposite of poor Pumpkin-face. He's got at least a head of height on me, boosted slightly by expensive shoes; his hair is dark, normally perfectly styled above his bright blue eyes. This afternoon, however, it was mussed, his royal blue shirt miss-buttoned right above his sculpted pecs. I just thanked my stars that he was wearing pants.

"Did you just have sex in the bathroom with that poor girl?" I asked. Mel lifted his hands in what he probably considered a delicate, beguiling shrug.

"I never kiss and tell, Gwen. But yes. We did. In several positions."

"Ugh," I grunted, shaking my head. I had to resist the urge to wipe the feeling of his pleasure away from my skin because it made me feel like he'd splashed me with acid. "That's so unsanitary. Both for you and the bathroom."

Mel frowned down at me, a spike of irritation clouding his otherwise happy psyche. He didn't complain, though. Something moved within his emotions that I didn't quite catch before he sighed, looking to the front of the line. The succubus owner of the café noticed us speaking, gave an amused little grin at our sniping, and then thanked the customer she was helping for coming in.

"Where were you the last two weeks? And why are you all beat up?" Mel asked, after a bit. I could feel worry in him and it reminded me we were friends, despite the fact that I could barely stand him. I also realized he'd effectively cut in front of three other people by joining me in my place in line. I didn't fight it, finding I'd sort of missed him in a weird, masochistic way that I didn't entirely want to examine or admit.

"I joined a secret, underground fight club. I came out on top."

"Was the prize a cake the size of the Space Needle?"

"Why do you think I won?"

"That's my girl," he said, making me laugh.

"Your girl, my ass," I spat back, still laughing.

"I've still got some time for your ass," he offered, as the customer ahead of us glanced back curiously, taking her credit card back from Madeline. "You wanna join me in the bathroom?"

"Gross." I spat apathetically, elbowing him. Mel laughed as we stepped up and Madeline glanced between us.

"Usual, Gwen?" she asked. I nodded, enjoying the gust of humor blowing through her, as it had the pleasant side effect of washing away some of Mel's caustic lust. "I could have it brought to a specific stall if you guys are going to be busy."

I wrinkled my nose at her suggestion. "Now you're not getting a tip"

"You never tip."

"I'll give you both a tip," Mel purred. Both Madeline and I looked at him, matching identical looks of disappointment on our faces. Mel only grinned, looking between us as if he had all the confidence in the world that one or both of us would break, yell, "Take me!" and strip off our clothes right there.

When neither one of us did, Mel just lifted his hands in dual finger-guns, shot each one of us in turn, and headed for the door. I turned back, tried to hand over my debit card, but Madeline waved me off.

"I heard about what you did in Montana. It's on me."

"You … how did you hear?"

"Word about you is getting around. You know," she said, her gaze taking on a serious intensity, "that you're so *helpful*. It's appreciated."

I heard the sound of glass sliding across wood and looked down to find that there was a fat slice of cake sitting in front of me on the counter. I looked back up to her, brows up. What did this mean, exactly?

"For being helpful," Madeline reiterated, letting the moment lie for a beat. "Now get out of the way, you're holding up the line."

"Oh," I said, grabbing the plate and stepping to the side. "Thanks."

I made my way to a table toward the back, staring down at my tasty gift and wondering if I should be happy about the free cake or worried that my name was being passed around the preternatural community. How wide did this go, I wondered. Was it local, just the Pacific Northwest? Did it go further? Should I have been worried about being accosted for help from some Southern belle mermaid hoping to bag a prince?

I was going to have to ask Chloe if I had anything to worry about—and if mermaids even existed.

I took a seat, lifted my gaze to the wall, and tried to decide how I felt about this development. It wasn't exactly like I had my hands full with my human clients. My schedule was pretty open each day. Did I want more trouble, though? Did I want creatures I didn't yet know about showing up at my doorstep asking for help? Would that be something I could handle, or would I just go completely nuts?

As I stabbed into the cake and shoveled a giant bite into my mouth, I considered that if this was how they paid me, I was open to the possibility either way.

Olivia R. Burton

About the Author

Olivia is a vegan thirty-something living in New Mexico with a clowder of cats and a stink of litter boxes. She enjoys vexing her kitties, cooking, watching action movies, and making up collective nouns for things that don't already have them (like a "stink of litter boxes"). You can find her and all information about her different series at OliviaRBurton.com.

Olivia R. Burton

Gwen Arthur Novels

Visit OliviaRBurton.com for more information

www.ingramcontent.com/pod-product-compliance
Lightning Source LLC
Chambersburg PA
CBHW072106170626
46813CB00004B/1473